Praise for *Insomnia*

"*Insomnia* is the perfect blend of everything I love in a
story. Suspense, twists, characters with many levels ... I
highly recommend this book to everyone, and I hope a
sequel comes soon!"

— James Dashner, *New York Times*
bestselling author of *The Maze Runner*

"Cleverly written and dangerously dark, *Insomnia* will
take you to the brink of insanity. A must-read for thriller
and romance fans alike."

— Elana Johnson, author of *Possession*

"*Insomnia* is suspenseful, fascinating, and completely
unputdownable. I've decided to nickname Jenn Johansson 'Scary McScarypants,' because she spooked me in
all the best ways."

— Carrie Harris, author of *Bad Taste in Boys*

"A riveting story of terror and despair that will keep you
up long past your bedtime."

— Jennifer Bosworth, author of *Struck*

INSOMNIA

Book 1 of
The Night Walkers

INSOMNIA

J.R.
Johansson

flux™
Woodbury, Minnesota

First Edition
First Printing, 2013

Book design by Bob Gaul
Cover design by Lisa Novak
Cover image: Man © dundanim/Shutterstock.com
           Black broken glass © iStockphoto.com/Hayri Er

Flux, an imprint of Llewellyn Worldwide Ltd.

Library of Congress Cataloging-in-Publication Data
Johansson, J. R.
  Insomnia/J.R. Johansson.—First edition.
    pages cm.—(The Night Walkers; book 1)
  Summary: Sixteen-year-old Parker Chipp spends his nights experiencing other people's dreams and getting no rest, so when he discovers that new friend Mia's dreams are different he becomes fixated on her until memory blackouts lead him to question exactly what their relationship is.
  ISBN 978-0-7387-3593-1
  [1. Dreams—Fiction. 2. Friendship—Fiction. 3. High schools—Fiction. 4. Schools—Fiction. 5. Mental illness—Fiction. 6. Soccer—Fiction.] I. Title.
  PZ7.J62142Ins 2013
  [Fic]—dc23

                         2013001174

Flux
Llewellyn Worldwide Ltd.
2143 Wooddale Drive
Woodbury, MN 55125-2989
www.fluxnow.com

Printed in the United States of America

To Ande, Cameron, and Parker—
thank you for making all my best dreams come true.

ONE

It had been over four years since I'd really slept, and I suspected it was killing me.

Tonight, finding someone other than Mr. Flint to make eye contact with before going to bed seemed like more work than it was worth. Besides, he was just an old man, the janitor of the Oakville Library. I'd seen the dreams of men like him before. The most exciting part was usually the new lawn mower they were using.

The instant his dream began, though, I knew I'd been dead wrong. This man was nothing like the others.

A woman sprawled across a bed with one thin arm thrown over her eyes, her jeans tattered at the bottom from dragging on the ground. Her white tank top was tugged up on one side, leaving her stomach bare, exposed. I thought she was pretty hot until I noticed the wrinkles around her mouth, the ring on her finger, and the clusters of gray hairs along her hairline. I groaned under my breath; sexy mom dreams are really not my thing.

The scene froze before me for a moment and I looked around. The walls were light green; there were tiny pink and blue flowers on the sheets. I heard the thunder before the smell of damp wood and perfume filled my nostrils. Each sense came like a wave, crashing over me.

Rain fell through the open window, pooling on the cedar chest below. The heavy green drapes rustled as they framed the darkness outside.

I knew I'd see Mr. Flint soon. The dreamer always showed up last, like the brain had to build the scene before thrusting the dreamer into it. It had taken me a long time to figure out even a basic knowledge of the way dreams worked. I didn't think I'd ever understand it all. I'd tried for months before I realized that no dreamers could see me. Even when I stood right in front of them and screamed at the top of my lungs—they never knew I was there.

Kind of ironic that I knew so much about people's dreams considering I never slept. Well, my body did, but my brain … not so much. The world of my dreams was no longer mine. It was forbidden and distant. I was just the guy that watched, a passive observer in the minds of others, seeing what they saw, feeling what they felt. I knew their dreams like I knew my own skin.

One thing I'd learned pretty fast was that all dreams had layers. Like the brain got too bored constructing only one dream at a time. There was always more going on under the surface. My brain tended to drop me in the layer closest to reality. At least, that was my best guess. I didn't know for sure, but it was the only explanation I could come up with for why I often saw fantasies and memories instead of the alternative. I still saw the bizarre stuff, but it was less frequent. Judging from the lack of leprechauns or talking furniture around me now, this dream was just another demonstration of that fact. I didn't get the subtext, the metaphors; I got the real thing.

The thunder sounded again and I sighed, waiting for him to appear. I could already tell that Mr. Flint's dream was a memory, and I just wanted to get it over with. I didn't like watching memories. Somehow it felt even more intrusive than watching fantasies. Everything in a memory was crystal clear, with very little of the haziness that literally hovered over other dreams I saw. After years of watching, I knew this level of focus, of detail, could mean only one thing. This wasn't a creation of Mr. Flint's mind; this was his life. His brain's twisted analysis of his past thickened the air around me, like a million observations given at once.

And then I saw him, in the doorway watching her. When his emotions hit, they crushed me, knocked the wind out of me. The janitor's desperate, churning passions swept me in wave upon wave of sadness, anger, and betrayal. Each one hit stronger than the last until the pain eclipsed them all, unbearable yet unchanging. Pain was life now. No hope remained. The pain smothered it along with everything else that reeked of happier times.

I crouched, clutching my side and panting. I knew better. The room was charged with an inexplicable energy as the physical pain faded in the shade of more ominous emotions: hatred, combined with blood-pumping adrenaline, turned into the purest kind of rage I'd ever experienced.

I clawed at the ground as Mr. Flint's fury ripped through me. His need to destroy, to make someone hurt the way he did, overwhelmed me.

As he approached the bed, something glinted in his hand. I narrowed my eyes for a closer look. He clutched a shining silver letter opener with a navy handle. Combined with the grim intent on his face, I'd never seen a more lethal-looking weapon.

I fought his emotions and struggled to move, to hide from what I knew would come, but it was no use. I couldn't leave. I could close my eyes, but the emotions of the dreamer were the worst part and I couldn't hide from them. If I didn't see what was happening, my mind filled in the gaps. Too often the disturbing images I came up with were so much worse than the nightmare I was stuck in.

He held a pillow over her head as he stabbed the letter opener through her tank top three times. Her gurgling screams pierced the air. Mixed with his grunts, her death created a horrific melody until all sound muffled to a whisper. The sudden stillness swallowed me. As I tried to control my breathing, her blood spilled from the triangle of wounds through her shirt and onto the floral sheets. My head hurt and my heart pounded in my chest.

His rage ended as abruptly as it came, leaving only despair behind. I could feel how much he hated her, hated himself. His absolute certainty that life was no longer worth living landed square on my shoulders and I shook under the weight of it. Mr. Flint held her hands in his and sobbed. He pulled the gold wedding band off her finger and held it to his lips. Wracking moans gushed out of his body, burying both of us in misery, barely allowing room for air.

I was horrified at myself for pitying him, even though it was impossible not to when I *felt* his emotions. The dream might have been a memory but Mr. Flint was actually asleep as it played out, hovering in that place where the boundaries between right and wrong blurred—I wasn't. Feeling sorry for a murderer disgusted me, but it didn't matter. His self-pity swamped me, overpowering my own revulsion.

My gaze darted between him and the woman, his wife. This wasn't the same man who'd first entered the dream. There was a change in him, so strong I could feel it. He was a murderer now. He would never be the same person again. There was no coming back from this.

He was a reflection of my ability—my curse. Having seen what I had, I'd never be the same again either.

———

I woke up coughing, my body covered in sweat. Curling in on myself, I wrapped one arm around my knees and tried to catch my breath. Why did I have to pick him? Why a murderer?

Being a Watcher sucked, especially when everyone else around me was a Dreamer. I didn't know if there were any more like me out there, but I knew that whatever lucky

Dreamer was the last to catch my eye, I couldn't break free of them. No matter how much I wanted to escape, I was stuck with that person for the night.

A loud thump rattled my door and I rolled out of bed.

"It's the weekend, Mom." My voice came out croaky and exhausted. I stumbled toward the bathroom, taking deep breaths and forcing myself not to think about Mr. Flint's dream.

In and out.

In and out.

"It's almost noon, your majesty," she yelled back from the kitchen.

I stopped in the middle of the hallway and rubbed my eye. "It's almost *eleven*. Stop exaggerating or I'll have to hire new help."

"Yeah, yeah," Mom muttered.

I fought the urge to tell her, to tell anyone, about what I'd seen. As much as I would have liked to go to the police and tell them I'd witnessed Mr. Flint murder his wife in a dream, I knew no one would believe me, and the psych ward wasn't my idea of a prime weekend hangout.

I grabbed the newspaper off the table in the hall and took it into the bathroom. The cold of the tile shot tingles through my feet as I flipped the pages. There it was:

Donna Marie Flint, born May 9, 1971, died last week during what appears to have been a failed burglary attempt. Friends and family may pay their respects at the Oakville Mortuary on Tuesday.

Tomorrow.

Mrs. Flint hadn't been dead very long, but it was still too late to save her. There was nothing I could do, nothing I could have done. The police were on the wrong track with the burglary, but they would eventually figure out what happened without my help. I had to believe that.

For one morbid moment, I wondered: If I was right about what was going to happen and this curse was slowly killing me, what would my obituary say? *Parker Daniel Chipp, a sixteen-year-old junior at Oakville High School, died of sleep deprivation.* Or would it be listed as something lame like *natural causes*? Either way it sounded pathetic.

I shuffled to the shower, turning the dials so the water was so icy it stabbed my skin like a thousand shards of glass. Most days it was the only way I could keep myself awake. The water raced down my skin in rivulets, carrying away images from the dream. Warm showers were a thing of the past now. After scrubbing my body raw, I turned off the water.

I wrapped a towel around my waist, trying to focus my mind on some of the happier dreams I'd seen. Other people's dreams took up so much of my life—and my brain—that it wasn't hard to reach into the pile and find a different one. They were each unique, and each equally exhausting.

The dream layers were often the hardest part. They could leave my head pounding for hours after I woke up. It was like the dreamer's subconscious brain had stretched its imaginative muscle and wanted to pack in as much as possible, just to torture me or something. Sometimes the other background layers were a haze, hovering over the main layer of the dream like a sheer curtain. Rarely, dreams were made of what felt like physical layers—some more reality-based, some more bizarre than an LSD addict's favorite hallucination—stacked above one another, and the Dreamer bounced between them like a ping-pong ball, like their brain couldn't decide what dream to have.

Then there was the mist of thought that twirled through the vivid memory dreams. If you stood in the curling tendrils of silver vapor, you could actually hear the Dreamer's brain thinking, reliving, deciding. The words and thoughts were so jumbled and convoluted, within a few seconds they'd make your mind spin. I'd carefully side-stepped the mist after my first experience with it.

The worst was when the other layers were so foggy that they were like background noise; it'd sound like a million bees buzzing in my head. I always had a terrible headache the day after watching one of those—the kind of headache no pain medicine could touch.

I took a deep breath and tried to focus on the task at hand. As I dried my face, I could actually feel the deep circles beneath my eyes, like they'd been there so long they'd hollowed me out. I shivered, pushed my messy black hair off my forehead, and tried to see if I looked any worse than the day before. My ice-blue eyes stared back. Yes, I looked like crap. But was there anything I could do about it? Nope.

I tugged on jeans and a sweatshirt and headed for the kitchen. It smelled like citrus and berries. Fresh fruit: Mom's favorite breakfast. She glanced up with a grin when I passed, but it slid from her face when her eyes met mine. I knew what she was thinking. Her constant worrying was the reason I only watched her dreams when I had no other choice.

"Did you sleep well?"

"Sure." I nodded and looked away from her concern.

Mom stepped in front of me and placed the back of one hand on my forehead. With a sigh, she brought it down and twisted her lips to one side. "Well, you *feel* fine..."

I grabbed her shoulders, smiled, and stared her straight in the eye. This early in the day, it didn't matter who I made eye contact with. I was safe, for now.

"That's because I *am* fine."

She stuck her fist under her chin and moved it back and forth as she watched me hunt through the kitchen for a snack. I knew that move. I'd seen her look at Dad that way so many times before he left that it was impossible to forget.

The first year he was gone, Mom had been so upset she'd thrown herself into her work. I was always fed and taken care of, but she'd never noticed how tired I was. That was over three years ago. I still missed those days. When she wasn't around, I didn't have to pretend to be normal.

I sliced an apple with the biggest knife I could find and fought the mixture of frustration and resentment that rose up every time I thought about Dad. I had enough problems without being forced to put up with the baggage he'd left behind.

I glanced up, ready to handle her the way I always did— with distraction.

"So, any appointments today?"

Mom grabbed her cell phone off the countertop and

scrolled through the calendar. "I have a couple of showings this afternoon and a few more tonight. I might be a little late. Will you be all right alone?"

"Yeah. I'm probably going to do something with Finn."

"That's all? No one else is coming? Just Finn?" She squinted at my face. Once again, she didn't believe me.

I popped an apple slice in my mouth and walked over to the window. This conversation needed to be over now. "Yep, just Finn," I crunched.

She nodded and turned back to her phone again.

I shuffled to my bedroom and pulled on some sneakers. If I didn't know any better, I'd think they were made of lead. Gravity was my enemy these days. Each morning my arms and legs—even my eyelids—felt heavier. I was amazed when the scale showed the same weight, or lately a lower one, than the week before. Each time I stepped on it, I was certain my head alone must be a few pounds heavier. It was so much harder to hold it up every day.

When I'd turned sixteen the previous month, I'd exhausted my final idea. I'd stopped by the gas station on the way home every night for two weeks, making eye contact with the guy on the night shift in the hope that I could sleep if my Dreamer was awake all night. But when I slept it wasn't real sleep. Watching dreams was like staying up all night watching totally immersive movies, and sleeping when my Dreamer was awake was like staying up watching static on a muted television set. It was peaceful to some extent, but my brain still wasn't sleeping. It was just my own personal void.

Nights like those helped me focus a little better during

the day, but not by much. So when Mom started freaking about me being out too late all the time, I gave it up. The nothingness got boring night after night anyway, like sitting in my own padded room. The irony of it made me smile; that was pretty much what I was trying so hard to avoid.

I'd tried everything I could come up with. I even tried not making eye contact with anyone all day—not as easy as it sounds. But even then I just saw the dreams of the last person from the day before.

Shoving my backpack toward the wall with my foot, I noticed that the main pocket was halfway open and the corner of a book was poking out. I picked up the bag and zipped it shut, then took a quick look around my bedroom. It looked . . . different. A couple of things had been moved, but it wasn't anything obvious. I sighed. She'd been in here again. It must've been while I was in the shower. Determination isn't something my family runs short on.

I drew in a deep breath and walked back to the kitchen. "Find any drugs this time?"

Mom didn't look up from her cell phone, but I saw her shut her eyes tightly before speaking; her voice tried so hard to be calm it wavered. "No."

"Won't keep you from looking next time, though, will it?" I sat down at the table and glared at her back. I had enough problems right now. Why did she feel the need to add to them?

Turning, she leaned against the counter and folded her arms over her chest. "What do you want me to think? You don't talk to me. You're losing weight…you…you just don't look good, honey."

"Way to boost a guy's self-esteem, Mom." I rubbed my hand against my eye and looked out the window across from me.

"Do you have a better explanation?" She waited a moment before continuing. "Because, believe me, I don't want to find drugs…but I don't know what else to think."

"I've told you." I shook my head and looked back at her. "I don't sleep well."

She lowered her chin and raised her eyebrows. "Parker, you sleep *all the time.*"

A hot wave of anger flowed over me. Why did she keep bringing this up? She never believed what I said, anyway. I stood up from the table and turned back toward the hall. "Well then, guess it must be drugs."

"Wait, please." She grabbed my elbow before I could get out of the kitchen but didn't speak until I turned to face her. "So, if it's sleep, we're going to a doctor. Today. Dr. Brown has an after-hours clinic on weekends. We'll go see him right now."

"Today?" I frowned. "But you have appointments."

"I'll reschedule. It'll be fine. This is more important."

A chill ran through me. I'd been avoiding this, afraid a doctor would confirm my suspicions, or worse, call me crazy and stick me in an asylum, but I had to be honest. I'd gotten as much information as I was going to get from my online searches…and I didn't like the answers they were giving me. It was time. I'd just have to be smart about it. I wouldn't tell him the whole truth, but I'd figure out a way to get him to give me the answers I needed.

"Okay, Mom, if you think it will help. I'm in."

TWO

Dr. Brown had been our family doctor for as long as I could remember. After sitting in the waiting room a few minutes, his nurse led us to a mustard-yellow exam room with pictures of fish on the walls. Now that we were here, I couldn't seem to keep still. I sat down, drummed my fingers against my thighs, stood up, looked at the pictures, and sat down again.

The door opened and Dr. Brown came in. He'd always been super thin and serious, and he always managed to take charge the moment he walked in a room. He smiled at my mom and shook my hand before taking a seat on his rolling stool.

"Well, Parker, we haven't seen you in a while." He bent over my chart and all I could see were the short brown hairs on top of his head. "With teenage boys, that's usually a good thing. What brings you in today?"

I crossed my arms over my chest. "I'm having trouble sleeping."

"That isn't all," Mom said. I wished again that she'd agreed to stay in the waiting room. "He's been losing weight."

Dr. Brown glanced at me and back at the chart. "Teenage boys tend to fluctuate a lot. You play soccer still?"

I nodded.

"I can give you some sleeping pills to help get your body back into a regular rhythm, but I don't want you taking them for very long. And you need to make sure you're eating enough to keep up with the exercise." He glanced at his watch and back to my chart.

"Okay," I said, trying not to sound as frustrated as I felt. Of course I'd tried sleeping pills. Over-the-counter, but still, they made the exhaustion so much worse. I'd be so groggy I could barely walk straight the next day. This wasn't going to get us anywhere, and I couldn't ask him anything with Mom in here. What a waste of time.

Dr. Brown squinted at me for a moment before turning back to Mom. "There's a new insurance form I'd like you to fill out while I chat with Parker. Just to make sure there isn't anything else going on, if that's okay with both of you?"

Mom glanced at me and I nodded. "Yeah, I'll be fine, Mom. Go ahead."

She stood and followed the doctor into the hall. I tried to prepare myself. I'd only have a few minutes alone with him. I was sure he had his own reasons for getting rid of Mom, but I had to control the conversation.

When Dr. Brown stepped back in the room, he handed

me a pamphlet: *Drugs and the Teenage Mind.* I groaned and shook my head.

"I'm not accusing you of anything, but when you've been a doctor as long as I have, you learn to read the signs." Dr. Brown had kind eyes. They were sympathetic, compassionate ... but it didn't change the fact that he was as wrong as everyone else. "You know that any drugs you put in your system can affect your sleep patterns as well."

I looked him straight in the eye. "Just for the sake of argument, let's say I am on drugs that are keeping me from sleeping."

His bushy brown eyebrows shot up. Clearly not the response he'd been expecting. "What are you on?"

"I didn't admit anything, and it doesn't matter." I shook my head and leaned forward, my elbows resting on my knees. "What I need to know is, what happens to a person's brain when they don't sleep?"

Dr. Brown shook his head. "Don't sleep at all?"

"Yes."

"Well, first they'd be tired, irritable, emotional, obviously." Dr. Brown shrugged, but he was watching my reaction closely. "And then there'd be tremors as the brain experienced stutters in its control of the body. Eventually the body would collapse from exhaustion and the problem would be fixed for the time being."

No matter how tired I became, I never collapsed and my brain never slept. I wasn't normal. I shook my head. "Let's say it didn't collapse. For whatever reason, a body kept going. What would happen next?"

He frowned. "That's not possible without external interference—and extreme stimulation."

"Okay, then with those things." I'm not sure when I stood up, but his eyes widened as he looked up at me. "What would happen next?"

"I don't understand. What's this about?" He rolled his stool back a bit.

I took a step closer but kept my voice low. I needed him to answer. "What would happen next, doctor?"

He frowned and stood up, but I still had a couple of inches on him. "The person would become psychotic, experiencing a variety of dangerous psychological symptoms, and then … well, then the person would die."

It felt like he'd punched me in the gut. The room spun a little and I crumpled back into my seat. My eyes glued to the carpet in front of me. The research I'd done … I was right. I'd been right. I didn't want to be right.

Dr. Brown sat back on his stool and scooted it closer to me. "Why these questions, Parker? You aren't saying that you—"

"No," I interrupted, looking up with a forced smile. "It's about a science project I'm working on."

"Oh."

He stared at me in silence and I could see that I now had his full attention, but I didn't want it anymore. I'd come for an answer, and he'd given it. I just needed to get out of there without Dr. Brown trying to have me committed.

There was a knock on the door and Mom poked her head in. "You guys about done?"

I nodded and got to my feet. Realizing I still had the drug pamphlet in my hand, I stuffed it into my pocket, but not before Mom got a look at it. Perfect. "I think the sleeping pills should help," I said.

Mom's shoulders slumped a little and she glanced over at Dr. Brown, her gaze piercing. "Do you think so, doctor?"

"I think it's a good place to start." He frowned, then continued. "But I want to check all his vitals...just to be safe."

After ten minutes of having me say "Ah," checking my reflexes and pupil dilation, and listening to my breathing and heartbeat, Dr. Brown handed me a prescription for some sleeping pills and a referral card to a shrink. His brow was furrowed and he looked like he was considering saying something else, but instead shook my hand.

"Take care of yourself, Parker. I'm here if you need me."

———

Mom and I barely spoke on the drive home. She grunted and almost snarled at the other drivers as we went. She clearly didn't believe me *or* Dr. Brown. I put on my headphones and turned up the music on my iPod. It wasn't like I was exactly happy with the results of the doctor visit either, and luckily, neither of us wanted to talk about it.

As soon as we were home, I headed to my room, shut the door, and called Finn.

He answered after the first ring. "Hey man, what's up?"

"Nothing. I need to get out of here."

"Okay. Are we talking out to a movie or a south-of-the-border kind of escape?" I could hear him munching on something in the background.

"A movie sounds good."

"Cool. Be there in a few." When I heard him hang up, I stuffed my phone in my pocket and flopped down on my bed. I pretended not to hear Mom whispering to Dr. Brown on the phone in the living room.

"Yes, but do you think he's on something?" A pause. "No, I know you can't tell for sure. I've never found anything in his room." A longer pause. "Okay, I'll let you know if it gets any worse. Thank you, doctor."

Dr. Brown's voice, as he listed the stages of extreme sleep deprivation, kept bouncing around in my head like a rubber ball with no means of escape. I'd already been shaking a lot, getting worse every day. I guess those were the tremors, so next was . . .

Become psychotic and then die . . . become psychotic and then die . . . become psychotic and then die . . .

Fear clawed at me. I wasn't sure anymore if knowing *was* better. I sat up and moved to my desk. The only thing I could do was be prepared. Time to do some more research.

I opened a search engine and typed in *Psychosis*. It came up with a definition: "Psychosis is a loss of contact with reality, usually including false ideas about what is taking place or who one is (delusions) and seeing or hearing things that aren't there (hallucinations)."

My stomach clenched. Psychosis made death sound like the better part of my future. I dreaded the hallucinations and delusions more than what would follow. I was most afraid of becoming one of the monsters I'd seen so often in dreams, of not being able to follow my own code, my own morality. Or worse, not being able to tell reality from whatever my mind made up … *that* would be the real nightmare.

I rubbed my hands together in an effort to warm them. My future felt cold, isolating. My kind of insomnia would be branded by everyone else as insanity.

The doorbell rang and I jammed my finger into the power button on my computer. I stuffed one hand in my pocket as I grabbed my jacket with the other. I needed to get my mind off of all this. I couldn't fix it, not right now, anyway. Finn was the perfect person to help me relax. Everything about him said *chill*.

"I'm going to a movie with Finn," I yelled down the hall. "I'll be back later."

"Okay. Please be safe … and smart." Even through her closed bedroom door, disappointment tinged her voice.

I bolted out of the house. The instant I saw Finn's face, the first dream of his I'd ever watched flashed through my head. Memorable, it was definitely memorable—I mean, he was a twelve-year-old, dressed like Superman, battling a giant bunch of broccoli. Finn's dreams were always … unique.

Even his most realistic dreams were never what I would consider "normal." That was the main reason I liked to watch his more than anyone else's. Finn's dreams were the closest I could get to what I thought my own dreams might've been like.

When we were thirteen, I told him I watched people's dreams. He immediately assumed I was joking, and, rather than try to convince him, I'd dropped it. He probably would have freaked out anyway.

Finn was leaning against the wrought-iron railing of our porch step. As I walked over I got a whiff of his deodorant; he smelled like old-man spice. His shirt read *I'd flex, but I like this shirt* with a remarkably muscular stick figure below it. I shook my head. That was Finn. His entire wardrobe was full of stuff like that.

"Glad to see you brought my car back." I plastered a smile on my face as I grabbed the keys from his hand.

"Is it my fault that my parents bought me a piece of crap that's only spent one week out of the shop since I got it last spring?" Finn flashed a grin and the spattering of freckles across his nose stood out like polka dots in the fading light.

"Well, it's definitely not mine."

Finn clutched his shirt in front of his heart. "Loyalty, man. Loyalty!"

The sun peeked through the dark clouds that filled the sky and I stretched my hands out as I walked toward the car, absorbing the fading warmth. The leaves were still undecided—half on the ground, half on the trees. I shook off the feeling that they were a little too much like me and stomped through some dried-up ones on the front lawn, enjoying the crisp, crunching sound the leaves made beneath my feet.

"The old theater first, right?"

Finn hopped down the remaining stairs and hurried to catch up with me. "First? Is there a second?"

I shrugged. "I've got to buy some new soccer cleats. Get them worn in before the season starts."

"As long as we catch that old craptastic Kung Fu movie, I don't care what else we do. And hey, maybe new shoes will improve your footwork. I'm tired of blocking all the goals when other teams steal the ball from you." He shrugged and climbed in the passenger side.

"If you blocked more goals, I wouldn't have to try to catch us up all the time."

Finn turned up the radio and pretended he couldn't hear me.

THREE

The sporting goods store always smelled like a gigantic rubber ball dipped in pine-scented cleaner. The store was pretty empty, but I noticed Jeff Sparks flipping through an issue of *Sports Illustrated* at the checkout line across from me. He was our senior class president. Everyone got along with him and he got along with pretty much everyone. He was definitely top dog, and had been the soccer team captain since junior high. There was a moment, when the team voted me co-captain of the soccer team this year, that I thought Jeff might not be down with sharing the spotlight, but so far he'd been cool.

"Any good?" I asked.

Jeff glanced up and smiled when he saw me. "Hey, man. Nah, my team sucks this year anyway."

"Dude, the Broncos suck every year."

He laughed, put the magazine back on the rack, and

placed a new pair of shin guards in front of the register. "And the Packers are any better?"

I shrugged and walked over to Jeff's register. My line wasn't moving anyway and I didn't like shouting across the girl ringing him up. "Always."

"Never took you for a liar."

"Then you haven't been paying attention."

Jeff paid and grabbed his shin guards. He walked backward toward the door and pointed one finger at me. "Soccer team meeting tomorrow after the assembly. Don't forget."

"I'll be there," I said as he left.

Jeff and I used to hang out all the time, but he was a year older so when he went to high school and I didn't, things changed. Sometimes I missed hanging out with him, but I'd been a little too distracted and tired to make an effort over the past couple years, and now I wasn't sure how to try again.

I hadn't watched his dreams in at least two years, but he used to dream a lot about hanging out with his mom. It seemed to make him oddly happy. Hard to look at our school's star soccer forward, not to mention my co-captain, in quite the same way when you know he's a serious momma's boy.

After buying my cleats, I glanced at the clock above the door and walked out into the damp night air. It was just after six. Not that I wanted to avoid Jeff's dreams, but I was glad Finn was waiting for me outside. His dreams were comfortable for me now. Besides, even his nightmares were too freaky to be considered scary.

He was sitting on a bench talking on his phone. The air

around us was thick and moist, but it hadn't begun raining yet.

"Yeah, we had to stop by the mall after the movie," he said.

I recognized his mom's muffled voice coming through the earpiece. He shrugged and said, "Fine, I'll ask him." He held the phone away from his ear. "Can we pick up Addie from the pool on the way home?"

I ignored his shaking head and laughed. "Sure, no problem."

He scowled and said goodbye. I wasn't going to be the one to tell Mrs. Patrick no. Besides, Finn's fifteen-year-old sister Addie was the coolest girl I'd ever met—although I'd never tell Finn that.

I'd avoided most girl Dreamers since the end of junior high, when girls got all weird. Addie was the only girl I'd ever been curious about, but I'd never watched her dreams. For some reason it felt like an intrusion with her. It didn't help things that last summer she'd turned ridiculously hot pretty much overnight. She even went to our school now that she was a sophomore. Too bad sisters of friends were off-limits. It didn't really matter, though—girls were so much work. It wasn't worth wasting the time I had left on them.

"Fine, we can pick up Addie." Finn gave an exaggerated sigh and got to his feet. As if we hadn't already agreed. "But I want to stop at a gas station for a drink on the way home."

"Okay." I shrugged and decided to change the subject. "Did you know about the soccer meeting after the assembly tomorrow?"

Finn nodded and tucked his phone in his pocket. "Yeah. Aren't we starting practices a little early this year? Spring's a long way off."

"Yeah, it's early. I think we should wait a few more weeks, at least until after Halloween, but it isn't worth arguing with Jeff about it."

"I don't understand half the stuff Jeff does, but it seems to be working for him."

"Guess so." I walked around to my side of the car, then cursed under my breath when my hands shook so hard I dropped the keys twice before managing to open the driver's-side door. The sky around us rumbled as it started to rain. Clumsy, dying, *and* soaked. Awesome.

"No rush," Finn muttered, pulling his jacket closed around him and glancing at the sky.

"I'd hate to get you wet, Princess," I joked as I reached a shaking hand over the center console to unlock the passenger side for Finn. The tremors always got worse near the end of the day. The way my coordination was slipping, but only in certain areas, freaked me out. In biology, they'd taught us about muscle memory—the difference between movements your muscles do out of instinct and movements you have to think about. I wondered if this was part of it. My brain was failing faster than my body.

"Good thing you picked soccer instead of football," he laughed. "Much better with your feet than your hands."

It was pouring before I even got the car in gear. Typical Oakville. Tremendous sheets of rain came on in an instant and made my car creak in unnatural ways. Like there was some kind of timer in the clouds, and every time it dinged, the sky exploded.

"When is your car getting out of the shop again?" I tried not to smile.

Finn glared out the window. "Actually, I'm supposed to get it back next month, but my parents are making me chauffeur Addie around until she gets her license in May."

I chuckled. "Maybe you're better off with it in the shop."

"Yep."

———

My car hadn't even stopped in front of the Oakville rec center when Addie ran out of the building. She looked up and grinned at the rain falling on her face, her auburn hair dripping wet. She climbed into the back seat and immediately dumped the rain water that had collected on top of her bag onto Finn's head.

"Oops."

Finn rubbed the water off his neck and scowled. "Are you sure we can't leave her here?"

I laughed as I pulled away from the curb.

Addie buckled her seat belt and leaned back. I tried to ignore the scent that always reminded me of her—oranges—this time with a hint of chlorine.

"How's the swim team this year?" I glanced in the rear-view mirror and met her eyes. She gave me a smile that said she knew I didn't care at all but was glad I asked anyway.

"Pretty good. We might make it to Regionals this year

if Gwen can learn to stay in her own lane." She sighed and leaned forward.

"She's not the only one who should learn to stay out of other people's space," Finn muttered before running his hand through his hair and flicking a few water droplets at his sister.

Addie held up the side of her jacket and ducked behind it. Her voice came out a little muffled. "What did you guys do today?"

Finn was still busy with his water revenge, so I answered. "Not much, really. Watched some kung fu. Got new soccer cleats. Ran into Jeff."

"Mr. Class President himself?" Addie grinned when Finn nodded. "That's always fun."

I glanced at Finn.

He shifted in his seat and turned to face her. "You know he's a total man-whore, right?"

Addie slapped his shoulder. "I'm smart enough to watch out for myself. Besides, it doesn't mean I can't enjoy the view."

I stared out the window in front of me, wondering why I felt so angry. But Finn was right—Addie should keep her distance. Jeff was a decent guy to his teammates, working hard and playing hard. Clean-cut, with his blond hair and brown eyes, he was your typical all-American jock. Unfortunately, with girls, he played the part. He always had more than one girlfriend at a time... usually more than two. Addie was way too good for him.

It was quiet for a minute. Finn shook his head. "Any girl who's okay with sharing their guy is crazy."

"Well, when it comes to Jeff, you realize that's half the

girls at school, right?" Addie twisted her hair up into a clip on the back of her head.

"You better not be in that group. And that's just one of the many reasons girls don't make any sense." Finn turned to face me. "You know he took Emily out last week?"

"Emily who?" I knew a few girls named Emily, and I'd never seen any of them with Jeff.

"Matt, from the soccer team—she's his little sister. Can you believe that?" Finn leaned back and shook his head. "Not cool, dude. You don't date your friend's sisters. I'd be pissed if Jeff tried to date Addie."

"Like I said"—Addie met my eyes in the rearview mirror for an instant before looking away—"I can take care of myself."

"Whatever. I'm just saying it's a fast way to ruin a friendship. You don't break the bro-code." Then he flipped on the radio. I couldn't decide if I wanted him to keep arguing with her about all the reasons she shouldn't date Jeff, or if I was just glad the bro-code conversation was over.

I pulled into the gas station parking lot and Finn hopped out. "You guys want anything?"

Addie shook her head and I said, "No, I'm good. Thanks."

I put the car in park and turned in my seat to face her. We were just friends, always had been, always would be . . . but that didn't change the fact that my heart sped up these days every time I was around her.

"So, how is your schedule this year?" Yes, it was lame, but it was still a conversation.

"Okay. I've been doing some training on sports medicine for the girls' soccer team and Coach Carter, just during gym and wherever else I can fit it in." Addie's eyes lit up and the gold flecks in the hazel seemed to glow. "Coach Carter says I'm pretty good at it."

"Sweet." I propped my elbow up on the seat. "You think you might want to do something with sports?"

"Doubt it." She leaned forward and we were suddenly closer than I could handle. I sat back, regretting every inch I was giving up. "But I'd like to do something with medicine. I'm also a nurse's aide this year."

"That's really cool, Addie." I glanced over at the store. Finn was paying at the counter. "I think you'd be great at something like that."

"Yeah?" She grinned. "Why?"

"Because you're smart and kind and . . ." I watched Finn walk to the door. "And pretty."

I heard myself say the words, and I clamped my jaw shut as I saw Addie's mouth drop open. *Seriously? Why did I say that?* I mean, it was obviously true, but still—*idiot.*

"All very important things in medicine." Addie winked and squeezed my arm. "Thank you."

Finn climbed into the car and I tried not to look as uncomfortable as I felt.

"What'd you get?" I put the car in reverse and did my best to avoid looking at Addie as I backed out of the parking space.

"A new concoction—might call it the Finn Supreme." Finn took a sip and smiled. "Sprite, cherry syrup, and vanilla syrup."

"Wow." I nodded, trying to keep from laughing. "High marks for creativity."

"Why do your drinks need names?" Addie looked out the window as she spoke, but in the rearview mirror I could see a small smile playing at the corner of her mouth.

Finn turned around to face her, looking surprised. "Why not?"

My headlights shined on Finn and Addie's yard as I pulled around the corner. The red-brick, two-story house sat on the edge of the cul-de-sac with a white picket fence around the backyard. Mrs. Patrick built little flower boxes under all the windows. The rain had eased a little, and mini-rivers ran down the gutters on the sides of the street.

Addie poked her head into the space between my headrest and the door. "Thanks for the ride." She smiled, then opened her door and got out.

I tried to ignore the bumps on my neck where her breath had warmed my skin. "See you, Addie." I watched her walk into the house.

"You want to play some PS3?" Finn asked.

I rubbed my palm against my right eye. I'd already been out too long and my eyelids were sagging. It was only eight, but definitely past time for bed. My brain was starting to freeze up, like an engine without enough oil. It wouldn't be real sleep, but at least the peaceful nothingness I hung out in before most Dreamers fell asleep would help smooth out my lurching thought-process a bit.

"Nah, need to get home. I've still got a few chores to finish before I can head to bed. Plus I should probably at least start the homework I've been stalling on all week. See you tomorrow," I said as Finn grabbed his backpack and jumped out of the car. It was a lie, of course. I never brought homework home. If I couldn't finish it during school hours, it wasn't getting done. It was hard enough trying to maintain any kind of social life when I felt like crashing by eight p.m. most nights; homework wasn't a priority. Especially now that I knew I probably wouldn't even make it long enough to *apply* to college.

After shutting the door, Finn bent down by the window and I could look him straight in the eye. "See you at the assembly," he said.

"Sure. Later."

As I pulled out, Finn pounded his shoulder with one hand, saluted, and then waved. I returned the weird farewell. He definitely kept things interesting.

The rain continued in a strange circular pattern on the way home: heavy, medium, light, then heavy again. The rhythmic thrumming made it difficult to focus on the road. My mind kept leaving the car. Alone again, I couldn't stop thinking about my future—or lack of one. As Mom would've put it, I was zoned—until I noticed the stop sign and the purple truck that was about to meet the front end of my car.

FOUR

I slammed my foot on the brake so hard my knee felt like it might bend the wrong way. I jerked the wheel to the left to avoid smashing into the little pickup directly in front of me. When my car finally screeched to a stop, I rested my head on the steering wheel for a moment. My breath fogged up the speedometer.

Leaning back, I glanced through the drizzling rain at the purple pickup and blinked. The seat was empty. Maybe it wasn't my fault after all—maybe the truck had broken down and was abandoned here or something. I considered leaving; there wasn't actually an accident, anyway. I didn't hit the truck.

A black motorcycle swerved around us. Correction, there wasn't an accident *yet* ... but if I sat here in the middle of the street for much longer, there would be. I leaned across the passenger seat to get a better look, but I still couldn't see anyone in the truck. When I reached over to put my car in gear, there was a sharp knock on my window.

I glanced up, and there was a girl standing next to my car. Her eyes met mine. They were such a deep blue they reminded me of the evening sky during a storm. Her hands pushed against her hips so hard she seemed to be using them to keep herself from exploding. She obviously wasn't hurt, but she looked extremely angry—and kind of like my mom in that pose. No need to check the clock this time; it was too late and I was too exhausted. I knew that unless I wanted to watch Mom's dreams for the zillionth time, I'd be watching this angry girl's dreams tonight whether I liked it or not.

I sighed, turned off the car, and climbed out. The ends of her long, dark hair curled out from beneath the hood of her jacket and her eyes felt as dangerous as a loaded gun's barrel. Dragging an umbrella out of the back seat, I held it over our heads.

"Hey, umm, that your truck?" I ran my hand through my hair, shaking away some of the water, and tried to charm her with a grin. She looked stunned for a minute, and I thought I might get away with it, but then she clenched her teeth and growled.

"A genius, huh? I half expected a stuntman from the way you were driving, but apparently you're a rocket scientist. Why is a prodigy like you driving a piece of crap like this?"

There was a hint of southern drawl in her voice that threw me off, and it took me a minute to realize she had insulted me *and* my car in under ten seconds. That had to be some kind of record. She kicked my tire with the pointy toe of one black boot.

"Come on. Leave the car out of it. You didn't even get a scratch," I said.

She crossed her arms over her chest. "No, but in your hands I'd consider even this oversized roller skate a lethal weapon."

I had a knack for "maneuvering" people, at least that's what I called it. Kind of like manipulation but not. It wasn't a separate ability, more like a side-effect from spending my nights watching people's expressions while feeling their emotions. It made it pretty easy to read people.

Most of the time, I used it on my mom. If I could tell her mood from her movements, her minute facial expressions, it was much easier to choose a good time to ask for things. One night, when she was feeling particularly guilty for working so much after my dad left, I ended up with a car. Not a great car, but a car. Considering I was only fifteen at the time, I didn't complain.

I tried not to maneuver people too often, but this seemed like an appropriate time. The girl's anger was getting us nowhere. This was a residential road that didn't see much traffic, but one motorcycle had already passed and I didn't want to be sitting in the middle of the intersection, in the rain, when the next car showed up. I opened my free hand, palm up, rolled my shoulders back, and focused on keeping my face calm and honest.

"Listen, I'm sorry—um, what's your name?"

After glaring at me in uncomfortable silence for a full ten seconds, she finally answered.

"Megan."

"Okay, Megan. I'm Parker, and I'm really sorry I ran that stop sign. I had a long day. I'm really tired, and it was totally my fault. I didn't mean to scare you." I kept my voice soft and level to show sincerity, then extended my hand to her, hoping the little hothead would accept my apology.

She seemed slightly mollified, took a deep breath, and glanced back at her pickup again before sticking her small hand into mine. When she finally relaxed and all the little angry lines on her forehead went away, I noticed a bruise and a few scratches near her temple.

"Oh, hey, are you okay?" A wave of guilt swept me and I reached a hand toward her face, but she flinched away from my fingertips. Her body language shifted so fast it nearly made me dizzy.

"No, that's a few days old. I'm fine. Anyway, I've got to go." Megan stumbled back around my car, but stopped when she got to her door. "Pay a little more attention, okay?"

"I will. Are you sure you're all right?" Something in her expression made me uneasy.

With a dismissive wave, she climbed into the truck and was gone before I could even get my car started.

I groaned and hit my head against my headrest a few times. I'd managed to do it again. No matter how I tried to avoid making eye contact with strangers right before going to sleep, it was impossible sometimes. At least Megan seemed fairly normal and about my age, instead of some creepy old man.

I drove down the last three blocks of cookie-cutter houses in a state of paranoid awareness. By the time I pulled into the driveway of our blue-brick split-level, every blink grated on my dry eyes. For a few minutes I sat alone in the cool stillness of our garage. Our house felt like a tomb, or maybe it was just like me—a dark life with a silent death waiting in the wings. Maybe it would be better to embrace it now. Give up and face what was coming on my own terms, by my own choice.

I shook my head and climbed out of the car. No matter how good it sounded, how much easier it seemed than this never-ending fight my life had become, it still wasn't what I wanted. There was so much more out there that I hadn't done yet. I wasn't ready to give up. I was just running out of options.

The kitchen was dark and silent. I could see a white note sitting on the dark green countertop like a small boat in a vast sea, but I didn't even glance at it. I already knew what it would say; I could find the leftovers without a note telling me how. I wasn't that hungry anyway.

Pain stabbed behind my eyes, as if I'd bruised the spot where they connected to my brain. I knew Dad used to get migraines. He always blamed it on fumes from the lab at the university—the hazardous life of a chemistry professor. I wondered if his headaches felt like this.

Sometimes I wondered if he might've been a Watcher too, but since he ditched us a month before I became a

Watcher myself, I'd never know. He probably wasn't, but I wished I'd gotten a chance to talk to him about it. I could always talk to him, about anything. You're supposed to be able to talk to dads about crazy stuff—but they're not supposed to walk out the door and never come back.

Crash, that was my plan. If I hurried, I might be able to catch a couple hours of nothingness before Megan went to bed and I joined her dream. Dr. Brown didn't exactly give me a time frame for this whole sleep deprivation/dying thing, but if I was brutally honest, I knew I didn't have much time left. My body couldn't take this much longer.

The quiet dimness of my room eased the throbbing in my head. The curtains were super heavy and dark gray, so even during the daytime, if you turned off the lights and closed the curtains, it was pretty dark. At night, you couldn't see your hand in front of your face—total blackness.

I collapsed on the bed. Who knew how much longer I could survive this way? It could be a year, but I doubted it— more likely less. Would I have time to explain, or at least say goodbye, to the people I cared about? How would my mom handle it? Or Finn and Addie?

I rolled over on my side and punched my fist into my pillow. I'd find a way to tell them goodbye. I wouldn't leave them wondering, the way Dad had left me.

———

The familiar rippling sensation came as I moved from my own dreamless white void into Megan's dream. A warm awareness slipped over me and I hoped the rest of her dream stayed this calm. Too bad I couldn't thank her for staying up late and giving me a couple hours of this peaceful solitude. I'd probably never see her again, and even if I did, that would be a really creepy thing to thank someone for.

I listened for a long moment to the thrumming inside my head. I used to wonder if it was my actual heartbeat that I heard or just some part of the dream that even the Dreamer wasn't aware of. I decided it must be mine. The Dreamer didn't even know I was here—why would they bother giving me a heartbeat?

Besides, I liked it better this way. It was the only thing I had control of in the dreams. If I breathed quickly or got excited, it would speed up; if I relaxed, the gentle cadence would slow. My heartbeat was my tether to reality.

I braced myself for the sound of her dream to come, waiting for it, but when it hit, I barely noticed.

Birds were chirping in the distance, and there was water sloshing around somewhere.

Smell hit next, sweet and earthy. It reminded me of a wheat field on a warm day. When sight arrived, it didn't disappoint. There were vivid colors everywhere. I sat in a wide pasture at the base of a tall purple mountain. The ground was covered with soft red grass. Nearby, a stream wound down to a wide silver lake. The sun hung high in the sky, but a soft breeze cooled my face and moved my hair.

Her emotions jolted me when they hit. A deep sadness, but it was less disturbing than it should have been—as though it was thinned by water, diluted to make it less painful. Still, I ached with an unexpected emptiness. It echoed my own day-to-day feelings in a strange way. Megan and I had much more in common than I'd have guessed.

Something felt different in her dream, though. Not bad, just different, unlike any other I'd watched. It nagged at the back of my mind, but I couldn't place it.

I turned, and froze when I saw her.

She stood a few feet behind me, wearing a white sundress and standing before an easel. Her left wrist twisted in circles, winding one dark curl tight around her pinky. She studied the canvas before her. She lifted her other hand and I expected her to paint, but instead she chewed on the end of the paintbrush. I had to admit, she might have acted a little psycho but she was also pretty cute.

I wanted to reach out and touch her, but I'd learned a long time ago that physical contact while watching wasn't possible. Whether it was the Dreamer or some other person in the dream, we just passed over each other. I couldn't interact. When I was twelve, the first year I started watching dreams, I must've tried to touch my mom a thousand times, begging her to help me understand what was happening. I'd tried to hold her hand, hug her, hit her, anything to make her see me, make her hear me.

It was probably better that it never worked. Just being here felt like a violation of the Dreamer's privacy—touching them was a line I didn't think I should cross.

I hopped to my feet and walked over to see her painting.

The canvas was blank, not even the slightest dot marred the white sheet before her. It was peaceful in her dream, but she was so focused she looked almost frustrated. She kept shifting her weight back and forth between her bare feet.

Strange. If there was any dream-world built for painting, this was it. And her deep sadness felt almost foreign in this place. Everything around us was so quiet, calm, and beautiful. This wasn't a memory, but it probably wasn't a fantasy either.

I closed my eyes and felt the sun on my face; a feeling of serenity soaked through my skin. What was so different?

In that instant, it hit me. This dream had only one layer.

I didn't think it possible: a single-layer dream. But it was so calm and real. It was like life, but enhanced somehow. Everything felt more vibrant.

But it wasn't just what was happening in her head that was different; it was what was happening in mine. I could feel it in some inexplicable way, a freedom in my thoughts—a flexibility in the way my mind wandered.

Hope seeped through the cracks of my carefully constructed wall. At that moment, Megan could've been Picasso and I still wouldn't have watched her any longer. If there was any dream I could sleep in—the true deep sleep I needed—this would be it.

I walked to a shady spot nearby. Rubbing my hands together to still their shaking, I took a deep breath. I could handle the disappointment if this attempt failed like all the others. It wouldn't hurt me anymore. Forcing my muscles to move, I reclined on the soft red grass, closed my eyes...

And slept.

FIVE

Waking up after a night in Megan's dreams—no, of *actual* sleep and *my own* dreams—was an incredible thing. I tried to hold on to pieces of the experience, the strange images floating through my own fragmented dreams. Finn had been there, and I think Addie and my dad. We were by an ocean. I wanted to tuck every detail away somewhere safe where no one could ever take them from me again.

It'd been so long since my brain had slept that I couldn't remember any of my dreams from before I became a Watcher. Now I knew what I'd been missing. Every part of my body felt rested and alive instead of dragging with the exhaustion I'd become accustomed to. Megan had somehow made it possible.

I lay on my bed, reveling in the refreshed feeling and dreamy oblivion. Sleeping was good. I loved sleep. Best. Thing. Ever.

Stretched out against my dark blue sheets, I didn't want to get up. I didn't want to ever move again. It was nearly impossible to think about doing anything except going back to sleep.

Thud. Thud. Thud.

"Parker!" Mom's shout shattered my happy haze like a bazooka. "Your alarm went off thirty minutes ago. You up yet?"

I bolted out of bed, fully alert for the first time in months—probably years.

"I'm up." A small grin crept across my face. I'd slept through my alarm? How ... *normal*.

Tugging a gray long-sleeved shirt and jeans out of the closet, I was through the door, past my Mom, and into the shower in under a minute. I would be late for school, but the sudden urgency that filled me had nothing to do with that.

It was Megan. I had to find her and make eye contact again. I had to find out if all her dreams were like the one last night.

My brain whirred as it sorted the information: her approximate age, where I'd seen her, what direction she was heading in and why. She didn't seem older than me, but I knew I'd never seen her before. That meant she could be new in town. She was old enough to drive, so chances were fifty/fifty she'd be attending my high school. I *would* find her.

Doubt flooded me as I stepped out of the shower. I forced aside nagging thoughts that maybe it wouldn't be that easy, maybe she was only passing through town. Maybe I'd never see her again. No matter what it took, though, I had to find her.

Why could I sleep in her dream? Could I do it again?

For a moment, the whirring in my mind stopped and my stomach clenched. What was I planning to do? Hunt her down? Force her to make eye contact with me? It felt wrong. But something else inside me spoke, something deep-rooted and instinctual. This was a possible means of survival. It could mean a real life for me.

I had to find out, but I'd need to be careful.

───────

I ran through the front doors of Oakville High School. Fifteen minutes late wasn't too bad. Everything seemed oddly hushed, though. I peered in the classrooms as I jogged down the hall, but they were all empty.

By the time I got to my locker, I wondered if it was some kind of holiday I'd forgotten about. My heart pounded and I racked my brain for what holiday it could possibly be. It was Monday, the first week of October. Why would there be no school?

I closed my locker and turned around, leaning against it to think. A mirror lined the back of the trophy case on the opposite wall, but my reflection looked nothing like me. There was color in my cheeks I hadn't seen in a year or more; my dark hair glistened. I looked almost healthy.

An eruption of laughter floated down the stairs at the end of the hall and I headed toward the sound. Then I smacked myself in the forehead. *Of course! The assembly. I'm a genius.*

All sports assemblies were the same at OHS. Technically this was a football assembly, since soccer season was still a ways off, but I knew that like always, it would somehow turn back to soccer. Soccer was like a religion for Oakville High students. No matter what group you hung with, no matter who your family was, no matter what else happened throughout the school year—we were all unified about soccer.

This actually might work out pretty well, I realized. The entire student body would be there, and it would be easier to find Megan when everyone was in one place.

I pushed open the doors to the auditorium. The smell of dust mixed with a hundred different kinds of cologne, perfume, and deodorant assaulted my senses. It took a moment for my eyes to adjust to the dimness of the room. There were three seniors on stage doing some kind of skit.

I saw Finn motion to me from a few rows up.

"Thanks," I whispered as I took the seat next to him. I glanced around, trying to spot Megan in the crowd. Finn watched me for a minute before raising his eyebrows.

"Who are you looking for?"

"Me? Nobody." I dismissed him with a wave as I craned my neck and squinted, trying to make out the features of a dark-haired girl a few rows behind us. My heart dropped to my feet with a nearly audible thud—it was Penny Charles, not Megan. We'd been partners on an astronomy project in junior high. Penny dreams an awful lot about fishing.

"Yeah, obviously—nobody." Finn laughed and turned

his attention back to the stage. He let out a low whistle. "Wow, check that out."

"Uh-huh," I said without even a glance forward. It had to be one of the many cute girls that Finn was into and I wasn't. In junior high, every girl I'd found interesting ended up having dreams about us getting married—even having kids. I hate watching myself in other people's dreams. No one should have to do that. It's like being possessed and having an out-of-body experience at the same time. What made it worse was my fear that the dreams were a lie—that I'd never live long enough to do either of those things. It was enough to cure me of any attraction I felt for the girls at school.

Yet here I was, pulling a stupid neck muscle trying to spot one at the assembly. And she wasn't even here.

I sighed and slouched back in my chair. The idea that I'd never see Megan again, never feel so rested again, was like a dump truck driving onto my chest and then parking there. Everything felt so tight around me that my vision swam, and it scared me. I needed to chill out. It was just one night, and it had probably been a fluke anyway.

Back to reality, Parker.

The stage was full of bouncing cheerleaders. Their swirling, colorful skirts made my head hurt. Jeff Sparks grinned and walked across the stage as they cheered. Leading the pep assemblies seemed to be Jeff's favorite part of being senior class president. It didn't hurt that it meant he could throw in at least one mention of soccer, whatever sport the pep rally was actually for.

Scattered around the stage, behind Jeff, stood more than

half the jocks at school. I was probably supposed to be up there—Finn, too, for that matter—but he was a slacker and I didn't care enough at the moment.

I watched Jeff, trying to distract myself from the misery that clung to my bones even after I could finally breathe normally again. He was perfectly at home up there in front of the entire school, smiling, his arms spread wide. I thought it was a little over-the-top, but he always said he liked putting on a good show.

"Logandale isn't even going to see our football team coming! The Oakville Boulders are going to pulverize them and head to Regionals!" Jeff nodded and pumped a fist in the air. "Then we can shift our focus to my personal favorite sport: soccer." He winked at the audience. "I have a feeling we'll have our best season yet this spring!"

A cheer rose from the crowd and a couple cheerleaders on stage jumped up and down with their pom-poms. Jeff was certainly entertaining everyone else, but not me. I wanted to go home. I sat forward, rubbing my shaking hands against my thighs to try to still a tremor. I felt better than usual, for sure, but one night of sleep wasn't enough to change my future.

"Now, it wouldn't be fair for me to take all this support and attention for myself. I may be Senior Class President, but our soccer team has *two* captains. And since I have some good soccer news to share, don't you think Parker Chipp should be up here to share it with me?"

Next to me, Finn laughed and elbowed me in the side. I blinked at him for a minute before what Jeff said sank in.

I shrunk down in my seat, hoping no one would see me. I couldn't take being the center of attention. *Please, not right now.*

The chanting started soft and got louder. "Parker! Parker! Parker!" It wasn't until people shoved me from the back that I finally got up, waved at everyone, and sat back down.

"Aww, c'mon, Parker. Don't be shy. Come up here!"

I growled under my breath but then stood and walked up to the stage. I spotted Addie as I went and mouthed the words "Help me." She giggled and rolled her eyes as the cheerleaders rushed down the stairs and pulled me up next to Jeff.

In one last, futile attempt, I threw a quick glance through the crowd for Megan again but couldn't see much. The lights were too bright, too hot—too uncomfortable. Jeff slapped my back and grinned.

He leaned over and spoke quietly in my ear. "Thanks, man. I know you aren't an attention hound, but we gotta get everybody pumped, you know?"

"No problem." I shrugged and stuck my hands in the pockets of my letterman jacket. Jeff turned back to the audience.

"Next Friday, the athletics department is sponsoring a bonfire rally out on Rush Beach. Everyone is invited to come and support our teams. Bring whatever you want to roast on the fire—as long as it isn't the Logandale quarterback. We don't need any extra help to beat them!"

A roar of laughter and applause filled the auditorium. I let out a small laugh too. One of the cheerleaders, Anna Connors, caught my attention with a little wave. I turned to face her, and she winked and beamed at me. Her long blond hair floated around her, hugging her curves. I waved back, trying to suppress a shudder. She was crazy hot, no doubt about it, but I still couldn't look at her without remembering a dream she'd had in junior high about French kissing her cat. I knew it was probably just a random bizarre dream, but it had cured me of any interest immediately. It was one of those unfortunate images that sticks with you.

Jeff took a step forward and continued. "As for the soccer news, I'm here to give you my personal assurance that the soccer season won't end only with my team winning State."

The auditorium quieted down and murmurs circulated.

"The girls' team is going to go all the way too!" Jeff nodded into the silence that followed.

Everyone knew the girls' soccer team struggled. They rarely even made it to Regionals, let alone to State. Like every other student in the auditorium, I watched Jeff, waiting for him to continue. What was he talking about?

"We have a secret weapon this year, and I'm happy to introduce her to you," he announced. "She's new. She's got amazing footwork, and I'm happy to say that even I have a hard time stealing the ball from her." He grinned at the crowd. "I can still do it, of course, but it's not easy."

He paused for dramatic effect. "Oakville's new star soccer player—Mia Greene!" Swinging one arm toward the cluster of people at the back of the stage, Jeff beckoned her forward.

I didn't even turn around to look. If Megan wasn't at the assembly, I wanted to either go home or drive to Logandale High and look around. Then I realized that everyone else was craning their necks to look past me, so I stepped to one side and followed their gazes.

After only a moment's hesitation, the same little brunette I'd nearly killed with my car walked out from behind the football team. She raised one eyebrow at me as she passed and took her place beside Jeff.

Megan—no, *Mia*—dreams of not painting.

Why had she told me her name was Megan? Then again, *random teenage boy who apparently looks like he's on drugs almost hits you with his car* ... I guessed I could see the reasoning.

I gave my head a quick shake. Who cared why? My heart almost burst from my chest. She went to my school! I tried to wipe the grin from my face, but it didn't work and I didn't care.

It wasn't until she was standing at the front of the stage that I noticed the clenched fists behind her back, and that in spite of the small smile on her face, she looked angry. I grimaced. Apparently she hadn't gotten over the near-accident yet.

Jeff moved to block Mia from my view and raised his eyebrows at me for a second. I realized I was staring with my mouth hanging partially open. I shut it with a click, and he gestured for me to come closer. Once I got to his side, he turned back to the crowd, throwing one arm around me and the other around Mia.

"This year, Boulders, we are unstoppable! Our football team will beat Logandale! Then we'll take State in girls' *and* boys' soccer! And we want to see everyone at the rally next Friday!"

The crowd yelled, "Boulders! Boulders! Boulders!" Then the burgundy curtains swung across the front of the stage, cutting us off from the burning lights and the chanting crowd. Jeff dropped his arm from around our shoulders and guided Mia a few steps to the right, smiling and asking what she thought of the assembly. I couldn't make out her response with the chattering of everyone else on the stage, but it didn't matter. My brain was still processing so fast I couldn't have focused on her words much anyway.

I swallowed. She was *here*. My hands stopped shaking and a warm gush of relief flowed through my chest, down my arms, and out through my fingertips. The only person who might be able to keep me alive was here, standing five feet away from me.

SIX

Addie and Finn came up the stairs on the side of the stage and trotted over to me. Finn was carrying his backpack on one shoulder and mine on the other.

"That was more than slightly awesome," he said, low enough that no one else would hear. "You should've seen your face, man. I mean, she's hot, but I didn't think you'd be into that."

Addie's face was neutral, but she was watching me closely. She was the only person I ever had trouble reading. It seemed like she only let me see what she wanted me to see. I wasn't sure why, but it made me nervous.

"Wha—why not?" I glanced over my shoulder and saw Jeff's back. He and Mia were deep in discussion, and she seemed to be getting more upset by the second.

"Well, I don't know..." Finn stared at his feet for a

minute before laughing and shoving me in the shoulder. "You know, because she's a girl, and . . . "

His face showed no sign that it was a joke. In fact, he appeared more uncomfortable than I'd ever seen him. Addie was staring at him now, too, her eyebrows raised so high they almost touched her hair.

"What are you talking about? You don't think I like girls?" I tried to keep my pitch from going skyward, but I wasn't very successful. I saw Jeff freeze and slowly turn in my direction.

"Come on. I didn't think you liked guys—I just didn't really think you liked *anybody* like that, you know?" Finn laughed, but it sounded hollow.

"Yeah, well, I don't. So you got that right," I muttered. Jeff and Mia were heading our way.

Addie stepped toward Mia and waved. "I'm Addie. Did you play soccer at your old school too?"

Mia nodded. "Yeah, I've been playing forever. You play?"

"No. It's never been my sport. I swim." Addie shrugged and started for the stairs. "Nice meeting you!"

The corner of Mia's lips curved up. "You too."

"Addie, come here for a moment please," Coach Carter called just before Addie was out of sight. She pivoted on one foot and jogged over to the coach with a grin that made me wonder why everyone didn't stand around staring at her all the time.

Jeff jolted me out of my gawking by punching me lightly

in the shoulder. "What was that all about, Parker? You've never seen a girl before?" He glanced over at Mia.

"No, I was just surprised. I nearly hit her with my car yesterday."

Finn barked out a coughing laugh and Jeff's brow lowered to match his voice. "You did what?"

"I didn't, though." I looked at Mia, but she seemed to be avoiding eye contact. "But I could've sworn she told me her name was Megan."

Now she did meet my eyes, and I saw a flash of a smile as she said, "Don't worry. It's a common mistake."

"You almost hit her with your car?" The muscle in Jeff's jaw twitched and he stepped between us. His response bothered me. Did he actually think he owned every girl in school?

"It was an accident. Besides, why do you even care?"

Jeff's eyes narrowed. "Because she's my sister."

"Duh-Duh-Dum." Finn put one hand up in front of him like he was holding a microphone and leaned forward with a grin. "That's it for today, folks. Tune in tomorrow for the next episode of *Days of Our Lives*."

Confused, I gave my head a little shake. "She's your what?"

Finn grunted and turned away, muttering, "Always wasting my best stuff."

"My foster sister. She's staying with my family."

That made sense. Jeff was an only child, and I knew the Sparks had done the foster thing before. But I was pretty sure the kids were usually much younger.

"Oh," I said, trying to glimpse Mia behind Jeff again. "Well, like I said, it was an accident, and she's fine. So, no big deal."

"It really was nothing." Mia stepped up beside Jeff, and I tried to look friendly when she glanced at me.

"Okay, cool." Jeff shrugged, then slapped my shoulder. "Why don't you set up a couple of chairs for the meeting, Parker?"

"Oh, right. The meeting." I pointed back toward the curtains. "Why don't we just have it down in the auditorium?"

"I want to get started right away. The faculty has only given us half an hour before we have to get to class, but it will take a while for them to empty the auditorium out. It might buy us a little extra time." He pointed to the stacks of chairs lined up off to one side. "We'll just have it up here on the stage. Keep it short and sweet."

"Right. Got it." I turned and grabbed some chairs, noticing that Mia was now talking to Addie and Coach Carter. *Of course*—this meeting was for both soccer teams. Despite having had a great night of sleep last night, my brain sure didn't seem to be keeping up this morning.

Finn took off his coat and threw it at to the back wall. His shirt said, *Come to the dark side. We have cookies.* I smiled as he grabbed a stack of chairs and started setting them out in a row behind mine. "You see who just walked in?"

I turned to the stairs Finn indicated. Thor, a monster fullback from the soccer team, was standing on the top step, nodding while Jeff spoke. I'd intentionally avoided Thor's dreams.

From the way he behaved, I was pretty sure they involved cutting people into bite-sized pieces.

"Perfect." I watched Thor's massive shoulders as he followed Jeff across the front of the stage. "Tell me why he picked soccer again?"

Finn frowned. "I'm amazed they let him on the team, after his stunt last year."

"No kidding." I shook my head and grabbed another stack of chairs. "Apparently when you're huge and fast, it doesn't matter if you break your teammate's leg your first time on the field."

"Good thing Jeff volunteered to teach him the rules." Finn pulled another chair off his stack and set it down a little harder than he intended. "He really wasn't getting the whole non-contact-sport part."

Thor's baseline emotional state seemed to be pure fury. It had really bothered me at first, especially since at his monstrous 6'5", he was six inches taller than me and built like a brick wall. But I'd gotten used to it. From his attitude and the dark pit stains on his shirt, I guessed God had given him a serious overdose in the testosterone department.

Addie walked up with Mia as Finn slammed another chair down. "Easy there. The chairs don't work as well when you break them in half."

Finn jerked his head toward Thor's back. "We're taking bets on whose leg he'll break this year. You in?"

Addie laughed, but then crossed her arms over her chest. "You wouldn't think it was so funny if it turned out to be you." She shook her head and lowered her voice. "Liv Campbell was crying in the girl's bathroom the other day—I swear I heard her say his name."

"What do you mean?" Finn turned to face her. "Why would she be upset about Thor?"

"Maybe he scared her?" Addie shrugged. "I didn't hear much, but she was really upset."

"See what I mean? Girls make no sense." Finn shook his head. "Liv is hot, but if she's interested in Thor, she deserves a special kind of padded room."

I saw Mia flinch, but then she laughed it off. "And you're an expert?"

"Yes." Finn looked at her for a second and then tilted his head to one side. "Aren't you?"

Mia smiled. "Do either of you even talk to him, or do you just hate him because he's bigger than you?"

I leaned over to grab another stack of chairs. "Because he's bigger than us. Besides, talking to him would require him to learn English."

Finn stood with his legs spread wide and an exaggerated look of anger plastered on his face. "Thor no need English. Thor God of Thunder!" He beat his chest with his fists.

As if on cue, thunder rumbled outside. The walls shook and both girls laughed.

I raised my eyebrows and pulled the last chair off the stack. "Nice."

"Thank you very much." He bowed with a grin. "I'll be here all week."

Mia took a seat and I sat down beside her. Addie stood in front of us with a surprised expression, then sat down on the other side of Mia.

"So, where did you live before this?" I asked.

Mia looked at the floor for a few seconds, her face hard to read. "Somewhere else."

I laughed. "At least you didn't lie this time."

Finn leaned down and whispered, "She's a foster kid, dude. Maybe she doesn't want to talk about where she came from."

I winced and nodded—total idiot.

Lowering my voice, I tried to sound casual. "Will you tell me why you told me your name was Megan, then?"

She pursed her lips, then they curved up. "I don't know. Stranger danger?"

"Fair enough." I leaned in. "But you're sticking with Mia? Because any more names might confuse me."

She shrugged. "For now."

Jeff walked to the front of the stage and motioned for everyone to quiet down. Members of both soccer teams started finding seats.

Finn flopped down on my other side and leaned across Mia and me to talk to Addie. "Please tell me you didn't join the soccer team, because I think that's the only thing that could make it any worse."

Addie raised her nose a little and ignored him, but Mia responded with a sweet smile. "Coach Carter asked her to stay for the meeting. She's helping with practices. Apparently she learned some awesome stretches to help us warm up and cool down. I really hope she doesn't teach any of them to the boys' team, though. You guys deserve a little pain."

Finn's eyes widened and he put his hands over his heart and groaned. Mia and I snickered just before Jeff started talking.

"Thanks for coming to this pre-season meeting on such short notice. I promise we won't keep you long. Just have to do a quick poll and discuss some schedule issues." Jeff smiled and glanced at the coaches, who nodded before he continued. "After a little begging, I convinced the coaches to let me lead some extra practices this year, before regular practice starts. This is my last year. The last year for all the seniors. And we should work even harder to make it our best year yet. Anyone have any thoughts or objections?"

The group was silent. I was watching Jeff's shoes and try-ing really hard not to tune him out. Finn elbowed me in the side and I glanced up to see everyone's eyes on me. I blinked, and then remembered I was co-captain.

"What do you think, Parker?" one of the midfielders asked from the other side of the room.

"I think Jeff's right," I said. "The state finals last year were tough. I'd like to feel more prepared going into it this year."

Several heads nodded and everyone turned back to Jeff. He smiled. "I'd like to start with one joint practice with the girls' team." A couple guys groaned, but he continued. "Teaching the girls some of the drills we run will only help us get them down better."

A couple of the girls crossed their arms over their chests and frowned. I sat forward, wanting to end any argument before it started. "Hey, the girls' basketball team always kicks butt, and they could give a ton of pointers to the boys' team if they wanted to. This isn't about gender; it's about a team that works and a team that struggles. Maybe we can help each other."

A few girls nodded, looking somewhat appeased. Everyone turned back and waited for Jeff to continue. He met my eyes for a second or two in the silence before he went on. I forced myself not to look away until he did, even though my instincts made me want to. It wasn't even lunch yet. I had plenty of time to make eye contact with Mia after the meeting. I wouldn't be stuck with Jeff tonight.

"Great. The joint practice will replace the individual practice we had tentatively scheduled for today after school. I want to see all of you there."

Jeff walked to a chair by Thor and took a seat as Coach Mahoney and Coach Carter stood up and started talking about new strategies and what they wanted us to focus on during Jeff's practices. Coach Mahoney wrapped things up by saying, "Coach Carter and I will attend the joint practice today. After that, your team captains will be organizing and leading the individual team pre-season practices. Any questions?"

He was already backing toward the stairs. He only waited a moment, then gave a quick nod and said, "Dismissed."

I stood and walked over to Jeff. He looked fine, but I

noticed the little things, like the way he kept stuffing his hands into his pockets and then pulling them out again. He was frustrated and I couldn't blame him—this was new territory, being forced to share leadership of the team. He didn't like that the guys had asked what I thought.

"Sorry about that," I said. "I think your plan's great. Guess the team just wanted to make sure we agreed."

Jeff's smile was tight, but he shrugged. "You're the co-captain." Then he turned to face a couple other guys from the team.

I went down the stairs leading off the stage and crossed to the auditorium exit. Mia and Addie were already there, watching the crowd make their way through the halls. I stood one step behind them, suddenly unsure of what to say.

Addie glanced back at me, then at Mia. She opened her mouth to say something, then clicked it shut again. I barely heard her muffled voice as she walked away. "See you guys later."

I watched her back until she disappeared behind some tall guy in a leather jacket. I couldn't help wishing again, for just a second, I could read her like I could most people.

"I'm happy to see you're less dangerous at school than behind the wheel of a car." Mia's voice was soft, a hint of humor behind it.

I stepped forward to stand beside her. "Yeah, it's harder to live on the edge here, but I try my best. I run with scissors constantly, and I gave myself a wicked paper cut this morning."

"Keep this up and you might seem fairly normal." She glanced at me and I felt a momentary rush when her eyes met mine. Then she smiled and shook her head. "I better go. See you around."

I grinned as she walked away.

"Hey, dude." Finn came up behind me. "I'm not your bellhop. Take your bag." I spun around, met Finn's gaze, and cursed under my breath. Then I remembered the soccer practice after school. I'd get another chance to see Mia at practice. If her dream last night wasn't just a freak thing, I had to find out—and the sooner the better.

"Please let me take it again," I pleaded.

Mr. Nelson frowned and I tried not to remember his dream. Watching that shiny bald head make out with my mom was not an image I liked to dwell on. "Sorry, Parker. You just need to try to do better next time."

"I can't have another failed test in this class." Mom might not have cared much when my A fell to a B, but she'd definitely notice a D.

"There's a physics tutoring group that meets in the library after school. You should join it."

I sighed. "Okay … thanks." I scrambled for some last way to convince him, and tried not to hurl when my mind came up with the obvious answer. Oh well. If I wanted to keep Mom off my back, sacrifices had to be made.

I walked halfway to the classroom door before pausing to rub my knuckles along the edge of a nearby desk. It was almost slick, worn smooth by years of use. "You know, my mom mentioned you the other day," I said, turning. Mom was going to kill me—they'd only been on one date and I knew, from experience, that the only man she ever dreamed about, even all these years later, was Dad.

Mr. Nelson whipped his head up so fast that the glare from the fluorescent lights bouncing off it was nearly blinding. "She did?"

"Yeah. Just that you were funny on your date."

"Really?" His eyes widened before he caught himself. "I mean, yeah. We had fun, but she was always so busy after that. I thought..."

"Oh yeah, her job keeps her really busy. Plus, when she has to spend time worrying about me and my grades, that's hard on her too." I shrugged and took a few more steps toward the door. "But I'm sure she'll have time again next summer or something."

Mr. Nelson's eyes narrowed. He wasn't an idiot, but he was also desperate. "Ever heard of abuse of power, Parker?"

I stopped and held my hands out, palms up, focusing on the emotion I wanted to convey—honest, innocent. "I'm not making any promises and I have no power, but what I'm saying about her being busy is true. And besides, what does it hurt to let me take the test again? It's not like I'm cheating or bribing you for a grade."

Mr. Nelson nodded slowly and closed the book in front

of him with a snap. "Tomorrow, during your study period. This is your last chance."

"Thank you. I really appreciate it." I smiled widely and hurried toward the door before he could change his mind.

Just before I got there, he muttered, "Improve your grades, kid, and you could be a freakin' politician."

SEVEN

Thor was right behind me on my way out to practice. Like *right behind*, so close he felt like a shadow. I slowed down for a minute to walk beside him, but when he glared at me with his little black eyes I decided it probably wasn't worth the effort. I jogged the rest of the way to the field.

"That's fun. You got to hang with Thor," Finn said with a chuckle when I stopped beside him and Thor ran past us to the bag of soccer balls near the goalpost. "You guys do anything new, or did he follow the routine and act like he wanted to put you in a blender?"

"Pretty much the usual. Though this time he mixed things up a bit and hinted about a pitch fork and a set of steak knives."

Finn laughed. "No actual threats this time?"

"No actual conversation."

"Sounds about right." Finn nodded as he adjusted his shin guard.

I took a deep breath and relaxed my muscles. Soccer was my primary escape. On the field, I could be normal. Adrenaline kicked in and kept me awake. Muscle memory made everything fluid and easy. It didn't feel like my mind and body were at war when I played. I didn't have to think.

We were the first ones on the field, but most of the girls' team was heading out the doors toward us. I strained to find Mia and spotted her coming out last. All the other girls were talking and laughing, but Mia was alone—until Addie jogged over from the side of the field and walked with her.

Great. Just what I needed—them to become best friends.

Within a few minutes everyone was on the field, and they were all looking at me. I groaned. Jeff seemed to be late to everything. The coaches weren't even on time.

"Okay, let's start with some laps: three around the field, and then five sprints from goal to goal."

Everyone started running and I caught up with Mia near the front of the group. "Did I hear right that they appointed you team captain ... as a sophomore? Did you come from some kind of top-secret Olympic training school?"

"Probably." She laughed and then grimaced. "But I think it had more to do with Jeff coming in and telling them to make me captain. I wish he wouldn't do that." A couple of girls from the team last year pushed past Mia and she stumbled into me. Before I could even try to help, she caught her balance and kept going, her chin high and her jaw clenched. "He's really not doing me any favors."

"Yeah, I can see that." We ran another lap in silence before I couldn't stop myself from asking, "So, what was the name of this Olympic training school? I feel like I should check it out."

She smiled but kept her eyes on the ground and didn't respond.

"Sorry if I'm getting too personal. I'm just curious—"

"No worries." Mia sprinted away before I could finish my sentence. I cursed under my breath. The last thing I wanted was to scare her off. Not before I could learn what I needed to know about her: why her dreams were so unique, if she had any odd pre-bedtime rituals I should know about. Admittedly awkward questions, but it didn't matter. She wouldn't even give up what high school she used to go to. The girl was a vault.

By the time everyone finished running sprints, the coaches and Jeff had shown up. Jeff paired each of our starters with two girls and had them run drills while we gave them tips and feedback. He put me with two sophomores I vaguely remembered from junior high, Kim and Christina.

They both had played in city leagues for fun but never competitively. I taught them a few of my best trapping tricks and then had them try to pass the ball back and forth as they dribbled past me without my stealing it. They got it past me the first two times until I learned their moves; then I took it three in a row.

"All right, I give." Kim sat on the ground next to the ball and glared at me. "How do you always know when we're going to pass it? It's like you're a mind reader."

I stopped in front of her and extended a hand. "Easy. I'll teach you."

She looked skeptical, but she grabbed on and I helped her to her feet.

"Now watch. Christina, try to get it past me."

Christina approached and dribbled the ball back and forth. I watched her movements and followed with my body, letting my muscles take over.

"You watch her feet, but it isn't her feet that will tell you where she's going."

Christina moved left but, at the last moment, dodged right and sent the ball directly into my extended foot. She shook her head as the ball bounced back behind her.

"It's her eyes." I turned back to Kim, but realized both teams had gathered around and were listening to me. I closed my mouth and looked at Coach Mahoney to see what we were doing next.

"What's her eyes?" Kim asked. Both coaches nodded for me to continue.

"Well, she won't make a move blind. If you watch her eyes, you can see where she's probably heading." I turned back to Christina and gestured for her to come at me again. "This time watch the upper body."

She moved toward me and feinted to the opposite side this time. Again, I stopped the ball and sent it flying back behind her. "See how she tilts just before she shifts? If her upper body and her eyes say she's going right ... well, then she's going right."

Everyone was silent as I went after the ball I'd just sent

toward the bleachers. Then I heard Coach Mahoney yell, "Pair up. Practice anticipating your partner's moves."

Just before I got to the ball, Addie scooped it up and handed it to me. "That was pretty good. You almost sound like you know what you're doing."

I smiled. "I almost *do* know what I'm doing." Glancing out at the field, I saw Mia running drills with Jeff on the far side. She was really good, but so was he. Neither of them seemed able to get it past the other. I turned back to Addie, but she'd already walked away.

I worked with Christina and Kim for the next thirty minutes, and by the end they were taking the ball from me as easily as I'd been taking it from them. The girls' team was much better than I'd expected; they just needed to figure out how to work together. And a few new tips didn't seem to hurt. Mia was definitely the best they had, though. If anyone could gain the respect of the team, she could, although the way Jeff forced her in as captain wasn't going to make that easy.

After another thirty minutes of drills, Addie showed us a few good stretches and the coaches sent us off to the locker room.

"You really think they can do it?" Addie asked, coming up beside me. Finn joined us on my other side.

"Do what?" I watched Mia's brown head bobbing a few feet ahead of me and knew I had to catch up with her somehow.

"Do you think the girls can win this year?"

"Sure, why not?"

"If you can get Jeff to schedule a few more of these joint

practices, they might stand a chance." Addie looked at me and smiled.

I shrugged. "Meet you guys inside."

Sprinting through the school doors, I took a quick sip from the water fountain and looked up just in time to catch Mia's eye on her way into the locker room. My timing was perfect. She smiled and then she was gone.

I couldn't help the huge grin that spread across my face as I slid on my sunglasses. Finn and Addie stood back near the doors waiting for the crowd to clear. I took another sip from the fountain before turning back to face them. I'd done it. All I had to do was make it home without making eye contact with anyone else, and I'd see if Mia's dreams were the same tonight. See if she could really be the answer I'd hoped she was.

"Stop it," Finn said as he passed me. "You look goofy."

Addie's smile fell from her face and she fought against the current of soccer players to get back out the door. I could barely make out her voice as she muttered something about waiting at the car.

———

The moment I entered her dream, I felt peace. For the first time in years, I let the hope of a different life make me feel better instead of dreading the disappointment it inevitably brought with it.

This one wasn't quiet, like her first dream. I could hear waves crashing violently, but it still soothed me. The water rolled over my frayed nerves and the knots in my back. The air tasted like the ocean, salty and wet.

My eyes opened on an angry sky above a cliff. The churning ocean was far below. Across the bay perched a beautiful white lighthouse. The small windows were framed in navy and the light cut through the fog like a scalpel.

My sense of touch came to life and I felt the stone beneath my feet settle into place. Even though the scene was entirely different from her previous dream, it still only had one layer. Everything felt so real without all the other layers creating chaos in the background. It was so similar to reality that I was almost certain I'd be able to sleep again.

Then the diluted sadness flowed through me.

I turned, searching for Mia. She stood behind me, again wearing the same white sundress. It whipped violently around her legs in the wind. It was a different setting, but everything else was the same. Strange … everything about her dreams seemed to break the rules I'd learned.

An easel, identical to the one in her previous dream, stood before her. She squinted at the lighthouse and bit her lip, then picked up a paintbrush and stuck the end in her mouth with a sigh. I moved to see the painting—again, blank. She stood motionless.

Her expression held so much frustration, it was almost painful to watch her. For a moment, I wished she could see me so I could ask her what was bothering her, but it was a dream. Her irritation and sadness probably weren't even based on an actual life problem. Besides, I knew why I was here, and I needed to know for sure if it would work again.

I looked around for a place to sleep. Excitement flowed through me, washing bits of Mia's gloom away. The most likely spot was near a rocky overhang where dark green vines covered the ground. They curled and twisted in around themselves, hiding from the rough weather. I felt them experimentally with my feet. They were soft, with no needles or thorns. I reclined on the vines, the overhang shielding me perfectly from the wind.

The sight of Mia, frowning at her painting, was the last thing I saw before exhaustion crashed over me like one of the rough waves far below, and I tumbled into the deep sleep I longed for.

EIGHT

After two nights of Mia's dreams, I felt fantastic, better than I remembered feeling ever. Her dreams could be the best thing that had ever happened to me. I was beginning to believe I might even be able to survive this curse with her help. Seeing her, making eye contact, her dreams…it was all I could think about. And now that I'd passed my re-take of Mr. Nelson's exam, it was all I had to think about.

I leaned against my car, the chill from the cool metal sinking through my shirt and into my skin. I thought about throwing on my jacket, but I liked being a little cold. I liked feeling so alive.

Occasionally I waved at one of the people passing me, but my attention was on the door to the school. I hadn't seen Mia all day, but she had to come out this way. I wouldn't miss her. At least I hoped I wouldn't. But already the parking lot was nearly empty. Some guy with a black leather jacket was standing at the bottom of the stairs into school, blocking my view. Lately, that dude always seemed to be in my way. Our school wasn't that big, and I knew most people by sight if not by name. So why didn't I recognize him? My hands shook and I moved a step to the left so I could see around him. Could I have missed Mia because of him?

I jumped when Addie grabbed my elbow, nearly breaking her nose.

"Watch it, Parker! Geez!"

"Oh, I'm sorry, Addie." I shifted my position so I could see her and the stairs at the same time. Reaching out, I put my hand on her shoulder until she looked at me. "Are you okay? Did I hurt you?"

She shook her head and rubbed the pointy tip of her nose that was already red in the cold air. "What are you doing?"

"What do you mean?" I dropped my arm back to my side and glanced over her shoulder at the stairs again.

"You've been staring at those doors since I came out. I called your name three times. What's going on?"

"Nothing." I shrugged and returned my eyes to the stairs.

She shuffled her feet and took a step away. "Who is it?"

"What?"

"Who are you looking for?"

I tried to find an easy explanation. "Jeff."

"Oh." I was relieved that her voice sounded more normal when she spoke. "He took Mia and left before last period. She had some counseling thing or something."

I couldn't stop my head from whipping around to her. "Is she in one of your classes?"

She bit her lip for a moment before speaking. "Oh ... it's Mia."

"What?" I shook my head, confused.

Finn walked up and leaned against the car. "What's Mia?" He pulled a Dr. Pepper out of his backpack and popped it open as he turned to me. "And why does she keep coming up?"

I ignored him and opened my car door.

"Parker likes her," Addie said softly. Her face was unreadable, like always.

Finn took a big gulp of his drink, then grinned. "Yeah? Is this the part where we sing Parker and Mia sitting in a tree?"

I shook my head, uncomfortable with the turn in the conversation. "See you guys tomorrow."

"Later," Finn managed to say around a mouthful of Dr. Pepper. Addie waved without looking directly at me and turned away.

Sliding into my ragged leather seat, I saw Addie hit Finn's shoulder as they walked toward the front of the school. I was glad she had swim team practice and Finn tutored in the library today. My mind was reeling from the last forty-eight hours and I needed some time to process—alone.

I'd already missed my chance for true sleep tonight. Realistically, Mia's dreams shouldn't be the same every night, but so far there seemed to be a pattern at least. It was far from a sure thing, but I had to admit it was possible ... her dreams might be able to save me.

Dread and fear of my future had been everything in my

life. Everything I said, did—even thought—was tainted by it. For years now, I'd been fading and doing it on my own.

Now everything was different. Maybe there could be an answer. Maybe Mia was the only way. A kind of manic hope and need was filling the emptiness in me. I tried to ignore the undercurrent of fear that still ran strong beneath it all.

It didn't matter. Nothing mattered now but the possibility of a different future.

———————

The woman at the checkout counter had pale green eyes. As with grass in wintertime, something had sucked the vibrancy away. They were sad even as she nodded and told me to have a nice day. Her nametag said *Agnes*, and she'd decorated it with stickers of small blue flowers. I hadn't meant to look her in the eye, but did it really matter whose dreams I watched anymore? If they weren't Mia's, then they were still bad news for me no matter who the dreamer was. I frowned as I loaded the groceries Mom asked me to pick up into the back of my car.

From the moment the dream started, I could feel them. Now that I knew what it felt like with the layers gone, they were more tangible than ever before. Like everyone but Mia, Agnes kept me locked in her dreams and away from my own.

I hated her and her stupid Pine-Sol-scented dream. Forcing down the urge to bash my head, or even her head, against the floor until I broke through the layers that kept me awake, I dug my fists into my thighs until I felt the anger dim. It wasn't her fault. None of this was her fault.

The sound of children's voices echoed down the hall. A game show was on the TV, but Agnes never turned to watch it. She kept dusting the same tables over and over, even though the room was spotless.

The detail was as clear as a memory but there were few items that overlapped. The same stack of coasters filled five separate places on the oak end-table. The game show had different contestants every time I looked at it but each was equally vivid. It was like several memories overlapping each other.

The front door opened and a thick man in a shirt and tie came into the living room. The emotion coming from Agnes shifted so fast I felt dizzy. Pure fear filled my body from my toes to my eyebrows, and I regretted the single violent thought I'd had against her. The sounds of the children down the hall silenced and I heard a door shut.

"Hi, dear." Agnes hid the feather duster behind her back. From my position, I could see the feathers twitching as her hands trembled.

He grunted and plopped into the recliner closest to the TV.

Agnes handed him the remote and put the feather duster in the closet. Within seconds she was back with a beer from the fridge.

He grabbed it and nodded without even a glance in her direction. "What's for dinner?"

"Meatloaf," she answered, backing toward the kitchen. "It will be ready in a few minutes."

Her fear was still there but she seemed to be feeling more

confident. I slumped onto the carpet and leaned against the wood paneling on the wall. She might feel better but I didn't. There was no question that he'd hit her before; it was impossible to miss the signs.

Agnes set the table and called for the kids to come to the kitchen. Two blond children came down the hall. The little boy was quieter than any child I'd ever seen. He couldn't have been more than five years old. His sister was maybe a year or two older, and she kept moving back and forth in front of her brother. It took me a moment to realize she was placing herself between her brother and her dad.

The kids sat at the table and Agnes brought a plate to her husband in his recliner. The family ate in silence. Everyone at the table stared at their plates. Agnes reached over to refill the milk in her son's cup. He lifted it but lost his grip. The glass fell to the table as if in slow motion.

Panic shot through the room like a lightning bolt. The little girl was back from the kitchen with a towel before I could blink. The boy stared in horror at the glass, but he didn't make a sound as his eyes brimmed with tears.

Agnes hurried to clean it up, but the moment her husband glanced back at her, she sent the kids to their room. I could hear their soft sniffles coming down the hallway as she continued to wipe up the mess with shaking fingers.

"I'm sorry, Ray."

He sighed and pushed pause on his DVR remote. When he stood, I stepped in his way. I didn't want to see this. *Please, no more.*

But he was an aspect of the dream, and I was just a

Watcher. He walked right through me and I felt nothing. I knelt on the floor, helpless, wishing I'd met the eyes of anyone but this poor woman.

"All I ask is that things be clean." His voice rumbled low and her fear spiked as she backed away from him. He grabbed her shoulder and shoved her against the wall. I watched her shrink to the floor. My arm exploded with her pain, but I didn't move or flinch. She didn't cry out, I would be strong with her, for her… even if she didn't know I was there.

"I know. It was an accident. I'm so sorry."

He reached under her chin, grabbed her throat, and lifted her to her feet. "Don't you want me to be happy?"

She nodded, gasping for air, and he threw her back to the ground. Everything ached. We gasped in air in unison, and I felt the will to fight seep out of my body, the same way it had fled from Agnes.

"Don't do it again." He walked back to his recliner and pushed play on the remote.

Agnes whispered, "I won't." Wiping tears from her cheeks, she got unsteadily to her feet. There was a cut on the top of her ear that was bleeding, and I could see the red outline of her husband's hand against her throat. She pulled her thin brown hair out of its bun with shaking fingers and tried to arrange it to hide her neck and ear. Carefully lifting the plates, she headed down the hall to her kids' bedroom.

As the dream faded into one of Agnes at work, I clenched my hands against my forehead. This was too hard. People had dark, disturbing secrets and every time I invaded their minds it dimmed a little piece of me. I could feel the darkness from other people's nightmares squirming into my brain. How long before it changed who I was—my idea of what was normal?

Or had it already?

———

I woke with my whole body covered in a cold sweat, and it only went downhill from there. I couldn't even think about food without wanting to throw up, and I couldn't stop shivering. It felt nothing like any flu I'd ever had.

The early morning rain fell in misty droplets on my car window as I watched the shadows outside the grocery store shift around in unnatural ways. I could almost see things moving in them, moving through them—things that I knew couldn't be real. I shivered as the well-lit interior of the store called to me. Hopefully the shadows couldn't follow me there, but what I planned to do inside wasn't any less scary.

My hands shook so hard I folded my arms and clamped my elbows down on them to make it stop. Sleeping in Mia's dreams seemed to ease the tremors, but now, after just one night without her, they were back full force. I didn't want to think about what it might be like if I missed her again today . . . or if her dreams were different tonight.

The store was nearly empty at this hour. I still had twenty minutes here before I had to head to school. Swallowing hard, I tapped on Agnes's shoulder. She whirled around to face me, her shocked face turning to a sympathetic smile when she saw me.

Agnes—dreams of being broken.

"Oh, dear, you don't look like you feel well. Can I help you find the pharmacy?"

Ever since I woke up, I'd been thinking about how to approach her. I couldn't help Mr. Flint's wife—she was already dead—but Agnes wasn't. I was done being helpless, done putting up with my curse holding me in this living nightmare against my will.

This time I would *do* something.

My jaw clenched so tight I couldn't speak. The paper in my hand was interfering. *I* was interfering in the most private parts of her life. My hand shook as I handed Agnes the list of shelters and women's rescues that I'd printed out the moment I'd gotten out of bed.

"It's a list of places that can help you."

Confusion crossed her features as she took my paper and glanced down at it. Within seconds she placed one hand to her mouth and started shaking her head.

"Agnes, they'll keep you safe," I whispered. I dropped my hands to my sides.

"I don't know what you're talking about," she muttered, her voice low. When she lifted her gaze to mine I could see pain and humiliation in her eyes. "Who are you?"

I shook my head, not knowing what else to say. Agnes pushed the paper against my chest and tried to turn away. I stretched my hand out to touch her shoulder, but she flinched and I stopped. This was exactly what I was afraid of. How could I help her? I couldn't even explain how I knew.

Stepping around to the counter in front of her, I laid my paper on her checkout stand.

"In case you change your mind." Then I turned and walked out of the store into the drizzling rain.

Once I got to the car, I kicked the tire. I rested my forehead against the cold, wet metal of the door and tried to push aside another intense wave of nausea. Why did this curse give me people's secrets without any way to deal with them?

I didn't understand it, but it seemed like getting real sleep through Mia's dreams was now creating a rebound effect that made me go downhill faster than before. If so, I needed to watch Mia's dreams as much as possible before it got any worse.

I climbed in the car and started the engine. As I was pulling out of the parking lot, I saw Agnes in the alley beside the store. She leaned against the brick building, wet and sobbing, clutching my paper to her chest.

At least I knew she kept it.

NINE

"It's for soccer, Mrs. Cooper." I smiled, keeping eye contact while telling a flat-out lie. "I wanted to talk to Mia about the upcoming season."

After Agnes, lying was not an issue if it meant avoiding another horrible dream like that. No more. I couldn't live that way, not when I knew there was a solution.

Last month, Mr. Nelson had let me make up an assignment by helping Mrs. Cooper, one of the secretaries, sort registration paperwork after school. She dreamed of school soccer games; a die-hard fan.

She bobbed her brunette head for a moment, the tight bun at the back bouncing with the motion, but she seemed confused. "And why can't you ask Ms. Greene herself for her schedule?"

"That's the whole problem. I can't seem to find her. If I knew her schedule, then I could at least track her down."

I glanced again at the clock, hoping I could convince Mrs. Cooper before Mia went to her next class. The smell of toner and paper permeated the office; my stomach was already churning with anxiety, and the smell made it worse. For now I was the only student in the room, but in just a few minutes the bell would ring and it would be packed.

"Yes, well—hmm ... " The school secretary turned her attention to her light blue sweater and tugged on a fuzzball clinging to the front. I needed to switch tactics.

"I understand." I raised my hands and took a step back from her desk in surrender. "I mean, there are probably privacy issues or something. I just wanted to talk to her about coordinating another joint practice. It'd be amazing if we could help each other. You know, take State with both teams this year."

Mrs. Cooper's eyes glazed over for a moment. I knew her weakness. No school in our state had won both the girls' *and* boys' title in over thirty years.

"I'll see if I can find her on my own." I shrugged and pulled my backpack over my shoulders. "Have a good day, Mrs. Cooper."

"Well ... " She cleared her throat and turned back to her keyboard. "I suppose if it's for the good of school sports."

The paper coming through the printer seemed to call to me. Everything else froze while it inched its way out. Finally, grabbing the sheet, she handed it to me with a sly grin. "Go Boulders."

"Thank you." I moved to the side of the office as other people pushed toward the desk. I'd been so focused on getting the schedule I hadn't even noticed the bell ring, but with how full the halls were, it must have.

I saw that Mia had PE next and then lunch. As much as I wanted to see her, I didn't think going into the girls' locker room was the answer. I would wait. It would only take one glance in her eyes, and then I'd be able to see her dreams again.

I folded the paper carefully and opened my backpack. After shuffling pencils and papers around for a minute, I found a folder and tucked the schedule gently inside. It was a lifeline—the last bottle of water on Earth.

Glancing up, I saw Jeff Sparks looking straight at me. Something in his expression told me he'd witnessed some of my conversation with Mrs. Cooper. I forced myself to meet his eyes in spite of the guilty shiver that ran down my spine. It didn't help that Thor stood behind him, looking as primed to pulverize as ever.

"Hey, man. What's up?"

"What are you doing?" Jeff's tone was casual as he glanced at the folder still poking out of my backpack. He knew *exactly* what I'd done.

"Just checking on some problems with my schedule."

"Hmm, I see." He slouched down and dropped his bag to the floor. Everything about him was so relaxed. I wondered if my guilty mind was playing tricks on me. Maybe he didn't know. "Did you get it figured out?"

"Yeah, I think it'll be fine." I took one step toward the door, but he moved to block my way.

Grabbing my shoulder with one hand, he stepped closer.

Everything casual about his expression disappeared and my muscles tensed in response. "Parker, be careful. I think you might—"

"Parker?" Addie's voice came from behind the office counter. "You're so pale. Are you okay?"

"Yeah, I'm fine." I nodded and tried to look healthy . . . until I realized I didn't know how.

Jeff's grin was instantly painted back on his face. He dropped his hand back to his side and picked up his bag. "Hey, Addie. What are you doing back there?"

She smiled and it made me take an extra breath. "I'm an aide for the nurse this period."

"Oh, that's cool." Jeff's grin widened and he winked. "I guess I know when to come in if I ever need someone to play doctor."

I liked Jeff well enough on the soccer field, but the way he acted around girls sometimes made me want to hurl. The fact that he said it to Addie made me want to hurl *him* through a window.

Addie laughed and rolled her eyes. "Right. Sure. That's gonna happen." She stepped out from behind the desk and stood next to me. Her hand brushed the back of mine for an instant and I tried to keep my breathing even. "Aren't you guys supposed to be in class or something?"

Jeff winked and tossed his arm around her shoulder. "Or something."

Addie glanced at me and this time I had a pretty good idea what she was thinking. I choked back a laugh. Jeff had picked the wrong sophomore girl to underestimate. She grabbed his hand and twirled out from under his arm like a ballerina, then stepped behind the counter before speaking again.

"I'll let Mindy know that you're into playing doctor again. She's an aide in here next period, right?" Addie propped her elbows on the desk, batted her eyelashes in the most ridiculously exaggerated look of innocence I'd ever seen, and then winked at him. "I've heard that sick room should practically have your initials carved on the doorway."

I coughed at the startled look on Jeff's face, but Addie didn't even flinch. Mindy was Jeff's on-again, off-again cheerleader girlfriend, infamous for her outrageous explosions of jealousy. Everyone knew the last time he kissed another girl she'd keyed the driver's side of his car, even though she'd never admitted to it.

Jeff cleared his throat, then tried to laugh it off as the bell rang.

"Um, I should go." I had a free study period and was in no rush, but they didn't know that. Besides, Addie could handle Jeff with both hands tied behind her back and probably put on nail polish at the same time. "See you guys later."

Addie gave me a little wave and I pivoted, walking out the door as Jeff called after me, "Practice tomorrow after school, don't forget!"

When I got to my locker, I reached into the folder and withdrew the paper I'd lied to get. Folding Mia's schedule carefully, I put it in my pocket. Feeling it there reassured me. I'd be able to figure this out. Everything would be all right now.

The mirror lining the back of the trophy case across the hall caught my eye again, but my reflection looked nothing like me. A chill ran through me. The guy I saw, his eyes were cold, calculating... desperate.

After rubbing my palms hard across my face, I glanced back at my reflection. It looked like me again. Just a trick of the light or something. Or maybe meeting Mia was changing me in more ways than I'd thought.

———————

"Mia?"

Her navy eyes met mine and I felt an instant surge of relief. Every lie I'd told in the office that morning was worth it for that one moment. I'd made eye contact. Now if I could just avoid meeting anyone else's eyes for the rest of the day, I'd be home free.

It wasn't even noon yet, though. Maybe I hadn't thought this plan through enough.

"Oh, hey." She looked down and grabbed a tater tot from her tray.

I took a seat across from her at the lunch table, heady from the adrenaline flowing through my veins. No more putting up with the tortured curveballs my curse was throwing at me. It was time for me to take control. Tonight, I would see Mia's dreams.

Glancing at my hands, she stopped short of popping another tot in her mouth.

"Aren't you eating?"

"Oh." My attention shifted to my empty hands and I realized they were shaking again. They still trembled against my legs as I thrust them into the pockets of my loose jeans and glanced over at the lunch line. When was the last time I'd eaten? Lunch yesterday, maybe? Trying to remember made my head hurt. It didn't matter anyway.

"Not really hungry." The words came out as a grunt and it surprised me. I didn't even recognize my own voice.

She raised an eyebrow but said nothing as she continued to eat.

The noises of the cafeteria flowed over us, clanking dishes and people talking. I wanted to kick myself for not planning better. All my focus had been on finding her and making eye contact—I hadn't considered what I'd do next.

"So…" I cleared my throat. "You like playing soccer."

Mia stopped trying to eat and tilted her head to one side. "Wow, you're a regular detective. You figured that out already?"

"Uh, yeah." I forced out a strained chuckle. The awkward silence that followed made my hands sweat as I tried to force my brain to think of anything else to talk about. This shouldn't be so hard. I talked to girls all the time and never had such difficulty. Maybe Mia was different because it was the first time I wanted—no, needed—something from someone in a very long time.

After waiting a few moments, she shook her head lightly and glanced around. Leaning forward, she whispered, "Listen, you seem like a nice guy. But whatever you're on—I'm not interested, and you should stop too. You look wasted."

I blinked, feeling a little stunned as her meaning sank in. "Wait, I'm not—"

Mia stood, and her eyes were sad. She shrugged. "None of my business, I'm just sayin'—rehab." Then she picked up her tray and walked away.

I watched her retreating back for a minute and sighed. Rehab.

I shook my head, wishing it were that simple.

The rest of the afternoon was painful. I was pretty good at making teachers think I was listening without making direct eye contact but I'd never had to do it with Finn before. With teachers, I'd just sit in the back and from across the classroom they couldn't tell if I looked at their eyes or the middle of their foreheads. Plus, I got average grades, so they didn't care much anyway.

Finn, however, was far more observant than I gave him credit for.

I kept rubbing my eyes as an excuse for not looking at him. After he asked me, "What the heck is wrong with your eyes?" for the third time, I finally gave up.

"I think I'm going home sick."

Finn's brow furrowed but he nodded, and I turned toward the parking lot.

I kicked a rock on my way to the car. It reminded me of my life as it bounced along trying to maintain stability— an impossible feat when even the slightest dent in the asphalt would alter its direction and send it crashing toward a new end.

The last thing I wanted was to cause problems with Finn. I knew he would get over it this time, but I needed a better plan than avoiding all eye contact besides Mia's.

———

Two nights of watching Mia's dreams later, my locker door slammed with a clang and Finn grinned at me from the other side. His shirt of the day said, *I'm schizophrenic. And so am I.*

"Hey, man. Feeling a little less bizarre now?"

"What do you mean?" I leaned back, looking around him, scanning the hall for the bazillionth time that day. Mia should've been heading this way now, but there was no sign of her.

"Let's see, you've been acting psycho. You went home sick two days ago. Then yesterday, you just disappeared in the middle of the day, skipped Jeff's practice and left Addie and me stranded here with no ride." Finn raised his eyebrows and moved his head, attempting to block my view of the hall. "No big deal. I mean, the nice truck driver we hitched home with seemed mostly sane—although I was a little concerned when I saw the shovel and all that rope behind the seat."

"Sorry, yeah—feeling better. Thanks," I muttered. I stepped around him, squinting.

Finn's hand pushed me back toward the lockers. Hard. I turned on him. "What was that?"

He sighed and glanced at the people streaming past us through the hall. "Listen to me. You've got to stop."

"Stop what? You're the one slamming me into the wall."

"It's no different than what you're doing to yourself."

"I don't have a clue what you're talking about."

"This whole Mia obsession. You need to lay off."

"What?"

Finn groaned and leaned back against the locker. "You're turning into a lunatic. I'm trying to help. Everyone sees you staring at her, always showing up wherever she goes. She'll never be interested if you don't stop acting like Ted-freaking-Bundy. It's even creeping *me* out."

My fists tightened by my sides. "It's not like that."

"Then what's it like, Parker? What's going on here? You've been acting really weird. And a word to the wise, girls don't like weird. Trust me, I know." He gave me a crooked grin and took a step back.

Anger bubbled inside me. He didn't have a clue what was happening. He'd never understand how painful it was when every cell in your body stopped talking to your brain. How scary it was to be dying and not be able to tell anyone. Why did he think he could tell me what to do?

"You can't understand, all right? So, just leave me alone."

I'd had enough. He didn't take me seriously when I tried to tell him about my curse before; I wasn't about to explain myself again. He needed to drop it.

As I turned to walk away, I was stopped abruptly by his hand on my shoulder. The anger inside me erupted, and I spun around and swung without thought. Only when I felt the pain radiating through my hand from where it had connected with his cheek did I realize what I'd done.

Finn slammed back against the locker, eyes wide. A gasp sounded in the hallway. The shock in Finn's expression jolted my system. His cheek had already turned an angry shade of red, and a few drops of blood dripped from a gash where his temple hit the locker. I felt my mouth drop open, and then closed it as my anger mingled with a sudden wash of regret. The two emotions clashed, leaving me in an argument with myself in my own mind. I didn't mean to hit him, but it wasn't like he didn't deserve it.

Finn shook his head and stood up straight. "What the hell, man? Talk to me when you decide to stop acting like such an asshole."

His back was so stiff as he walked away that he didn't even look like himself. For some reason that made me sadder than anything else. I glanced around to see everyone frozen, staring at me.

"What?" I demanded.

Almost in unison, the crowd found something more interesting to look at, whispering to each other as they made their way toward their classes.

Then I was alone—and I felt alone.

I leaned against my locker, waiting for my pulse and breathing to regulate. What was wrong with me? This wasn't like me. Finn didn't deserve that. What was I thinking? I'd been doing things I'd never have done before Mia. I was out of control. All week, I couldn't seem to think of anything but seeing her again. I couldn't focus in my classes. I'd memorized her schedule, but needed to keep the crumpled paper in my pocket to feel secure. Nothing mattered if I couldn't find a way to see her.

Was this what addiction felt like?

I'd gone so long without deep sleep that I'd forgotten how incredible it could be, and now that I'd tasted it again, I was addicted to it. My situation was so much worse than I'd thought.

I stepped forward and caught a movement in the mirror of the trophy case. When I glanced up, I saw two figures instead of one: me, and some guy standing just behind me.

I whipped around, but there was no one. I was still alone in the hallway.

My heart pounded, loud in my ears. Pivoting in a slow circle, I turned back to the mirror, but it was just me now. My reflection was pale, panting. For the first time I could remember, I looked as scared as I felt. I was beginning to hate that mirror.

Drawing in a deep breath, I walked toward my next class, trying to shrug off the icy feeling in my gut and rubbing my palm across the small lump in my pocket that held Mia's class schedule.

No matter what, I had to sleep.

TEN

I'd found ways to make eye contact with Mia over the weekend, but at school the next day I kept missing her. When
the final bell rang, I was trying not to think about the withdrawal that would hit me like a semi if I couldn't find her.

Hauling back, I kicked the soccer ball as hard as I could.
It flew a good ten feet over the goal and bounced up the
grassy hill beyond. Jeff's soccer practices had fallen to the bottom of my agenda, especially after what had happened with
Finn. Practice sounded like a pain I didn't have the energy to
deal with right now.

Still, kicking the ball had always been the best way for
me to work out my stress. So here I was, missing shots on the
barely upright, unguarded goal at the empty park a few blocks
from my house—pathetic. Was there a stronger word than
frustrated? Because I was way beyond that at the moment.

I sat for a minute on the cold, dead grass as the sky

above me began to darken. Whose dreams would I watch tonight? Clearly not Finn, and oh please, God, not my mom. I'd had a little too much of her cocktail of real estate and worry in the past months. But a random stranger was too much risk. I'd proven that many times.

Pulling a handful of yellowing grass, I chucked it into the air, but it only floated for a moment before returning to the ground. Nowhere near the violent effect I'd been going for. Look at me—even my explosions of anger were pathetic.

I heard a soft thud and looked up just in time to duck a soccer ball hurtling toward my face—*my* soccer ball.

"Oh, oops." At the sound of Mia's voice, my heart pounded so loud in my head that it crowded out all thought.

"Oops," I repeated.

"I thought you were supposed to be good." She dropped her own ball from under her arm and dribbled it back and forth toward me. Watching her feet snapped me out of my fog. My muscles flexed instinctively in response and I got to my feet.

"I am good." I walked closer, mimicking her movements.

With a swift, unexpected move, she swept her left leg wide and kicked the ball just out of my reach and into the goal behind me. She stared me in the eye and frowned. "Maybe if you ever went to your practice..."

I pivoted and ran to get both balls. Tossing hers back, I stood behind mine. Direct eye contact from her sent my blood pumping. I needed a moment to catch my breath.

"Has Jeff been complaining?" I closed my eyes and

relaxed into my body, feeling my muscles ache to take over. When she answered I opened my eyes to watch her.

"Not to me, but I overheard him talking to Mahoney today. He wasn't exactly quiet." She kicked her ball off to the side with the toe of one shoe and motioned for me to bring mine closer.

"I see." I picked up my ball and tucked it under my right arm as I walked over.

"So, what is it exactly? Too good to practice with your team, so you do it on your own?" Her brow furrowed, but a smile curved the corner of her mouth.

"Yeah. I try not to mingle with the little people." I dropped the ball to the ground in front of me but didn't touch it—not yet. I needed this moment to last.

"Makes sense." Mia nodded, then her eyes turned cold. "I heard you punched Finn, though. Your best friend? Not so cool ... even for a celebrity like you."

I felt the muscles in my jaw clench and sparks of anger flared inside me. Instead of answering, I moved my attention to the ball, trying to work through the emotions before I said anything I'd regret.

My muscles moved without thought, without orders. Seamlessly working together to move the ball forward—left to right, right to left, front and pull back, then forward again. Mia's eyes watched and her mouth closed as she stopped talking and tried to keep up with my footwork.

Back and forth we moved in sync, and then I saw it—the brief flash of triumph in her eyes. She saw an opportunity, but so did I. I feinted to the left and she took the bait. When she lunged for where she thought I was going, I flipped the ball around her to the right and into the goal.

Mia studied me as I came back with the ball. Her arms folded across her chest, her brow was lowered in confusion. "You *are* good."

"Thanks. So are you."

"I know." Mia rubbed her hands up and down on her arms. The sun had set and even I was getting cold. "I just don't get you, Parker. One minute you seem cool, normal even. The next you're acting all crazy."

My defenses kicked in and I felt angry … again. Crazy? I was really starting to hate that word. "What do you want from me? An explanation? Because I don't have one."

"No." Her expression tightened and she jogged over to pick up her ball. "I want you to get over it. Accept the fact that I'm not interested. Leave me out of your mess."

"I wish." My laugh came out so cold and hard she flinched and I wanted to take it back for an instant. Instead, I lowered my voice and finished, "You *are* my mess."

"Whatever." She took a few steps backward, her eyes guarded before she sighed and turned away. Her fists were clenched by her sides as she walked out of the park. I resisted the urge to catch up with her and apologize. But what did I have to apologize for?

———

The heavy clouds churning above Rush Beach made the sky dark long before sunset. Groups of students crowded around the bonfire, trying to keep warm. The air smelled rancid, like dirty fish in boiling water.

After four full nights of amazing sleep, I felt great. I leaned back on my hands and stretched my legs, damp from the wetness of the sand. Water was seeping through my jeans, but I didn't mind. I didn't want to move closer to the fire yet; I had a better view of everyone from here. I hadn't planned to come—most of the team had been looking forward to this bonfire since the assembly last week, but I wouldn't even have shown up if I'd seen Mia earlier in the day. This was my last chance.

And it paid off. Mia was standing back near the tree line, talking and laughing with Addie. I didn't realize how close they'd become, so quickly. Probably because Addie had stopped speaking to me a week ago when she found out I'd decked Finn.

Addie caught my eye with a cold stare before turning her back on me.

I picked up some sand and threw it as hard as I could. The wind cut it in two different streams before it fell back to the ground. Apologies weren't my strong suit, but I knew I needed to talk to Finn, tell him I was sorry. I just didn't know how to explain the way I'd been acting. And telling him the truth wasn't an option.

At least I still got occasional angry glares from Addie. Finn hadn't even looked at me this week. He was now standing next to the bonfire talking to Anna Connors and Jasmine Blackwell. Jasmine and Addie used to hang out all the time in junior high. She had more nightmares about drowning than I considered healthy, and I was kind of an expert. It was weird to see her on the beach. I wondered if anyone else noticed the nervous glances she kept throwing out at the water.

The white letters on Finn's dark shirt glowed in the firelight: *Cancel my subscription. I'm tired of your issues.*

I couldn't help but laugh, even though I suspected it was aimed at me. Lying back on the sand, I felt small amounts of it trickle down the neck of my shirt. The clouds above were moving so fast it was almost hypnotic. Every once in a while a star would peek through for a moment before its light was swarmed and choked out by the roiling mass.

A few guys stood around a huge cooler of punch that was on a table to one side of the fire. I saw Matt and Leroy from the soccer team lift the lid and pour something in the top. I shook my head. No more punch for me. I had enough problems keeping my body and brain in check without any … additives.

Matt caught my eye and walked over. Swinging myself upright, I checked my watch out of habit. It was getting late, but it didn't matter. I knew whose dreams I wanted to watch and I was going to make it happen. He sat down between me and the fire. We'd been friendly at practice and games last season, but I wasn't here for conversation and he was blocking my view.

I picked up a jagged rock about the size of my fist and squeezed it for a moment. The rough edge dug into my palm a little and I loosened my grip. Pulling it across the sand, I dug a crevice in the ground between us. We were divided. I was separated from everyone else. Couldn't he see that and just leave me alone?

"So, what's up with you, man?" Grabbing a handful of sand, he let it fall through his fingers, ruining my line. When half of it blew back into his face, I forced myself not to laugh.

"Meaning?"

"You haven't been showing up to practice and Jeff seems pissed." He turned to face me.

"And?"

"Look, I just wanted to warn you. He says if you don't get it together before the season starts, he's going to talk to Coach Mahoney about replacing you." He looked out at the water and fidgeted. "I just think you shouldn't be a co-captain if you don't even bother to show up."

I watched him for a moment before leaning back to get a better view of Mia. "You want my spot, Matt? Is that it?"

His face turned bright red and I could see I'd hit my mark. "Screw you, Parker. I was just trying to help." He stood up and walked back to the fire.

It wasn't that I didn't care about soccer. With the way my grades were falling, it had always been my best shot at getting into college even though I'd never really believed I'd live that long. Now, with Mia, there was a chance I could survive even longer than I'd hoped—and that possibility was so much more important than Matt wanting to take my place as a starter that it was almost ridiculous to waste time thinking about it.

My gaze pulled back to Mia, again and again. She was like a magnet. I was planning to stop her when she left, but the fear that she'd get away without making eye contact suffocated me. I couldn't approach her with Addie standing there though. Her anger was bad enough from a distance. I couldn't stand to feel it close-up, especially since I deserved it.

I pulled my shoulders up tight and then released them, trying to relax the tense knots in my neck as I pushed the guilt aside. I needed to focus on Mia.

She wore a big jacket she'd probably borrowed from Jeff. I liked the way her small hands barely poked out from the long sleeves. If I hadn't been so drawn to her dreams—and if I ever decided to break my own rule about girls—I might've been interested for other reasons. As it stood, one addiction at a time was plenty.

I didn't realize I'd been staring at her for several minutes until I caught Jeff's eye as he released one of the cheerleaders. He walked toward Mia, moving to block my view. Taking her hand, he tried to pull her toward the bonfire. She froze up and didn't move a step. I could see her legs trembling and she shook her head violently. Addie laid a hand on Jeff's arm and smiled, said something in his ear, and turned him back toward the fire. Jeff laughed, shrugged, and walked back alone.

My arm started to hurt, and I realized I'd kept digging the trench without realizing. It was now almost a foot deep. I dropped the rock and the muscles in my hand ached. The stone gleamed red in the light from the bonfire. As I leaned back on my palms, pain shot through my hand and I brought it closer. There was a shallow cut and a few reddish-black drops of blood from gripping the jagged edge of the rock too tight. I'd sliced up my palm and hadn't even noticed. The redness on the rock was my own blood.

Rubbing my hands on my dark jeans, I tried in vain to get the sand and blood off. Why did this Mia thing have me so messed up? It was hard to believe it hadn't even been two weeks since I'd first watched her dreams. Sometimes I didn't even feel like the same person as before. If I'd been smarter, I could've handled the whole thing differently, better, but it had caught me off guard.

I glanced back just in time to see Mia waving at Addie and moving toward the parking lot. Jumping to my feet, I ran to cut her off. I only needed a minute, one glance, and then I'd let her go.

I skidded to a stop in front of her, my feet tingly and raw as I realized I'd left my shoes back on the beach. Mia jumped away and gave a little squeak before glaring at me.

"What on earth is wrong with you?"

"Sorry, I..." My mind went blank.

"Seriously, if it weren't for Addie telling me you were just acting weird lately, I'd wonder if someone should have you committed." She laughed a little, but there was a hard edge behind her voice I hadn't heard before.

I'd have to thank Addie for defending me—assuming she would ever speak to me again, and even though a very strong argument could be made these days for a padded room and a white jacket. I put my hands on my knees and feigned panting, trying to buy time to figure out what to say.

"Look, I'm flattered, really." Mia's voice was a little softer when she spoke again. "I mean, you're really cute, but let's be honest. You keep showing up everywhere I go, and the way you act—you're starting to freak me out."

I stood up straight. "What?"

"Come on, Parker. Do you really think I don't notice you staring at me? The way you came by my house to talk to Jeff last weekend? Am I supposed to believe you didn't know he was at a meeting with Coach Mahoney? A meeting, Jeff told me, that you were supposed to be at? Seriously." She shuffled her feet and looked away. "And just now, I thought you were going to bore a hole through my head back on the beach."

"I'm sorry. I just really like your...your eyes?" I'd meant it to come out as a statement, not a question. I wanted to kick myself.

She stared at me, unblinking. "My eyes?"

"Yeah, you have pretty eyes."

Mia flushed and looked over my shoulder. "Oh, thank you."

My mind grasped for something, anything to say in the stillness. "So, uh, I heard you paint."

The moment it slipped out, I recognized my mistake. Her dreams were the only reason I knew about her painting. I really hoped it connected to reality somehow.

Her gaze turned cold. "You heard wrong." She shook her head and looked away again. "I don't paint anymore." She focused on something behind me and her eyes widened. Her voice was so low I could barely hear it when she spoke.

"Uh-oh."

"Uh-oh, what?" I asked just before Thor grabbed my shoulder and pinned me against a nearby pine tree.

"Hello to you too." I focused my eyes on his neck as I struggled against his grip. I didn't know why he was involved in this, but since Jeff was the only person he didn't seem to hate, I guessed it made sense. Jeff stood next to Thor, arms folded across his chest.

"Let him go." Jeff sighed and pulled Thor's shoulder until he released me. He seemed irritated, but nothing compared to the anger radiating from his buddy. "Seriously, Parker, what's going on here?"

My shoulder hurt where it'd been scratched against the rough tree bark. "What do you mean? What's *his* problem?" I nodded my head toward Thor and he growled.

Jeff stepped forward and pulled me a few steps farther away from the small crowd that was gathering nearby to watch us. He ducked his head, forcing me to meet his eyes. I thrust my hands in my pockets, mostly to keep myself from strangling him.

"Look, can't you see you're scaring her? You need to lay off, man. I think everyone is a little tired of the way you've been acting lately." His eyes flashed but he kept his voice low. I could see another emotion in them, something darker, but it was gone before I could place it.

"Jeff, it's not that big of a deal." Mia's voice came from behind him. I looked for her but found Addie first. She'd never looked at me like this before. With disgust. With her gaze on me, it was hard to remember to breathe.

Shaking her head, Addie turned and stomped back

toward the fire. It took me a second to remember to look for Mia. I met her eyes for one life-saving instant before she looked away.

Jeff waved his hand at her. "Go home, Mia."

"Fine, I was leaving anyway." Mia huffed. "Not that anyone asked my opinion, but I wish *all* of you would leave me alone."

She walked away. I'd have to leave soon to avoid eye contact with anyone else. The anticipation of another night of Mia's dreams was sweet, and I was desperate not to lose it.

For a moment, no one spoke. Jeff shrugged and watched Mia's truck pull out of the parking lot. I kept my eyes carefully trained on the ground. The small crowd at the edge of the beach was getting larger, watching us in silence. When I saw that Finn had joined them, I decided to try and smooth things over with Jeff. Besides, Thor could probably break most trees in half. Who wants trouble with someone like that?

"I didn't mean to cause a problem, man. It was a misunderstanding." I stared at a spot just to the side of Jeff's eyes and shrugged.

"No worries," he said, loud enough for everyone to hear.

As Thor walked away, Jeff gave me a lopsided grin, flopped one arm across my shoulders and whispered in my ear. "Just chill it, okay?" Then he released me and jogged back toward the fire.

The others followed Jeff. Before he was even halfway back to the bonfire, his arms were around two giggling girls and he was joking loudly with Matt.

Finn was the only one who didn't move. He stood staring at the ground, and I waited. I was rooted in place, torn between missing him and my overwhelming desire to bolt from the parking lot before Finn could look up and ruin my chance to sleep tonight. But he never raised his eyes. After a few seconds of awkward silence, he just turned and walked back toward the fire. I hated myself a little for feeling relieved.

I started back for my shoes but froze when I noticed that same leather jacket guy, the one who was blocking my view in the parking lot the other day. He was wading up to his ankles in the edge of the water—totally insane. It had to be ice cold. I wondered who was that crazy, but it was too dark to make out his face.

He turned and my skin prickled. In the darkness, I could feel his eyes on me.

Thor stoked the fire with a long stick. Several big sparks soared up in the air and pulled my attention away. The jacket guy didn't move from the water, but he watched me while I grabbed my shoes and walked to the parking lot, until I was out of sight.

ELEVEN

Over the past three weeks, I'd gotten more sleep than I had in years. Mia wasn't exactly making it easy, but it was worth the trouble. I'd awaken with my mind filled to the brim with images and memories from my *own* dreams, which I hadn't been capable of for years. I felt whole in a way I'd never believed possible. Funny dreams, bizarre dreams, even nightmares—I loved every one of them. Mia had opened up a new world to me, a world of my own creation, and she didn't even know about it.

My dreams didn't show me problems I couldn't fix. They didn't fill me with emotions I wasn't prepared to deal with. My dreams happened and then went away. They were temporary, fleeting, relaxing.

Seeing the fluidity and randomness of my own dreams confirmed my theory that when I was watching the dreams of others, I was stuck in some more realistic layer. Really, it wasn't surprising. My brain was technically awake. My conscious mind was finding the slot with the most reason and stuffing me into it, the layer that it could force into some box that made sense and at least partially obeyed laws of nature.

I hopped out of bed and smiled at the fading circles under my eyes in the mirror on the back of my door. Life with sleep was incredible. I could think. I could focus. And most of the bad memories and nightmares I'd witnessed in other people's heads were fading away. Even my coordination was better— all thanks to Mia and her incredible dreams.

Outside of the dreams, things with Mia weren't at all pleasant. That first week, she'd been annoyed at how I'd waited outside her last class every day and she hadn't been afraid to tell me so. But ever since the bonfire, she'd stopped telling me off and just tried to get away from me as quickly as possible. The mere sight of me seemed to scare her now. I tried not to make it worse than it had to be—I'd meet her eyes and then leave. The less complication, the better.

Flopping down at my desk to gather my stuff for school, I glanced up and saw my sixth grade soccer picture hanging on the wall. Finn was grinning so wide I could almost see every one of his teeth, and he had one arm flung around my shoulder. I missed him, but every time I thought about apologizing I realized how much easier it was to see Mia's dreams when Finn wasn't around to distract me. That alone had made the decision to stay away from Jeff's soccer practices, and Finn, an easy one.

Reaching up, I took the picture down and stuffed it in

one of my desk drawers. I didn't want to think about him right then. I hadn't talked to Addie either, though it was harder to keep away from her somehow.

In fact, everyone at school seemed to be giving me a pretty wide berth now. Probably a bad sign, but it didn't matter. I ignored them along with the voice inside my head that kept telling me this was wrong. Pushing it deeper into my subconscious was easy when everything inside me felt so much more alive.

Shaking off the doubts, I jumped in the shower. I slept and it was wonderful. And that was all that mattered.

———

The next day, after barely making eye contact with Mia at the end of school, I stood in a bathroom stall, waiting and listening. Once the halls were silent and I thought everyone had gone, I snuck out the side doors to the parking lot, keeping my head low and my sunglasses on. I couldn't risk making eye contact with anyone else on the way out.

I'd almost reached my car when Matt ran into me in the parking lot, hard. My backpack fell off my shoulder, and my sunglasses went flying and broke against the asphalt.

"Oops." Matt barely controlled his laughter. If it didn't require looking at him, I might've punched him. I regretted what happened with Finn; I wouldn't think twice about Matt.

"Not cool, man." I muttered without a glance in his

direction. Pulling my backpack up, I left my shades where they were and kept walking. Just a few more feet and I could get away from this moron.

I stumbled as Thor's hulking frame stepped in front of my car door. He caught my shoulders with both hands, but he did it so roughly I could feel the bruises down to my bones. Red-hot anger boiled inside my chest, and I jerked my head up to find myself staring into his small dark eyes.

Matt stepped up beside us and laughed. "He didn't want you to fall."

I'm not sure what made me more furious: them giving me a hard time or the fact that Thor had forced me to meet his eyes. I brought both elbows up as hard as I could and broke his grip on my shoulders. A low growl erupted from his chest, but he stepped aside when Matt waved him off.

"Watch yourself, Parker," Matt said as I climbed in and started the car.

I drove aimlessly for a while, needing to be moving, to think. This was just perfect. If I didn't want to see a dream featuring my decapitation—not exactly at the top of my to-watch list—then I needed to find a way to see Mia again. *Tonight.*

Slamming my forearm against the steering wheel, I kept driving. This wasn't going to be easy. Her reactions bothered me—but not enough for me to change anything. It wasn't my fault that I had to go to such extremes to get the sleep everyone else took for granted. My curse controlled me; it wasn't by choice.

I was pretty sure Mia would be working at the mall tonight. Glancing around, I couldn't suppress a shudder. With my "aimless" driving, I'd managed to go straight to her. I was a block away from the mall without even consciously deciding to go there.

Whether I wanted to resist or not, her dreams kept me coming back. Every night, they amazed me. Each setting was more beautiful than the one before, each equally worth painting. Yet she never touched her paintbrush to the canvas, every time looking just as frustrated. I got the feeling that if her sadness hadn't been dimmed by her strange dreams, it would have been impossible to even breathe under the weight of it.

I wished I could do something to help her, especially if her sadness and frustration were somehow tied to reality. Even unknowingly, she'd helped me more than I could've ever imagined.

Pulling into a nearby fast-food joint, I killed some time eating dinner and playing games on my phone. When there was just an hour until the mall closed, I drove slowly through the parking lot, searching up and down the rows for her purple pickup. Once I saw it, I parked my car a few spots away.

Leaning back in my seat, I rolled down my window, turned on some music, and propped my feet up on the dash. There were worse ways to spend an evening. Besides, she was worth the wait.

Just as I was relaxing, a black motorcycle blew past my car and parked near the front of the lot. I sat up straight when I recognized the rider with his black leather jacket—the same guy I'd seen before. It was getting dark, but under the bright lights I noticed a patch on the right shoulder of his jacket that I hadn't been close enough to make out before. It looked like a pirate skull, but instead of one eye patch, it wore two—one over each eye.

My skin crawled and I had a vivid flash of memory. My dad, standing in his room with me bouncing on the bed. He'd chuckled and asked me to hand him his wallet. When I grabbed it off the nightstand, I saw the same skull—two eye-patches carved into the well-worn leather. I'd asked him what it was. I could still hear his rich voice echoing in my head.

"It's to remind me about people."

"What about them?"

Taking the wallet, he'd stuffed it in his back pocket before lifting my chin until I looked in his eyes. "That a blind skull sees more than you think."

The memory faded and I drew in a shaky breath. It had been a long time since I'd thought about spending time my dad. The jagged pain in my chest was the reason why. Leaning out the window, I tried to see the rider's face, but he didn't take his helmet off until he was walking through the mall doors and out of sight.

I should know who he was. He obviously went to school with me, but I just couldn't identify him, at least not without seeing his face. The patch was probably the symbol of some old band or something, but still, I needed more information.

I vowed to pay more attention at school the next day, see who had the jacket with the blind skull.

Pushing him out of my mind, I focused on what really mattered: Mia. I turned up the radio and tried to bury my memories of Dad under a heavy drumbeat and wicked guitar solo.

When she finally appeared, the parking lot was nearly empty. She carried a small silver purse and swung it around, singing softly to herself. I waited, trying not to feel like a cat ready to pounce. I stepped out of my car as she approached and moved between her and the truck. Raising my hand, I waved.

The moment she saw me, she froze. Her terrified expression told me I shouldn't have come. She swallowed hard, then reached in her purse.

"I have p-pepper spray." Her voice shook so hard it was difficult to understand her.

"Whoa. I just wanted to say hi." I took a step back, but then stopped. I wanted to leave her alone, but she was looking down. I wasn't certain I'd met her eyes—I had to be sure. Why couldn't she just give me what I needed?

I'd never seen anyone look so scared—no, I had. Agnes had had the same kind of fear in her eyes that Mia's held now. Was I no better than that loser husband of hers? If I had nightmares now, I knew what they would be about.

Frustration, anger, fear, and guilt flowed through me. I wanted to comfort her and force her to meet my eyes at the same time. An idea infected my mind like a parasite; if I had a weapon—it might make her do what I wanted. I choked back the bile that rose in my throat. I was disgusted at myself, but the desperate need drove me on.

Fighting the urge to look away, I stepped closer. "Mia, please. Calm down."

She gasped and thrust her hand back and forth in her bag searching for something, probably the pepper spray. I stopped where I was and she finally looked up.

Her eyes were so filled with terror that I flinched, but something dark inside me took over. It didn't allow me to even glance away. It made sure I got a solid look in her eyes before releasing me.

"Okay, I'll go. I didn't mean to scare you." My legs felt wobbly as I retreated to my car. Even as I left the parking lot, I could see her small form in my rearview mirror. She put her face in her hands and trembled from the tip of her head to the heels of her boots.

I parked around the corner. The car felt stuffy and claustrophobic. I dragged myself outside and took a few ragged breaths. My fingers tugged on my hair and I banged my fist against the roof of the car. Battle lines were being drawn in my head. How could I choose which side to take? Hardly a fair conflict: my life or her fear?

Part of me argued that it wasn't Mia's fault. Why should she suffer because of my problems? Another part of me raged about the situation. Anything I did was justified. I'd been calmly awaiting my terrifying future for so long, who could blame me for seizing an opportunity to avoid it? Was it my fault I'd been forced to such drastic measures to stay alive? Sleep wasn't optional; I'd learned that. I had to have it.

There was no way out of this situation, and every time I bent a rule, the darker part of me broke it in half. I could feel it now, could see where it had come from. It was the part of me that had kept me sane when I'd developed my curse, had helped me deal with Dad leaving and Mom working all the time. The part that helped me survive through nightmare after nightmare. But it didn't care about anyone else, just about keeping me alive. Each step I took that I wouldn't have taken before seemed to strengthen the instinct. It cared about survival, and only survival. Any moral problems weren't a consideration. I didn't want to give in to that, I didn't want to be that guy ... but if I stopped, I would die.

No matter how much I hated myself for it, my life was still more important than her fear. She would live through being afraid sometimes.

Maybe this could be good. Mia might fear me, but I could watch over her. Walking through an empty parking lot at night all by herself, she could run into someone much more dangerous than me. If I made sure she was safe, it could make up for any pain I caused. I could keep her out of any real danger. After all, I wouldn't physically hurt her.

I dragged in a few more deep breaths and the war within me stilled. It only bothered me a little that I wasn't sure which side had won.

———————

The next day, I felt better. I had a plan. It had been a huge mistake to wait for Mia in the parking lot after work. Looking back at the situation, no wonder she'd been terrified.

My new plan was different. It would work.

By the time I found a parking space and climbed out of my car, it was 8:50 p.m. Only ten minutes before the mall closed. I tried to contain my smile; still plenty of time to get to her store and do a little shopping.

I figured that this way, in public, she wouldn't be so afraid. I could shop around the store, make eye contact, and then leave. I'd even be willing to buy something if it let me meet her eyes without freaking her out.

It was a temporary fix. I certainly couldn't go and buy something every day without running out of money—and fast. For now, though, it was the only idea I had.

I walked through the front mall entrance and ran right into Mr. Blind Skull himself. But now I could see more than just his old leather jacket. He had spiky brown hair that made him look kind of wild, and muddy-brown eyes. He was an inch or two shorter than me…and I'd never seen his face in my life. Was he new to the area?

"Excuse me," he said, looking quickly away as he stepped around me and jogged toward the parking lot. I didn't even have time to apologize for plowing into him, let alone ask him about the blind skull patch, before he was out of sight. I shook my head and got back to business.

When I got to Mia's store, I was surprised to find it empty. I checked my watch and groaned. It was only a few minutes before closing; the entire mall was pretty much deserted.

Making my way inside, I tried to appear casual. I stopped at a rack here and there, but my eyes continually scanned for Mia. I'd nearly given up when I made it to an alcove near the back of the store and saw her.

She had her back to me as she meticulously folded and straightened a table full of jeans. I couldn't help myself. She was so close. I took a step and she visibly stiffened. Still, she didn't turn, just continued to work. For a moment I wondered if it was even her. Moving slowly around the table, I caught sight of the side of her face—definitely Mia—but still she wouldn't look at me.

Half the lights in the store went out. I glanced out into the mall and saw it was the same there. It must've been a signal to remind customers it was time to leave. The sudden dimness made everything a little eerie. I needed to get this over with.

I took a deep breath. It really didn't have to be so difficult. Why did she make everything so hard?

Without raising her eyes, or acknowledging my existence at all, Mia turned and moved to straighten the next table. I cursed under my breath. With the dim lighting and the empty store, this was no better than the parking lot—except here she didn't have her pepper spray.

With a shake of my head, I grabbed a pair of jeans in my size from the nearest table and stepped forward. "Hey, Mia. Could you help me with this?"

She didn't respond.

"Mia?" I reached out and touched her shoulder with the jeans.

She whipped up and away so violently that I jumped. Her whole body recoiled like I'd struck her. I watched, gaping, as she fell backward into a metal rack. The resounding clang from her head hitting the hard edge echoed in the empty store. Her body crumpled to the floor, and I thought she'd knocked herself out until I heard her moaning. She lifted her face toward the ceiling and mascara-tinted tears rolled down both cheeks.

Nausea churned in my gut. I didn't know whether to help her or run away. So I did nothing. I simply stared at the disaster I'd created.

Over and over, she moaned the word "no."

I looked at Mia, at what my actions had caused. She was broken and it was my fault.

"I'm—" My voice caught on the words. "I'm sorry. Let me help you," I mumbled as I took a step toward her. She cried harder, wrapping both arms around her knees and burying her face in her jeans.

"Hey, what's going on here?"

I turned to see an older man walking back from the front of the store. He had on a black-and-white-striped shirt and a nametag that read *Chad*.

"I—she—" Finally, I gave up and closed my mouth. There was no way to explain.

Chad stepped around to Mia, touching a blossoming spot of red on the back of her head. I shuddered. He turned on me immediately, grabbing a walkie-talkie from his belt.

"I'm calling security."

Everything had gone so wrong. I was screwed. I glanced at Mia again and found her dark blue eyes resting on me. She flinched when she met my gaze and quickly turned away.

"I'm so sorry, Mia."

Then I ran.

TWELVE

I focused on meeting the eyes of every shopper I passed on the way out. After what I'd done, I didn't deserve the rest that Mia's dreams provided. I was a freak, a monster. When I glanced at my reflection in the store window, I met the cold eyes I'd seen before in the mirror at school. Only this time it didn't surprise me as much.

And when I blinked, he didn't go away.

Once outside, I couldn't hold it in any longer. I threw up in the bushes in a dark corner of the building until I shook. I'd become something horrible. And worse, I didn't know if I could stop myself. Already the darkness in my traitorous mind was searching for another way to see her. I'd given over control to that darker side, far too much control.

I had to take it back.

I drove to Finn's house out of reflex. This was the end. I needed help and he was my only hope at this point. I needed a friend. I just hoped he could still be that friend after everything I'd done.

Addie answered the door. Her face fell the moment she saw me, and it felt like a hole being ripped through my gut. I was stupid to have come.

"What do you want?" She folded her arms over her chest, looking about as welcoming as a *Closed* sign.

Clearing my throat, I tried a smile, but it actually seemed to make her angrier.

"Finn—I need Finn," I said, glancing over her shoulder. "Please?" I sounded pitiful but I didn't care.

Finn walked into the room behind her. His sweatshirt was a vibrant blue. It had been a long time since I'd seen him in a shirt that didn't make a literal statement. When he saw me, he pivoted on one foot and turned to leave.

"Please." I pushed past Addie and into the living room. "I really need you to listen. I was wrong." Everything I said was true, but only because it was my last hope. I'd lie through my teeth if I thought it would make him talk to me again. Even worse, I'd tell him the truth.

He stopped with his back to me, and I waited. After a full minute, he turned to face me, his expression cold. With a long sigh, he walked past me to the door, rubbed Addie on top of the head, and finally spoke.

"I'll be back. Have to at least hear the idiot out."

Addie nodded but still glared at me as I walked out behind him. At the last second, she grabbed my arm and squeezed, hard. "If you hurt him again, I swear, I'll deck you myself," she hissed, too low for Finn to hear. She was such a little thing but her eyes were dead serious.

"Don't worry, Addie. I've been stupid—to both of you. I won't do it again."

"I know the way you've been." She took a deep breath and released my arm. "This isn't you, Parker. You're not like this—this person."

I hoped she was right. "I'm trying to fix things."

She nodded and whispered "Good," then placed her hand on my chest and pushed me gently out the door.

Finn sat in the driver's seat of my car. The knots that were tying up every muscle in my body loosened a little. Maybe I hadn't broken things beyond repair. Finn would listen. If he would only *believe* me, I wouldn't have to figure this out alone.

And I was so tired of dealing with everything alone.

Climbing in, I tossed him the keys. "Where we going?" I asked.

"If I have to look at your ugly face, you're going to at least buy me a shake while I do it." His voice was tight as he turned the key and the car came to life.

"I owe you at least that much."

"Yeah, you do."

We drove to the Shake Stop in silence. It was a quiet night, no rain or wind and very few other cars on the road. Everything around me was the exact opposite of the turmoil inside my head.

Wave after wave of panic hit me at the thought of telling him I was a Watcher. I had to, though; I needed his help. I needed him to help me figure out what to do with the mess my life had become. Shame washed over me, and I tried to shake it off by focusing on every dream of Finn's that I could remember. I'd need to provide specific details to have any chance of convincing him.

The biggest problem that stood in my way was that many people don't remember their dreams. I knew Finn did— at least sometimes. He'd told me about some of his funnier ones—it was weird to hear his take on what he could remember. I'd seen them too, and since I wasn't sleeping, I usually remembered a lot more than he did. I just hoped we both recalled some of the same details.

Finn picked a corner table away from everyone else. He sipped his chocolate-chip shake before staring at me pointedly. "So? Get on with it."

"First, I'm really sorry for punching you and for the way I've been acting." He looked away with a non-committal grunt and I went on. "Seriously, man. There's no excuse. I was an idiot, plain and simple."

"Idiot sounds about right." He seemed to relax a little and nodded for me to continue.

I cleared my throat and popped the knuckles in my right hand before speaking. "Okay, this will sound insane, but it's true, so hear me out."

Finn nodded without a word.

"I'm not like everyone else—I mean—I don't sleep the way you do."

I paused for a response from Finn, but there was none. He waited for me to continue. This was hard. It was awkward.

And I had no reason to think he would ever believe me. I squared my shoulders and pushed on anyway.

"When I go to sleep at night, I see other people's dreams."

Finn's eyes clouded and the corner of his mouth jerked as though uncertain how to respond. "You told me this joke a few years ago…"

"I know, and I know I said it was a joke, but it wasn't. It sounds crazy but I'm serious. It's been going on for four years, and I can prove it. I've seen more of your dreams than anyone else's. Not counting the past few weeks, do you remember any of your dreams?"

Finn shook his head; his voice was a low growl when he spoke. "Un-freaking-believable. I came out here thinking you had something important to say, and instead you bring up some old punch line? You used to be cool, man, but now everything is just a big joke to you."

"I'm serious, Finn. Please. I remember one from a month ago!" I practically yelled as he stood up from the table.

He stopped and sat back down with a sigh. "I don't know why, but I'm going to give you about thirty more seconds. You better impress me—quick."

"Okay, you had a dream that you were boxing with a shark—while you were surfing."

Finn's expression didn't change but his shoulders straightened. "Go on."

I pushed my fingertips hard into my forehead, searching for the details I never expected would be important. "Oh! Another one—it was a while ago, though—maybe six months? You were the king of the mer-people and I was your servant. And—and there was this mermaid. She was smokin' hot. Her name was Cassie, or, um, Cassa—"

"Cassandra." Finn's reverent whisper interrupted me and his eyes got huge. His mouth opened and closed like a guppy before any sound came out. "How—h-how? Did I tell you?"

"No. I saw it."

"I don't remember telling you." Finn spoke slowly but finally shook his head. "But I must have. That's just not possible."

He looked like he was thinking about standing up again, so I spoke quickly. "Fine, you ask me about one. One you're sure you never mentioned to me. Just make sure it's not from the last three or four weeks."

"Fine." He hesitated, taking another slurp of his shake. "I had a nightmare a few times last year. I thought about telling you but I never did. It started out on an island. Tell me what happened."

"I know I saw that one." I closed my eyes tight and tried hard to remember details. "The island was deserted. I don't know how you got there, but there was this cruise ship that picked you up and it was haunted. A bunch of undead freaks turned you into one of them and made you entertain them." I stopped there because I didn't want to embarrass him. It'd been the creepiest rendition of "Copacabana" I'd ever seen.

Finn whistled, his eyes wider than seemed humanly possible. I wondered how wide they could get before there was danger of them falling out. "H-how did this happen?" he finally asked.

"I don't know. It just started."

"When?"

Relief washed over me, and I could breathe freely for the first time in what felt like ages. "Four years. I can't tell you how glad I am you believe me—I wasn't sure how many more of your dreams I could remember."

Finn shook his head. "Not so fast. One more. It was my favorite dream from a few months ago. I remember I had it on a night when you slept over. I was a pirate."

I nodded with a grin. As if I could forget that.

"What was my name?"

"Finn the Amazin'—you liked it because it kind of rhymed," I said without batting an eye.

"You were in the dream too. Who were you?"

I closed my eyes before answering. "Patrice—the barmaid."

Finn hooted and slapped one hand down on the table. "Dude, how do you *do* that?"

I shook my head. "I don't know, but really—it's not a good thing."

"How can you say that? It's awesome! So, tell the truth, do the cheerleaders ever dream about me?" Finn leaned back and nodded with confidence.

We both laughed and stared at each other for a minute. I think it was still sinking in with him. I'd never expected how good it would feel to tell someone. Never had I anticipated an outcome that didn't include a straitjacket.

Finn *believed me*. He'd listened and now he would understand. I wasn't alone. Laughter seemed to release the pressure like a hole in a balloon. If this situation could be fixed, Finn would help me do it. He always did.

The restaurant around us had emptied. There were only two other tables occupied now, one with a family and the other an older couple. Finn was quiet for a long time, and then he took a sip of his shake.

"What?" I was pretty sure I knew what was coming, but I wanted to make sure he got to get it all out.

"Well, it's weird, but it still doesn't explain why you turned into such a freak with Mia. You know she called Addie crying yesterday." His face hardened. "She said you were waiting for her in the parking lot after work. If that's true—you're seriously messed up."

I grimaced, knowing he hadn't yet heard the worst of it. "It's true."

"What were you thinking? What's your problem when it comes to her?"

"Mostly, I'm an idiot, but there is an explanation. The massive downside to being a Watcher is that I don't get regular sleep. It's like I'm awake all the time. I forgot what it was like to get real sleep, and honestly—it was starting to kill me—quickly."

Finn's eyes widened. "What do you mean you're a 'Watcher'? Are there others like you?"

I shook my head. "I don't think so. I just call myself that. At least I've never met or heard of any, but it makes sense to keep it quiet, if you know what I mean."

"Yeah, I guess." He was silent for a moment before continuing. "No real sleep, though? That really sucks. Sleep is, like . . . my favorite activity."

"Yeah, sleep rocks." I grabbed his shake and took a sip. "Sleep is what caused the problem with Mia."

"How?"

"For some reason, in *her* dreams—I can sleep. I actually fall asleep in the dreams. For the first time in four years, I'm not tired. You have no idea how incredible that feels. I need it. The problem is that I only see the dreams of the last person I make eye contact with before I go to bed. I had to see her last, every day—"

"And she had to see you."

"Right. There lies my problem." I sighed.

Finn nodded and stirred his shake. "I'm pretty sure sleep was one of the needs they listed in biology. Food, water, sleep. Something like that. I don't remember if there were more." He paused. "But you have to stop stalking her. There's got to be another way."

"I know. You should've seen her face when she saw me." I swallowed and glanced away. "It was so, so bad. I'd never hurt her, but she's terrified of me. It's horrible."

"Geez, man. This sucks." He put his head down on the table for a minute, rolling it from side to side. I was shocked at how well he was taking my strange news, but that was Finn. He always surprised me.

Suddenly, something that had bugged me for a long time rose to the surface. I'd never been able to talk to anyone about this before. Now seemed as good a time as any.

"Hey, can I ask you a question?"

"Sure."

"Does it bother you? Knowing that I've seen into your head so much for the past four years?"

Finn watched me for a minute before shaking his head. "Nope. Should it?"

"I guess not." I shrugged. "I just always feel like I'm intruding."

"I figure since I have no control over what I'm dreaming, it's not like I can be embarrassed." He took a long sip of his shake. "Besides, I find my dreams quite entertaining."

I laughed. "As you should."

He nodded, then rubbed the knuckles of one hand across the tabletop. "So are you sure Mia is the only one with those dreams? The ones you can sleep in?"

"Not necessarily, but I've seen a lot of dreams from a lot of different people ... none of them are like hers."

"Any idea what makes her different?"

"Not a clue." I held my breath for a few seconds, then breathed it out slowly. "I really don't get it. I wish I did."

His head jerked up and he looked at me funny. "Four years? Don't take this the wrong way, but how are you still alive?"

I dropped my gaze to the table and studied a crack in the vinyl surface. "I don't know. I really didn't expect to even live this long."

Glancing up, I saw Finn's face pale and he stared at me until I cleared my throat and looked away.

"But that's crazy. The last year or so I thought maybe

you looked kind of sick, but you rarely miss school or anything so I blew it off. I never believed you could be dying." He seemed sad, and I had an overwhelming urge to talk about anything else.

"Anyway, it doesn't matter." I shrugged, trying to think of another subject to change to—but I couldn't come up with anything.

"You said you're *dying*." Finn gaped at me. "How can it not matter?"

"I can't change it—and you said it yourself, this whole Mia thing has to stop."

He closed his mouth and scratched his jaw while he watched the cars on the street outside the window. "You know, she and Addie are really good friends now. She's over at my house all the time."

I didn't know what his point was. Of course I knew they'd been hanging out a lot. You learn those kinds of things about a person when you follow them everywhere they go. I choked back a wave of nausea and nodded.

"Maybe if we can convince her you're not a freak, you could see her at my house a few times a week. No following, no stalking—just hanging out." Finn pulled on his right ear, the way he always did when he was thinking.

A dark corner of my mind screamed *"YES!"* at any opportunity to be around Mia, but I ignored it. Anything that dark part of me wanted, I had to assume was a bad idea. At least for now, though, it was the only plan that would work until I had more control and could start to trust myself again.

"I don't know. It might have been a good idea to start

with, but I've ruined any chance of it working. She doesn't want to be anywhere near me, and for good reason."

"Well, we can't have you croaking from lack of sleep. We'll figure something out."

And that was it, right there.

Warmth spread from my chest and down my arms. I never understood how badly I needed that. Someone else who knew I was dying and wanted to try and stop it from happening. That was what I'd longed for but couldn't find. I wanted someone else to know . . . and care.

I wanted someone I could say goodbye to.

Clearing my throat, I shrugged and stood up. "If you say so."

It was the worst kind of lame but I wasn't sure what else to say. Some sappy speech would only make both of us uncomfortable. Still, I wanted to say something to show my gratitude.

Finn got up and threw his cup in the garbage. He pulled my keys out of his pocket and walked out the door. I caught up with him as we got to the car.

"Hey, umm, thanks for believing me."

He grinned and punched my shoulder. "Hey, umm, thanks for not really being psycho."

THIRTEEN

This was a terrible idea. I paced in Finn's kitchen, wiping my damp hands on the front of my jeans for what felt like the millionth time. I'd only resisted my darker urges for what, twenty-four hours now? Total fail. Even knowing this was Finn's plan didn't make me feel any better. I needed to stop making decisions based on what I needed and start making them based on what Mia needed—and right now, that was for me to stay as far away from her as possible. I never should've let him talk me into this, no matter how good his intentions.

Finn slouched at the kitchen table. It looked like he was sleeping. He hadn't moved a muscle in ages, but his baseball cap was pulled so low on his head it was hard to tell. I jumped when he sat forward.

"Parker, you need to chill. You're making me sweat and

that's really saying something since you left the door open and it's practically snowing in here."

"Oh, sorry." I walked over and kicked the bottom of the back door the rest of the way closed with my left foot. "When will she be here?"

"I don't know. Her truck has been breaking down lately, so Jeff is dropping her off." Finn leaned back in his chair. "You freaking out isn't going to make her get here any faster."

With a shrug, I plunked down in the chair beside him, rolling my head back and forth in a vain attempt to relax my tense muscles. I grabbed an orange from the bowl on the table and flexed my fingers around it. "I don't know if I want her to get here at all."

"I'm telling you. This is going to work." But he chewed on the end of a pencil as he glanced toward the front door.

"You don't know that."

"No, but were any of your ideas this good?"

I swallowed hard and tapped the orange against the top of the table. My ideas sucked. My ideas had made everything infinitely worse—possibly unrecoverable.

Finn tried to play it off, but he seemed almost as nervous as I felt. His hands were a dead giveaway. We were opposites: when he was happy, he couldn't stay still. At the moment, his arms were crossed over his chest with each hand pinned under the opposite biceps. Keeping them motionless was the only thing he could control.

Finn watched me, his expression frozen halfway between laughter and fear. His eyes were glued to my hand. Only when I looked down did I notice that I was still hitting the orange against the table—hard. Juice oozed out of cracks in the peel, dripping over my fingers and onto the table. I stood, threw the smashed orange into the garbage, and grabbed a napkin to clean up the mess. I had no idea what was going on with my hands these days. They almost had a mind of their own. I sat back down across from Finn.

"Sorry. I wasn't paying attention."

"No, really? If you wanted juice, you could've just asked." Finn glanced over at the blob of orange peel in the garbage can and grimaced. "You all right, man?"

"Yeah, fine."

That wasn't the truth and we both knew it. This was it. If we couldn't make this work, there wasn't much point in trying anymore. I would leave Mia alone. She deserved that much after everything I'd put her through. It was the only option I would allow myself to consider. But I hoped I could find someone else like her before it was too late.

I shook my head. That thought was so absurd it made me want to laugh. There was *no one* like her, no one who could do what she did.

I'd managed to alienate and terrify the only girl who could help me. Classic.

A car pulled into the driveway and I jumped up from my chair. The doorbell rang. I heard Addie bound down the stairs in the front room to answer the door. She hadn't said a word to me since I'd come to apologize to Finn the night before. But somehow, after I dropped him off, he'd convinced her to invite Mia over today while I was here. I had no idea what kind of dirt he had on Addie to make her do it, but it must've been really good. On top of that, Finn must've begged me half a dozen times today, "Don't be a freak."

Yeah, because *that's* an option.

If Addie would give me a chance, I'd show her I was still the same guy I used to be. I would not let myself hurt Mia again. I couldn't.

My heart pounded in my ears and I nearly bolted out the back door. It was so strange; my feet were rooted to the spot but my flight instinct pushed me like a freight train.

"Casual, remember?" Finn whispered, pushing me back down into the chair and grabbing a pack of Uno cards from the kitchen counter. I took them from his hand, needing something, anything, else to focus on.

I heard Addie open the door as I slid the cards out of the box and onto the kitchen table, hanging on every word, every breath, every creak of the floor.

"Hey!" Addie said, but then her voice hushed and she spoke with quiet concern. "What happened now?"

I froze, my hands hovering in the air, the Uno cards quickly forgotten. I'd carefully avoided Mia all day. It couldn't be about me this time.

"I—I don't know what to do." Mia's voice sounded so small and scared. Even though I couldn't have caused it, I was still crushed by a wave of guilt. It might not be me this time, but I was certain I'd made her feel this way before.

The sound of the door closing echoed in the still house, and I feared Addie had taken Mia outside until I heard her speak again.

"After school today—I got an e-mail." Her voice shook with every word.

I glanced at Finn and saw a look of confusion on his face that must've mirrored my own. He tilted his head to one side and pointed at me with his eyebrows raised. I shook my head. I didn't even have her e-mail address.

"From who?" Addie's voice sounded tight. I knew she was probably thinking of me. After my behavior, who else would she assume sent Mia something that upset her so much? I held my breath, silently praying Mia would clear my name.

"It's pretty obvious, but I can't be sure. He didn't exactly sign it." Mia's voice sounded muffled, like she had her hands over her face. Bitterness and fear dripped from her words. Guilt felt like a weight balanced on the dull side of a blade and each time she spoke it plunged deeper into my chest. "He said things—terrible things. He w-wants to hurt me."

My breath came out in a gush, refusing to let me hold it any longer. I heard a gasp in the other room, and Finn stared at me like I was an idiot. I felt like an idiot.

Mia was off the couch and in the kitchen in a heart-beat. When her searching eyes met mine, I couldn't suppress a shudder. Her skin paled but she didn't look away. Dark smudges made paths down her cheeks where her tears had fallen. Addie came to stand behind her, shaking her head and glaring back and forth between Finn and me.

My mind whirled through what had happened and I could think of only one thing I could focus on. I had to help her, to prove to her it wasn't me this time. "Mia, let me see the e-mail."

Her eyes widened and her face contorted with anger before she spoke. "You're really messed up, you know that? What's wrong with you?" She raised her hand and rubbed the back of her head, and my mind pulsed with the vision of the blossoming blood last night. The twisted satisfaction that filled a dark place within me made my stomach turn. I'd seen her eyes, and the darkness within me was satisfied.

What had I become?

"How is your head?" I kept my voice as calm as I could.

Mia's face contorted with anger and fear. "I d-didn't need stitches. Sorry to disappoint."

Addie placed a hand on Mia's shoulder but the moment she touched her, Mia whirled.

"You knew he was here?" The expression of betrayal on Mia's face was heart-wrenching, and Addie flinched.

"No—I mean, yes. It was a mistake. I'm sorry." Addie glared at me, and I couldn't meet her eyes.

"Mia." Finn stood, trying to somehow fix this mess.

"Don't talk to me. You're sick by association if nothing else."

Finn's face fell, and he slouched back down at the table with a sigh. His plan had failed spectacularly.

"It wasn't me," I said softly. For the first time, Mia appeared to actually be listening. I wanted everyone to stop staring at me like I was a monster. And even more, I wanted to believe that they weren't right. That I wasn't slowly becoming everything they thought I was. "I don't want to hurt you."

Mia looked like a statue as she watched me. Only her hands moved, and they shook so much I was surprised it didn't jolt her whole frame. I had the sudden impression that I was watching a time bomb about to go off.

I wanted to grab her hands, to stop them from shaking, but I knew that would be a huge mistake. Her gaze was too guarded to tell if she believed what I said or not. And if she didn't, grabbing her wouldn't exactly go over well.

A bit of anger and resentment filled me. I was trying so hard not to be the bad guy. If someone wanted to hurt or scare Mia, I wanted to help. I *needed* to help—it was the only way I could prove everyone wrong.

I knew it would be stupid to touch her, but I walked into the living room and retrieved her backpack. Using slow, deliberate movements, I walked back into the kitchen and placed it on the table. The others looked more like portraits than real people. Only their eyes seemed alive, following my every move.

"Please, let me help you." I reached for the zipper, hoping she might've printed a copy of the e-mail to show Addie.

Before I could get it even halfway open, Mia snatched it from my hands.

Her whole body shook with rage and fear, but she stood her ground and glared up at me. Her eyes locked with mine and the fury in them looked ready to boil over. When she finally spoke, her gritted teeth twisted her voice into a low growl. "Stay. Away. From. Me."

Then she ran out the front door.

In the stillness that followed, every muscle in my body retreated in on itself. I surrendered, crumpling into the chair and laying my head on the table. I didn't even move when Addie thwacked me on the back of the head.

"What is wrong with you? Don't you see what you're doing to her?"

"He isn't doing it, Addie." The sadness in Finn's voice mimicked mine.

Addie sighed. "I don't want to believe he sent the e-mail either, but he certainly isn't innocent here."

I didn't lift my head, but when I heard her turn to leave I spoke. "I need to see the e-mail. I want to help."

Addie froze in the doorway, or at least it sounded like it, and when I heard her speak again she sounded on the verge of tears. "Parker, I never imagined saying this to you, but please do us all a favor. Stay away from Mia—and our family—until you get some help."

For a few minutes after she left I couldn't bring myself to move. Every hope, every dream that life could be better had been sucked out of my body. It was over. Why try so hard for a life that couldn't last much longer and would only be filled with exhaustion and pain for everyone I ever cared about?

I didn't know which hurt worse—Addie's lost faith in me or Finn's continued hope. They were two of my favorite people in the world and one of them had to be wrong. If Addie was wrong, did it matter? My life was done anyway. If Finn was wrong, then the best I could hope for was a quick death, the only way I could stop myself from hurting anyone else on my way out.

It was so quiet I would've thought I was completely alone if Finn hadn't shifted his weight in his chair every once in a while. I groaned. How was it possible that even when we were trying to make this better, it still got worse?

When I sat up, I was surprised to see that Finn had his sunglasses on. I didn't have the energy to ask why so I just raised my eyebrows.

"Yeah. I wear my sunglasses at night. I'm that cool."

"What are you doing?"

Finn shrugged. "You need to see her dreams tonight."

I shook my head and reached for his glasses, but he dodged aside.

"I won't let you give up—especially not now."

Frustration seeped through my veins, and I couldn't keep my voice level anymore. "Why not? We tried, and look where it got us. Giving up seems infinitely better right about now."

"Because you can't give up." Finn shrugged and stood up. "At least watch them tonight. Maybe her dreams will give you a clue about who really sent that e-mail."

"You heard her. She wants me to leave her alone. It's none of my business." My voice sounded cold, even to me. As much as I didn't want to let my bad instincts win, it was hard to argue with the only person who believed me.

"After everything else you put her through, don't you at least owe it to her to make sure this guy isn't a real threat?" Finn opened the back door and pushed me out of it. I knew he was manipulating me, but he had a point. I did owe Mia at least that much.

Before I could say anything else, he spoke again. "Tell me what you find out tomorrow. Addie won't forgive me if we let anything happen to Mia after this. And since you're the prime suspect at this point, you'd probably end up in jail. Which I hear sucks." He closed the door and I barely heard his muffled "Good night" as it locked.

FOURTEEN

Mia's dream jolted me to the core the instant it began. Gone were the peaceful scenes and ease of entry. Her dream layers vibrated around me so hard it felt like she'd hit me with them. The impact jarred me until my teeth ached.

I tried to orient myself in the madness. The nightmare swirled around me in chaos. Mia and I were wearing all black, dressed in shadow. She hugged her knees on the ground beside me, sobbing and rocking back and forth. All around us swirled other levels of the dream—bits of visions, nightmares, and memories in a twisted soup of confusion. Every noise reverberated a thousand times over.

My mind recoiled from the barrage on my senses, unwilling to accept the nightmare that had overtaken my sanctuary. Mia's dreams weren't like this. There was nothing peaceful or beautiful here. I knelt to the ground beside her, shoving my fists against my ears in an effort to regain some sanity. I wasn't causing this... was I?

The noises quieted until I could hear only a faint crackling. The smell of something burning filled my nostrils. I was relieved until Mia's sobs intensified and I was hit with her emotions. They were twin trains of misery and fear, leaving me wide-eyed and panting. My brain couldn't think under the mad pain of it. What was going on?

The swirling halted, leaving us in a grassy front yard. The other levels must have separated for the moment. The house before us was dark, but I watched as fire quickly spread to each window. In what felt like seconds, it was engulfed in flames.

That's when I heard the screaming.

I thought it was Mia, but then realized it came from the top floor of the house. Mia rolled to her side, wrapping both arms around her head. Her misery flowed into me as it escalated. Ending it was all that mattered. Unable to close her eyes or truly block out the sound, she thrashed about, trying to turn away.

The screaming in the house got louder, and I forced myself to face the blaze. If Mia had to witness it, so would I.

There were figures moving inside. I saw faces in the upstairs window—a man and a woman, both older. The woman had long brown hair, and the man haunting dark blue eyes. They had to be her parents. I watched them pound on the window. The man fumbled with the latch, trying to open it.

Smoke clouded the view and I couldn't see. Then both

figures were highlighted as the flames surrounded them. With their arms wrapped around each other, they melted into the fire, and within seconds, all was quiet.

Mia's gasping breaths filled the stillness, and I crouched down beside her. My gut twisted. I knew my tears matched the ones that drenched her face. So much agony. I hoped to God this wasn't a memory, but deep down I knew it was. The clarity of the sky, the stars, the vividness of the heat, the smell—it was too well defined to be just a dream. This was real. No simple nightmare was this solid—this terrible.

Mia had watched her parents burn.

Sitting beside her, I buried my head in my hands, knowing how much I'd added to her problems. No wonder she never answered any of my questions about her past. I'd never in a million years imagined she could've witnessed something so horrifying.

I knew I couldn't touch Mia in a dream, but this was too much. I couldn't just watch her, not alone in so much pain. I reached out and wrapped both arms around her shaking shoulders. I gasped when I felt the soft fabric of her shirt with my hands and she relaxed against me, sobbing into my chest. Then she wrapped her arms around me and clutched me so tight I had to work to breathe. I could feel her pain as it eased. It was so strange and it made no sense at all, but somehow, I was helping her through the nightmare. Somehow my touch didn't pass right through her.

I held her for hours as the swirling layers came and went. We sat on the grass, and Mia cried into my chest until the flames burnt the house to ashes. I absorbed her sadness and brushed her soft hair with my hand. She smelled like salt and flowers. Trying to soothe her eased my own guilt, even if I didn't deserve it.

After the flames died out, the house and yard faded to blackness. She still clung to me, but her sobbing had stopped. Her breath came in quiet puffs, but they were slowing in frequency as she regained control. The other layers of her dream faded to the background and I knew I should try to sleep, but I couldn't—I wouldn't—leave her. Not in this nightmare all alone. I owed her that much. Especially when I knew she could feel me here.

"Thank you," Mia whispered.

Her small hands rubbed my back, sending a shiver down my spine. She was trying to figure out who I was. Her hands ran up to my shoulders and down along my biceps until she pushed her face away from my chest and looked up into my eyes.

Her expression went from curious to horrified, and in a split second she was on her feet. I lay back on the ground as her panic ran through every nerve ending in my body, transforming them into something raw and terrible. The moment she broke physical contact with me, she seemed confused. She spun back and forth, her eyes searching and her arms held out in front of her for protection. I realized she couldn't see me anymore. I froze, trying to breathe through the fear. I'd hoped maybe I could show her who I really was, that I didn't want to hurt her—if only in her dreams. But it was no use. This was my fault. My actions had caused her terror. I didn't resist as it cut like a scalpel, tearing my insides apart. I deserved every slice.

Before I knew it, the dream changed and swirled around us like fabric in the wind until we settled inside our school. A thunderstorm vibrated the building. Mia ran to the wall and flipped the light switch. Nothing happened. Typical nightmare scenario. My muscles tensed, sensing this dream wouldn't get any better.

A low, dreadful chuckle came from the end of the hall, followed by the sound of footsteps. I squinted and Mia stopped, standing still as a statue, both of us trying to make out who it was. The figure stayed in shadow.

The footsteps quickened and a primal growl filled the air. Mia's flight instinct made my hair stand on end, and she sprinted down the hall away from the figure. I was jerked along with her until I got my feet under me and ran beside her.

The hall seemed to go on forever, the pursuer coming closer with every breath. Mia ran until she was panting and clutching her side. My heart pounded in my ears from my own exertion. We came to the end of the hall, but instead of the doors that led out to the back parking lot, there was another wall of lockers—a dead end.

Mia searched for something to defend herself with, but there was nothing. She tried to open a locker to hide in, but they were all locked.

New emotions flowed with the fear now, a spike of anger and confusion. My own anger mingled with hers. I wanted so much to help her, protect her from any more pain. Watching her parents die and having creepy me following her around? She'd been through enough. If anyone deserved to have peaceful dreams, it was Mia.

The footsteps slowed, and again the disturbing laugh echoed around us.

"Please—leave me alone," Mia whimpered.

"You know I can't do that." The voice from the shadows was deep, distorted and gravelly. "I told you how I feel about you."

"Threatening someone isn't love." Mia spat out the words.

"Maybe you don't know what real love is."

The pursuer was mere feet away now, and their conversation sent a chill through me. I wasn't sure I wanted to see who it was anymore. He lit a match, and I choked as I watched a darker, colder version of myself lift up a torch and light it. No, this couldn't be happening.

The sneer on my face and cold light in my eyes were darker than I'd ever seen in a mirror—almost inhuman—but still, I could see him for what he was. Mia knew me better than I thought, and better than she should. She could see the darkness within me, and she'd brought that part of me to life in her nightmares.

And here, I couldn't even try to control it.

Fear pulsed from Mia as she cowered away from the torch's flames and Darkness walked closer. I didn't want to see what Mia thought I was capable of, but I couldn't drag my eyes away. As I stood in the corner, my entire body shook with the fear I'd inspired in her.

Darkness reached out and touched her face. She cringed and he grabbed her hair, smashing her head into the locker. My skull exploded with her pain. Mia screamed and blood ran down the side of her face.

"You'll learn to love me—and no one else." The voice was mine now, not the gravelly distortion of before. But it didn't make any sense…it couldn't be me. I'd never said anything like this, nothing about "loving" Mia. Unless, of course, the threatening e-mail said these things, the one she'd thought was from me. I felt ill, overwhelmed by every emotion and image around me. The dream might not be me, but it came from the reality I'd created for her. My actions made her believe I was this guy.

Mia whispered something too low to hear, and Darkness brought the torch near her face. She froze like a deer in the headlights, unable to move with the flames so close. My spine stiffened as I felt her cold fear. After seeing the nightmare of her parents' deaths, I knew why. No wonder she'd refused when Jeff had tried to bring her closer to the bonfire at the beach.

I watched as I—*he*—grabbed a strand of her hair and touched it to the fire. She squeaked when the flame leapt up, almost reaching her head before Darkness squished it between two fingers. He laughed. He enjoyed torturing her.

I knew I had to stop him, but I couldn't. My fists passed right through him. Apparently I could affect the Dreamer—at least with Mia, I could—but I was as helpless as everyone else when it came to the dream itself. Thunder shook the building from outside like a reflection of all the frustration I felt.

Darkness—this other me—opened a locker and pulled some kind of metal stand out. I swore under my breath and took a step back. That locker had been locked when Mia tried it just a moment ago. Darkness put the torch in the stand, the flame positioned far too close to Mia's face. Her entire body was trembling so hard that the locker behind her made a strange rattling noise that echoed in the empty hall.

Darkness grabbed the hair on the back of her head with one hand and crushed her face to his. His other hand wandered freely over her body and she screamed in protest.

I shuddered and backed away from the scene. I couldn't do it—couldn't feel this—couldn't be a part of this.

No matter what he did, Mia couldn't seem to move. Her eyes locked on the fire, paralyzed. My worst fears played out before my eyes and I felt her terror—the terror of *my* victim. How could I have let myself become this monster in her life? Was it within me, aching to get to the surface?

No, it was worse than that. I knew it had already gained some kind of control over me.

Darkness rammed Mia's head into the locker again, growling, "Kiss me back, or I'll make you wish you had."

Mia didn't blink. She didn't lift her eyes from the flame, but she was still in there—striving to fight back. Her anger flared as she opened her mouth and brought both lips inward until only a thin strip of pink remained. Mia had strength. She was still herself.

Darkness roared, a sound of fury unlike anything I'd

ever heard before. He rammed Mia's head against the locker again. Ruby blood dripped down to the floor. He did it again. Again. And again. Her eyes were still open, but they appeared unfocused as the dream began to blur.

"Stop!" I felt my voice tear lose from my throat. My brain was smashed by wave after wave of pain. "Stop hurting her!"

Nothing changed; no one heard. I kept yelling until my throat went raw, pounding my hands against the locker behind me until they bled, but it made no sound. I crouched deeper into the corner, quaking and sobbing as I watched myself beat Mia to a bloody pulp. Her face was unrecognizable except for her dark blue eyes. They weren't watching the flame anymore. It seemed like they were staring straight at me. The *real* me. And with one final bone-shattering smash against the locker, they closed, releasing me from my own private hell.

FIFTEEN

When Mom heard me puking in the bathroom, she told me to stay home from school. It was Friday, so I knew I'd be missing a history test, but I didn't care. I wasn't really sick, of course—not exactly, anyway—but staying home sounded good. Every time I blinked, I saw images from Mia's nightmare and they made my stomach roll.

So here I was, at home in the daytime. Alone again. I'd tried to sleep, to go into my white void—if only to escape the pictures that kept pelting my brain like BBs fired at close range. But for the first time in years, I couldn't.

Reliving what I'd seen in Mia's nightmare was the last thing I wanted to do, but it wouldn't leave me alone. Every flash of it brought up more questions and worries. Who sent her the e-mail? What did it say? What had started the fire that killed her parents?

Addie had said that Mia went to therapy during the

first week of school. That was good. If that fire was a memory, especially a recent one, she would need all the therapy she could get. But I'd have to get Mia to talk to me to answer the questions I had, and the likelihood of that happening anytime soon was less than zero.

Besides, the dream had brought up more questions, beyond those just about Mia. Like, how had I been able to touch her? Was this another aspect unique to Mia? I hadn't tried for years to touch a Dreamer, so what was different now? Could I touch anyone? Had she actually seen me? Would she remember it after?

I growled and punched the throw pillow on the couch. Just once, I'd love for something to be easy.

There was a knock on the door. I glanced at the clock on the microwave. School was over, and I figured after last night Finn would show up at some point.

When I opened the front door, the grin dropped from his face. "Whoa, you're really sick? I figured it was an excuse, but you look terrible."

"Not sick, but I feel terrible." I leaned against the counter, grateful Mom wouldn't be home until later. If Finn thought I looked bad, Mom would probably freak.

Finn pulled a chair out and sat on it backwards, facing me. He crossed his arms over the chair back and frowned. "What happened?"

"I don't know." I shook my head. "Do you know what happened to Mia's parents?"

"No. Addie might, but she hasn't talked to me since yesterday. Her parents were in the dream?"

"Part of it." I walked to the table and pulled a seat out for myself. My body was too heavy to hold up anymore. I crossed my arms on the table and slumped down in the chair. "In the dream, she sat on the front lawn and watched her parents burn in a house fire."

Finn glanced away, not speaking for a minute. When he did, his voice was quiet, somber. "You think that actually happened?"

I considered denying it, but what good would it do? "Yes."

"That must've sucked." Finn walked to the fridge and grabbed a Dr. Pepper. He held one out to me, but I shook my head.

"The dream only got worse from there."

Finn fidgeted as he popped the top on his drink and sat back down. "What's worse than watching that?"

"The watching wasn't as bad as the feeling," I mumbled.

Finn sat his drink on the table in front of him. "Huh?"

"I could feel what she was feeling. That's not new; it's always been that way with Dreamers. It's not that bad, usually." I rubbed my knuckles across the surface of the table and looked up. "But this time was terrible."

"Oh." Finn gulped his drink, eyes huge. "Wow."

We were quiet. His slurping gulps echoed through the room. The clock on the kitchen wall ticked the seconds away. No more secrets. No more dealing with everything alone. I needed to tell him everything.

"Someone chased her down the hall at school. I think she's afraid of fire—which makes sense, if that really happened to her parents." Everything spilled out in a rush, like a poison I'd been holding inside—like it could kill me if I didn't. "Anyway, when the guy caught up with her—it was me."

Finn winced. "You were chasing her? Why?"

"It wasn't really me. She dreamed it was me. She thinks I'm the one who sent the e-mail, and so in her dream ... " I traced the grain on the table in front of me with my finger. "I had to watch myself be the bad guy."

Finn sipped the soda and pulled on his ear. He stood and walked out of the room. He came back a few seconds later with my basketball. "Come on. Let's go shoot while we talk."

I shrugged and followed him outside. Finn stood at the foul line we'd painted on my driveway when we were thirteen. He took a shot. Nothing but net. "So, did the other you catch her?"

"Yes."

"And?" He retrieved the ball and tossed it to me. I took a shot, but missed—I didn't care. My mind filled with flashes from the nightmare.

"She thinks I'm a monster. Whatever that e-mail said, it must've been bad." I pushed my hands into my hair, tugging on the roots. The pain made me feel better for some reason. Maybe because I deserved it.

"What happened?" Finn gripped the ball so tight his knuckles stood out, bright white, against the rest of his skin.

I took a breath and spoke quietly, looking anywhere but at Finn. "In the dream, I held a torch to her hair and beat her head against the locker until she was so bloody I couldn't see her face anymore." A shudder ran through me and I swung my arms back and forth to shake it off.

Finn let out a low whistle before making another shot. "Did the other you say anything?"

I thought back, trying to remember. "Something about making Mia love him."

"Okay, so we know the psycho e-mail guy probably said that." Finn dribbled through his legs while he talked. "And with that kind of violence, we can assume he included some pretty horrible threats too." He pivoted on one foot to face me. "Do you have any idea who it might really be? Anyone else ever popped up in her dreams before?"

"No, it's always been just her alone, until now. Her dreams were pretty repetitive until last night."

"Is that normal? To have the same dreams over and over?"

"Well, nightmares might repeat because of the strong emotions tied to them, but I've never seen that with other dreams. Then again, there are a lot of weird things about Mia's dreams." I grabbed the ball from Finn and fired off another shot from the top of the key—and missed. "Like last night, she cried during the fire, and I hugged her. I've never been able to touch the Dreamer before. But when I held her, she could feel me. That's definitely new." I rubbed my eyes and blinked a few times. They didn't want to focus anymore.

A grin spread across Finn's face. "Dream action—sweet."

I tried to laugh, but it sounded forced even to me. "Yeah, until she saw my face and freaked out—that was when the other part of the dream started."

Finn's smile fell a little but he kept dribbling. "And you're sure you've never touched anyone in a dream before?"

"No. I've tried, but it's never worked. It's been a while, though. Maybe something is different now."

"But what?"

"No clue, but I've been doing this longer now. Maybe I have more control?" I shrugged. "There's really no way to be sure."

Finn nodded and made a lay-up. Then he grabbed the ball and turned to face me. "So, how are we going to figure out who really sent the e-mail?"

I stared at him. I hadn't really expected Finn to help anymore. After last night I felt useless—maybe everyone would be better off if I just left, ran away and never came back. Although, if the e-mail freak was serious and did anything to hurt Mia after I was gone, I'd never forgive myself.

Of course, I'd probably be dead soon—but I'd be a totally pissed-off ghost.

Snagging the ball from Finn, I made my first basket. "We have to start by figuring out who might want to hurt her." I dribbled the ball for a minute and then shrugged. "I've been following her around and I have nothing. The only people I see her with are Jeff and Addie."

"Yeah, we might need help to figure this out."

"In that case, we have two choices. Ask Mia, which is not really an option, or somehow get access to her computer. Getting the e-mail and seeing the address would be a good place to start."

"Three, actually." Finn picked up the ball and dribbled it

a bit before taking a three-point shot—*swish*. "We could see if we can convince Addie to help us. She and Mia hang out all the time. If we can get her on our side, she could help figure out who sent it, and maybe even get her hands on the e-mail."

I frowned. "She's not even speaking *to you*. What makes you think she'll help me?"

"It's Addie. If anyone can convince her, you can. She's been friends with you almost as long as I have. Trust me. She wants to believe you aren't bad."

I wasn't so sure, but I shrugged. Anything would be worth a try at this point.

Finn nodded. "Do you ever watch her dreams?"

"No."

He grabbed the ball and held it still. "Why not?"

I searched through my mind for a better reason than the real one. I knew Finn wouldn't like it if I said his sister was the only girl I'd ever really liked, and I didn't want to risk ruining that. Even if it hadn't been against the bro-code, after hearing what Finn thought about Jeff dating Matt's little sister, it was clearly off the table.

"I don't know," I finally said, then shrugged and grabbed the ball from him. Great answer. Smooth.

"Well, you need to—tonight." Finn grabbed the ball back. "Then, tomorrow, you can tell her too."

It felt insane to even consider telling anyone else I was a Watcher. It wasn't that I didn't trust Addie, but she already considered me nuts these days. It would be risky to discuss the dreams with her. I clenched and unclenched my fists a few times, allowing the tension to flow out through them.

"Without any other option besides breaking and entering and then hacking into Mia's computer, I guess it's worth a try." I met Finn's eyes. It was disturbing to see him looking grim. So un-Finnlike.

I took the ball and dribbled for a minute, enjoying the controlled feel of it in my hands. "One night won't work, though. She might not remember enough from one night of dreaming for me to persuade her. I need a couple days to be safe."

"You better get started. We'll need her to help convince Mia that you're innocent."

My next shot bounced off the backboard, but Finn jumped and pushed it back up and in.

"You suck. Why aren't you on the basketball team again?"

"I'm humble." He grinned. "Don't like to steal all the glory, you know? Try to spread it around to losers like you."

I laughed. "Wow. So generous."

He shrugged. "It's how I roll."

I tucked the ball under my arm and headed toward the house. I felt much better having a plan, even if it did feel crazy to tell Addie. After last night, doing nothing wasn't an option anymore.

SIXTEEN

Getting Addie to meet my eyes was a bigger feat than I would've expected. When Finn and I got to his house, she was in her room and didn't come out until dinner. At the table, she stared down at her food, fuming. I could practically see the steam rising from her forehead. Mr. and Mrs. Patrick knew something was going on but didn't seem to have the details. They kept asking Addie questions and exchanging concerned looks when she mumbled the answer without glancing up.

After the fifth question, she sighed and asked if she could be excused.

"Are you sure you've eaten enough?" Mrs. Patrick asked while eyeing Addie's barely touched spaghetti.

"Yep. I'm full." Addie pushed away from the table and walked out the door into the backyard.

"Don't worry, I'll clean up." Finn grabbed her plate

and pushed the spaghetti and sauce onto his with a grin. His parents laughed. Finn elbowed me in the stomach while I tried to swallow my last bite.

I coughed. "Thanks for dinner. I'd better head home."

"You're welcome, Parker," Mrs. Patrick said with a smile.

"Anytime." Mr. Patrick waved.

Finn nodded and kept eating as I walked out the back door.

Addie sat on the porch swing. She glanced up and I finally caught her eye before she groaned and turned away.

I'd gotten what I needed, but it didn't seem like enough.

"I know you don't want to hear it," I said softly. "But somehow I'm going to make this better." I started down the steps, but she cleared her throat and I turned back to face her.

"It's not that I don't want to hear it." The disappointment trickling from Addie's voice hurt more than I wanted to admit. "I just wish I could believe it."

———

The first night, most of Addie's dreams took place in the music store at the mall. Random bands kept showing up and playing mini-concerts. Great when it was Neon Trees or Daughtry—not so great when it was one of those Disney girly bands. Still, at least it wasn't boring. From her emotions, she seemed to enjoy most of the same ones I did. Not surprising, but it racked her up some additional points on the coolness scale. Not that Addie needed any.

On the second day, I ran into her, literally, on her way out of the grocery store. She huffed a little, but when I helped her pick up the bread and lettuce I'd knocked out of her hands and said I was sorry four times, she calmed down.

In her dream that night, Addie was walking through the park alone. The moonlight made everything shimmer. Her pale skin glowed. She was beautiful. I did my best to pretend she still looked like a skinny ten-year-old, but she didn't ... the way her hair curled over her shoulders, the small waist that curved out to her hips. On top of her ridiculous hotness, Addie was one of the prettiest girls I knew, and by far the most awesome. It was almost a punishment to know her so well and not be able to do anything about it.

We walked through the park in silence. There was apparently no destination or reason to be here. The cool wind kicked some mist off the creek and it obscured the path before us. It was peaceful. The other layers of the dream were distant and quiet. I almost wondered if I could sleep here, but the slight humming of the layers in the background kept me from even trying.

Addie crouched and turned as a sound echoed behind us. It was low and foreign, like a growl mixed with the sound of grinding metal. I couldn't see a source and after a moment it was quiet again. Addie bit her lower lip, her eyes scanning the dark shapes around us. She felt fear, but also a confidence that surprised me. Whatever had made that sound, she was prepared to handle it.

Eventually she turned back around and began walking.

The noise never sounded again, but she was a little jumpy for the rest of the dream.

Everything around me faded to black and then I heard the wind. I blinked and could then see the few remaining leaves undulate in a tree near me. The wind forced them to obey, and with each gust more leaves blew off and fluttered to the ground. I watched them move, and it took me a moment to realize I couldn't see Addie anymore.

I was sure I'd been in her dream, but now I was here... and as far as I could see, she wasn't. Still, if I'd learned anything lately, it was that I didn't really understand how my curse worked. I'd rather believe that I just couldn't see Addie than that I'd somehow sleepwalked up a tree.

As if I didn't have enough problems.

I didn't know where I was or how I'd gotten here, which was a pretty strong argument for the invisible Addie theory. The cold cut through me like a knife, but I knew that didn't matter. Everything could seem very real in dreams. I was pretty high up. The way my curse worked, if I jumped I would probably shift to a new spot on the ground before I hit it. I'd watched enough falling-off-a-cliff scenarios to learn that much. But if it wasn't a dream, I'd probably shatter the bones in my legs. Not worth the discovery.

Light spilled from the left second-story window of the house before me. It seemed familiar, but in the darkness it was hard to tell. I blinked a few times, trying to see if the figure moving around in the bright light was Addie. When the dark hair fell across her face as she pulled the hood on her sweatshirt back, I gasped. It wasn't Addie.

It was Mia.

I watched, mesmerized, as she sat on the foot of her bed. Her shoulders jerked back when she tugged off her shoes and socks. I couldn't see her face until she grabbed a brush and began pulling it through her hair. She was crying.

Each stroke of the brush seemed to soothe me. If this was real and she saw me, then she'd probably send Jeff and Mr. Sparks after me—or call the police—but she never glanced toward the window. And how could this be real? Why couldn't I see Addie anymore? How could it still be her dream when I couldn't even feel her?

It made no sense, but I couldn't deny how good it felt to be able to look at Mia without worrying. It was peaceful to watch her and not be plagued with guilt. Everything about it made me sad, but I wasn't sure whose sadness I was feeling.

I don't know how long I sat there—long after Mia had gone to sleep. I shifted position a little against the rough bark, wondering when I would transition into another one of Addie's dreams. My conviction that this wasn't real wavered enough to make me careful when I crawled down from the tree. I sat at the bottom and shivered until the dream ended and I was forced back into my void.

Why cling so hard to a life that was so similar to a nightmare that I couldn't tell the difference anymore?

———

The next day was Sunday, and I didn't realize until noon that it was also Halloween—my mind had been so caught up in worrying about the weird Addie/Mia dream that I'd forgotten about my favorite holiday. I was used to not having answers about my curse, but still … something about the dream really bothered me.

I didn't get to watch Addie's dream that night. She'd gone to a scary-movie marathon with Mia, and since my mom had been nagging me about never being home, I spent the evening playing Scrabble with her and handing out candy to the neighborhood trick-or-treaters. Then I got to watch one of Mom's boring dream presentations. She was selling beach-front property, and it was more an auction than a sales presentation. People kept jumping up and offering her money.

She seemed to enjoy it. Me? Not so much.

By the next day, I'd passed the point of exhaustion. My withdrawal symptoms seemed to be easing a little, but I was so much more tired than I'd been before I met Mia. When I let my guard down and my mind wander, visions of Mia's bloody face and the fire creeping up her hair still plagued me. Addie's dreams had been a welcome relief, but still not something I could sleep through.

There was some weird game show on at Finn's house after school. We watched it with his dad while we waited for Addie to come home from swim practice. Each of my eye-lashes felt like it was made of iron—so heavy. It was impossible to keep my eyes open while sitting on their comfy couch. Rather than get up and try to stay awake, I relaxed back, not sleeping but resting my eyes.

Flashes of Mia's nightmare kept rising to the surface no

matter how many times I pushed them away, so I decided to stop fighting and see what they wanted to show me. Fear clouding Mia's face as she turned to run. A shadowy figure sprinting after her, but she couldn't see him—she could only see me. She cried every time she glanced back at me, but I couldn't stop following. I couldn't let him get her. He chased her, so I chased him. My breath grew ragged. I got close, but I couldn't seem to catch him. I knew if I didn't, he would kill her. I had to save her. I had to save Mia.

———————

"Parker." I heard a girl's voice whisper by my ear, her hand squeezing my shoulder. "Parker."

"Mia?" I mumbled, trying to convince my eyes to open. The hand tightened briefly and then fell away. When I finally pried my eyelids apart, Addie knelt before me, her hazel eyes sad. She looked more hurt than angry.

"Sit up. Everyone else went to pick up dinner, and you were breathing so hard I was afraid you might have a heart attack." She glanced down at the carpet poking between her fingers and muttered, "I probably should've let you."

I wanted to stand up for myself, but my sluggish brain was having a hard time formulating thoughts, let alone comebacks. What just happened? Not a real dream—I was sure I hadn't actually fallen asleep. I'd just stopped fighting the images. Some kind of daydream, maybe? Like my subconscious was trying to tell me something and didn't have any other way to do it. Weird. "Wha-what time is it?"

"The clock is on the mantel. Check it yourself." Addie shrugged and grabbed her backpack, seeming like a completely different person than the girl I used to tease. Behind her, the clock read 6:57 p.m.

"Come on, Addie. Don't do this." I reached out for her hand to stop her from going anywhere, but she jerked it away and my fingers closed on empty air.

"Me? *I'm* doing this?" She struggled with her backpack, trying to pull it up and over her shoulders as she turned toward her room. "You aren't even close to the person I thought you were. And I'll never forgive you if you drag Finn down with you."

I stood up and blocked her path. "It isn't what you think."

Addie gave up on her backpack, dropping it to the floor behind her. Her hands clenched into fists. "Oh really? What did I get wrong? Did you not go psycho? Did you not go all super-stalker on the first girl you ever liked? She's been through enough, you know." Her shoulders bobbed up and down with her breathing.

"I'm sorry for acting like a freak," I said, stepping closer. "But not for everything else. Sometimes you should trust me. Sometimes you're wrong."

Addie stood up on her tiptoes and looked me straight in the eye. The anger was still there, but now tears slid down her cheeks. "Then you should stop proving me right."

It hurt to see her pain. I reached up with my thumb and brushed one of the tears away. Her skin was so soft. I ran my fingers over her chin and down to her shoulder. I stared in her eyes, wanting more than anything to make her understand.

"Mia isn't the first girl I ever liked. I never even *liked* her. It isn't like that. She isn't... she isn't you, Addie."

Addie blinked, but she didn't step away. She was so close. My hand squeezed her shoulder and the urge to pull her against me was almost overpowering—but I couldn't, not now. If I would ever have a chance to earn back her trust, I had to prove I wasn't the one hurting Mia... not anymore, anyway.

The back door opened, and the sound of Finn and Mr. Patrick arguing about which Chinese noodles were the best floated into the house. I dropped my arm to my side. Addie wiped the tears from her cheeks, opened the front door, and looked at her feet as she gestured for me to walk through it.

I stood on the front step alone, wishing I knew what she was thinking. Addie's eyes met mine for only a second and then she closed the door, leaving me alone in the dim porch light.

————

This had to be the last night. Mia needed help—and we needed Addie.

Her dream began with her body in shadow, watching herself as a kid—maybe five or six. The younger Addie sat on the old metal swing set they used to have in their backyard. Her auburn hair was longer and the waves fell down her back. Mini-versions of Finn and me were kicking a soccer ball back and forth. The whole scene looked familiar. It had to be a memory, but we'd hung out like this a hundred times—I didn't know why she'd remember one specific day so vividly.

She started swinging, humming to herself. Clouds moved in, cutting us off from the sunlight. The wind picked up, tossing Addie's hair around, but she didn't seem to notice. A few minutes later, the air exploded in one of those abrupt Oakville storms. The rain came down in sheets, drenching everything in seconds. As younger Finn and I bolted inside, the smell of electricity filled the air and a massive boom rattled the windows. Then I finally realized what memory she was dreaming about.

Addie was alone outside, getting colder and wetter by the second. She cried on the swing, her tiny body trembling, and one long curl tangled up in the chain of the swing. She called out for Finn, then for me, but her small voice was drowned out by the raging storm.

Minutes went by as she pulled, yanked, and twisted her hair, struggling to get it free. I kept waiting for the younger version of myself to show up to help her, as I vaguely remembered doing. Time stretched endlessly while she tried and tried to free herself, sobbing and jumping every time the sky lit up and the thunder boomed around her.

Finally, Addie gave up. She sat in her swing crying and shivering, her arms wrapped around her head in a vain attempt to hide from the worsening storm. That was when seven-year-old Parker finally came to the door. He ran outside, grabbed her arm, and tried to pull her with him. She squealed in pain when her hair pulled tight. He reached his fingers up, trying to untangle it. Her petite arms wrapped around his waist as he worked at the knot in the rain. Finally, he managed to free her. They ran inside and watched through the window. Seconds later, the lightning hit the swing set, leaving Addie's swing scorched and mangled.

I glanced over at Addie as she watched her dream. A slight smile curved the corner of her mouth, and I knew I had to try. Reaching out, I touched her shoulder and she turned to me. There was no hint of the anger I'd seen lately. She almost seemed to be expecting me.

"You were pretty cool that day." She spoke softly, almost like a thought. She moved closer and wrapped her arms around my waist, exactly as she had in the memory.

I put my arms around her and pulled her close, like I'd imagined doing so many times. She felt even better than I'd hoped. Our bodies seemed made to fit together. I rested my chin on her head. She smelled like she did in real life, and an unexpected happiness sank deep into my skin.

"I'm not as bad now as you think I am." I hoped she could hear and feel me, but I wasn't sure.

"In my head, I always called you Hero. From that day on, that's what you were to me." Addie frowned. "At least, until you turned into the bad guy."

Her eyes got sad and she moved to turn away, but I wouldn't let go, afraid of losing the connection.

Something about the way she spoke was different too— so simple and young, like part of her was still that girl on the swing. She could hear me, could see me. In her dreams, she still trusted me.

Maybe it was time I started using this curse to my advantage.

"Addie, I need you to promise me something."

She glanced up at me and raised her eyebrows. "What?"

"Tomorrow, if I come to you and ask you to listen, will you try to remember this memory and this conversation? Will you try to listen?"

Her eyes met mine for a moment, and then she nodded. "Okay, I will."

I took a deep breath and released her. She turned toward another memory, oblivious of me now as though I'd never been there. As if this entire thing never happened.

Crossing my arms, I pushed them down against my rib cage, trying to control the wriggling hope inside my gut.

Tomorrow, I'd find out if I could affect a Dreamer.

SEVENTEEN

The next day dragged by so slow I only survived my last class by thinking up a hundred different ways to destroy the clock on the wall. Since we were in different grades, Addie and I had zero classes together, which made the day feel even longer. I knew what the stakes were. She could decide I was crazy, or she could believe me. The help of Mia's best friend would be a huge asset in resolving my crisis, but it was more than that. I wanted Addie back on my side, in my life. I needed her to believe in me again. And if she could tell me what the e-mails said, or even convince Mia that I wasn't the one sending them, that wouldn't hurt either.

On top of that, I had to know if she remembered me from her dream. If she did—well, that could change everything too.

I leaned against the lockers outside the chemistry lab in an effort to stop myself from pacing. Chemistry was Addie's last class of the day. I hoped I could catch her on her way to the parking lot and convince her to talk to me.

I'd have to see if I could get my keys from Finn. He'd been doing most of the driving lately. After about the fourteenth time I'd heard him mutter about wanting to live long enough to go to college, I threw my keys at him—he'd never given them back.

I was so tired. Every day that passed seemed to add ten pounds to each eyelid. I could barely keep them open— keeping them focused was impossible.

It was like my body had readjusted to real sleep with Mia and was acting more like a regular person's. And now, after only a week without Mia's peaceful dreams, the four years of sleep deprivation had caught up with me. Without her dreams, without real sleep, I knew I couldn't keep this up much longer.

A guy turned the corner at the end of the hall and I caught a glimpse of that same spiky brown hair, but when I glanced up he ducked into the next classroom. He didn't have the jacket on, but I could swear it was the Blind Skull guy. With everything going on with Mia, I'd forgotten about finding him and figuring out who he was.

The bell rang and I jumped about a foot, making a couple of sophomore girls across the hall giggle. I grinned and shook my head as they waved and smiled. Addie was halfway down the hall before I realized she'd passed me. Hefting my backpack on my shoulder, I hurried to catch up with her, but people kept pouring out of the classrooms between us, slowing me down.

Coach Mahoney turned the corner at the end of the hall. "Parker! I need to talk to you."

Addie was already out the door; I didn't have time to stop. Besides, missing a few—okay, most—of Jeff's practices wasn't the same thing as missing Coach Mahoney's practices. "I'll stop by your office tomorrow, Coach!" I called over my shoulder, speeding up. I'd been around Mahoney long enough to know he cared more about performance on the field than politics off it. And he'd never had a single complaint about my performance.

"Parker!" he shouted again.

I sprinted through the door, down the stairs, and still didn't catch up with Addie until we'd reached the parking lot.

"Addie, wait!" I yelled when my feet hit the pavement fifteen feet behind her.

Addie froze, then pivoted around to stare at me.

Addie—dreams of spontaneous concerts, spooky walks in the park...and me.

At first, a look of disbelief and anger filled her face, but when she opened her mouth nothing came out. She closed it, confusion filling her eyes, and she waited. It took me a full minute to realize she was giving me a chance to speak.

"We need to talk." Everything about the way she glared at me screamed that she wanted to say no, to tell me off. I rushed on. "It's really important. Please."

With an exasperated sigh, she jammed her hands onto her hips and walked toward me. "Fine. What?"

"Could we go somewhere?" I really didn't know where to start. I hadn't actually expected her to agree, and the middle of the school parking lot didn't seem like a prime location to chat.

"Great idea!" Finn appeared from out of nowhere and pushed Addie and me toward my car. His shirt of the day said, *See you all at my intervention.*

I might have to get one of those.

"We're *all* going?" Addie scowled.

"We'll hurry. I promise." I opened the front passenger door for her and then climbed into the back seat. My mom used to flick me in the shoulder any time I didn't open doors for girls. It didn't actually hurt, but it got her point across. It was an old habit now. Finn drove us out of the parking lot and I tried to get my thoughts together.

Addie only gave me about thirty seconds before she spun around in her seat and said, "Okay, talk."

"Do you remember what you dreamt about last night?"

Her eyes widened before her face went blank. "No, why?"

I opened my mouth to respond, but I wasn't sure what to say. From her expression, I was pretty sure she was lying, but I didn't want to get my hopes up.

Addie turned to Finn. "Where are we going?"

"Nowhere," he said with a grin. "I'm just making sure you can't run away from this conversation."

She leaned against the door and crossed her arms over her chest before turning her glare on me. "So? You're just wondering about my dreams?"

"Not exactly." I paused and decided at first it would probably be best to avoid mentioning Mia altogether. "I have this kind of … talent … I guess."

"A talent?" Addie raised one eyebrow, but she seemed more curious now than angry.

"Yeah. I can see other people's dreams. And for the last few nights, I've been watching yours."

Her eyes darted back and forth between Finn and me, like she thought maybe she missed the joke. "Uh—huh?"

"Prove it. Give her examples." Finn slowed to a stop at a red light. He glanced at his sister. "Although she'll never believe you if she doesn't remember the dreams."

Addie followed our conversation with her eyes, looking more frustrated by the second.

I shook my head. "I'm pretty sure she does."

"I'm right here!" she snarled. "If you want to talk to me, then talk to me. If not, then take me home. Now!"

"Sorry." I ran through her dreams in my head, trying to decide where to start.

"A couple of nights ago, you had a dream you were at the mall—shopping in the music store." I watched her face carefully, but she didn't betray any emotion. "All these bands kept showing up and playing songs. It was actually pretty awesome."

Addie sighed and rubbed her hands over her face. Finn kept glancing between her and the road. After a minute, she leaned back against the door again and looked at me, her eyes sad.

"All you've proven is that you're every bit as creepy as Mia says you are—and maybe more than a little insane." She scowled at Finn. "He's supposed to be your friend. Can't you get him some help? Tell his mom?"

"I believe him."

"No. You don't." Disbelief and contempt took turns stamping their way across Addie's expression.

Finn pulled into a park across the street from the elementary school. He turned to face his sister and looked more serious than I'd ever seen him look. "Yes, I do."

Gratitude welled in my chest. Someday I'd have to pay him back for all this.

Addie threw her hands in the air before resting them on her knees. "Well, then you're both nuts."

Something in her expression seemed more concerned than angry. Like she feared what we were saying could possibly be true. I needed to go for it—no holding back.

"Another night this week, you had a dream you were in a park. Something was following you, but it never caught up." Something inside told me not to mention the dream outside of Mia's window. I still wasn't sure what that was and any mention of Mia would probably make Addie shut me out completely.

Finn laughed and banged his fist on the steering wheel. "What were you afraid of? The squirrels?"

She punched him in the shoulder. "Shut up."

I frowned and shook my head at Finn. He couldn't make fun of her, not right now.

He nodded with a shrug, catching my hint. "I need some air anyway." Finn got out of the car and walked toward a nearby pavilion with a drinking fountain.

Addie lifted her eyes to mine; they were a sea of confusion. Her hands were clenched tightly around the hem of her purple-and-gray-striped shirt. "I remember that park dream. How did—how did you know about it?"

"I told you. I watched it." I took in a deep breath, hoping she was coming around.

She shook her head. "To be honest, I don't know if I even want to believe you. If it's true, then I'm bugged. My dreams are private, and I don't want you snooping around in them. But if it's a lie, then you're insane and really messed up."

"Oh." I was an idiot. This was the exact reason I'd avoided watching Addie's dreams up until now. Somehow I knew she'd react this way. I put my hand on the back of her seat, resisting the urge to touch her. "I'm sorry. If it makes you feel any better, I never watched your dreams before this week. And I won't ever again if you'll just belie—"

She raised her gaze to mine and cut me off, her eyes intense. "Do you ever—I mean, do the people know you're there? Do they see you? Talk to you?"

"If I'm touching them, then they can see me and I can talk to them. But I'm not sure if they remember it." I paused, nervous to ask, but dying to know the answer. "Last night, you dreamed about when we were younger and your hair got stuck in the swing during that storm. After the memory, I touched you—"

Addie gasped and her hand flew to her mouth. Her other hand grasped mine tight, searching for support. Whispered words snuck through her fingers.

"I remember you."

The implications of her words shot through me, quick and unexpected like a desert storm, leaving a dump truck worth of sand strategically located in my throat. After about four attempts to swallow, I finally managed to respond.

"From your dream?"

She nodded tightly, one hand still covering her mouth as though refusing to let her speak anymore. Her other hand trembled. I wrapped both of mine around it and held on tight.

"What, exactly, do you remember?"

Addie lowered her hand from her mouth to her lap and bit her lip. "Everything, I think." She closed her eyes and leaned back against the passenger seat. "I remember you being there after the memory. It's weird, though, because at the time you totally blended in, like you were part of it."

She opened her eyes. "But when I saw you today I remembered you being there, and something about it felt different, separate maybe."

"So, you remember our conversation? What I said?" I tried not to get my hopes up. This only mattered if she remembered everything, and if it happened with everyone and not just her. Still, it was incredible that she remembered me at all.

Addie scrunched up her forehead. "I think so. We talked about the memory—and you asked me to remember our conversation if you talked to me about it later. Right?"

The breath I hadn't noticed I'd been holding rushed out. "Yep, that's pretty much it."

She took a deep breath and frowned. "Well, since that doesn't explain—or justify—all the crap you've been pulling lately, I should go." She pulled her hand out of mine and clasped hers in her lap.

I cleared my throat. "There's more."

Addie relaxed back against the seat and turned her eyes to meet mine. She looked relieved. "I hope it's good. Tell me."

It only took a few minutes to explain the way my curse worked, the lack of sleep, and the way Mia's dreams had changed everything. When I finished, she sighed.

"That's why you look exhausted all the time." She bit her lip, and then put her hand on my arm before continuing. "I'm sorry. I didn't know ... I said some pretty bad stuff."

I shrugged. "It's okay. I did some pretty bad things."

"I know, but ... " She squeezed my arm tight. "So, you'll probably die if ... if we can't figure this out?"

I nodded, and her face fell. I didn't know what to say. I'd never reassured anyone about my possible impending death before. Maybe it was wrong, but the look of devastation on Addie's face made me feel less alone. It was a simple comfort, and not one I'd ever experienced before.

If I died, I would be missed ... and not only by my mom and Finn.

Finn knocked on the window and we both jumped. She rolled it down.

"So, it's cold out here. If you two are done making out—"

"Bite me," Addie interrupted him. Finn laughed, walked around the car, and slid into the driver's seat, but Addie didn't remove her hand from my arm. "So, I appreciate you telling me, I really do, but what do you expect from me? Why did you tell me?"

"We were hoping you might help us with Mia." I tried to read her expression, but it clouded over and became un-readable.

"So you aren't actually the one sending the e-mails?"

"No, it's not me. Wait—e-mails? She's gotten more than one?" I felt a shiver run down my spine, remembering her nightmare again.

"Yeah, she's gotten one every couple of days. She has at least two or three now." Addie released my arm and rubbed her fingers over her knees. She appeared more nervous than she had during my whole confession.

"What's wrong?" Finn looked as confused as I felt.

"It's just … if it *was* Parker"—Addie glanced at me and then back to her brother—"I never believed he'd actually hurt her. I thought he was messing with her head, which was bad enough. But if it's someone else … who knows what they might do."

"Exactly." I nodded. "We need your help figuring out who's really sending the messages."

Finn draped one arm over his seat, angling his body to face us. "If we can do that, maybe we can find enough proof to show Mia it isn't Parker."

Addie sighed and bent her head over the dashboard. "You really came to the wrong person."

My gut fell to my feet. "Why?"

"Ever since that day she came over and you were there, Mia won't talk to me about the e-mails. I mean, she tells me if she got one, but if I ask what it says or if she still thinks it's from you, she totally freaks. Literally has a panic attack—she shakes her head and starts breathing really fast. Then she bolts. After three reactions like that ... " Addie shrugged. "I stopped asking."

My body slumped against the back seat as one more weight landed on the thousand already there. Sure, Addie believed me, but it wasn't going to help after all. Every time I got close to an answer—to things getting better—someone built a huge rock wall right between me and the finish line.

I was getting really tired of running into rock walls.

Glancing up, I saw Addie and Finn both leaning over the front seat, watching me. They looked sad ... and scared.

"I'm sorry," she said.

"It's okay. We'll just have to think of another way." I closed my eyelids tight, then opened them again. "I'll watch her dreams again—see if I can get any more clues."

"No, bad idea." Finn shook his head. "You don't want to go through that again, man."

"Go through what?" Addie glanced at me, but I shook my head and looked out the window at the park. I couldn't tell anyone about the nightmare again. Reliving it in my own head was bad enough.

"Mia had a nightmare about the guy who's threatening her. Parker was the bad guy in Mia's mind. Not fun to watch yourself being all evil, you know?"

Addie winced.

"Are you sure we can't just figure it out? Is there anyone you think could be sending the e-mails?" Finn asked, tugging on his ear again.

"No, I have no idea." I shifted my weight uncomfortably on the seat.

"What about Thor?" Finn turned back to face me, his expression hopeful. "He's crazy, has anger issues, and hasn't he been pretty weird about Mia?"

"He scares pretty much everyone without even trying." Addie nodded at Finn. "It could be him."

"Plus, he seems to enjoy it." Finn rummaged around in his backpack.

I shrugged. "Maybe, but I think he's only involved because she's Jeff's foster sister. He doesn't seem all that interested in Mia unless he's trying to keep me away from her, and we all agree that's pretty justified."

"So, let's start with a list of suspects." Finn fished a pen and paper out of his bag.

Addie covered her mouth and tried not to laugh.

"What?" Finn looked up. "I've played Clue."

I shrugged. "Go for it."

"We should include every guy we've seen her with." Finn scribbled *Thor* on the paper and *Jeff* underneath it.

"There is some guy that knows her from work at the mall. Chad." It felt lame, but it was the only other person I could come up with. Finn scribbled the name on the list and looked back up expectantly.

It was quiet a minute, and Addie sighed. "It's hard to imagine anyone we know doing something so terrible. But it doesn't even have to be someone we know. It could be someone from her old school." She leaned her head back against the seat and groaned. "I wish she would just talk to me."

"I'll find a way to watch her dreams. It doesn't matter if it's hard on me," I said, even though my stomach told me it did—a lot. "If that's the only way to get any clues, I'll do it. She needs our help."

Neither of them argued. They simply watched me. I knew they wanted to help, but I was the only one who could really do anything. Besides, they were already helping more than they knew. It was nice just knowing they believed me.

There was no choice anymore. The only chance I had to make up for what I'd done to Mia was to save her. Even if it killed me, I'd make sure she wasn't in any real danger. Besides, I'd always known I wouldn't be able to live like this forever. I might as well do something worthwhile on the way out.

"I can keep trying to convince Mia to talk, or at least to show me the letters." Addie's voice sounded small.

I leaned forward. "Yeah, but don't freak her out too bad. She needs a friend."

Addie nodded, looking helpless. "I think I could at least make the eye contact thing easier." She looked so soft and sad it made me ache with a need to fix it.

"Maybe I can try what I did with you and see if I can get through to her in the nightmares," I said. "That might work." I tried to sound optimistic, even though my history with Addie was perhaps what made it possible.

With Mia, I was simply her nightmare brought to life.

EIGHTEEN

"Just a little farther." Addie's eyes sparkled as she tugged on my hand again. I didn't think I had the energy to move as fast as she wanted me to. But she didn't stop until we got to the back door of the nurse's office.

When we walked through the door, Mrs. Allison stood up from behind the desk. Her hair was like a fluffy brown football helmet but she had a kind face. "Hello, Addie." She glanced at me with concern. "Oh, dear, you don't look like you're feeling very well, do you?"

I glanced at Addie quickly, then back to the nurse. "No. I guess not."

"Parker's been having a hard time with um—headaches lately. He has free study this period, and I wondered if he could use one of the empty sick rooms to study. All the other students make it hard for him to concentrate in study hall." Addie glanced at me and gave me a little nod.

"Oh, yeah, migraines actually." I raised one hand and rubbed the back of my neck. "It's so hard to focus in there."

"You poor thing." Mrs. Allison placed the back of one hand across my forehead. After a moment she nodded. "Those migraines can make life terrible, can't they?" I nodded as she sat back in her chair. "Addie, be a dear and show him to the back sick room. It's mostly used for storage anyway."

"No problem." Addie practically bounced as she led me down the quiet hall to a room half full of boxes. She walked inside, dropped her backpack, and stacked some of the boxes against the far wall.

"Addie"—I dropped my bag and started helping her— "why do I need to study here?"

"You don't." She flashed me a wide, beautiful smile and stacked another box against the wall.

"Oh." My mind went blank. I had no idea what to say. When she was so close, I couldn't think straight.

"Excellent response." Addie laughed and turned her attention back to the boxes. She didn't seem to want to tell me what her plan was until she finished reorganizing, so I relaxed and followed her lead. Within a few minutes the room was straightened and I sat on the cot in the corner, confused.

Addie pushed the door closed behind her and came to sit beside me on the bed. I was uncomfortably aware of how good she smelled and the way her leg was resting against mine. I didn't know why, but that's all my brain seemed capable of focusing on. She smelled fresh, like soap and orange juice. The smell of her soaked up anything useful in my head and turned it into a sponge. I closed my eyes and took a deep breath.

"That's exactly what I was thinking."

My eyes flew open and I stared. There's no way she was thinking what I was thinking.

"It is?"

"Or maybe not?" Her brow furrowed, and she continued. "This will be good, right?"

I nodded before I could even stop myself. "Probably?"

Addie tilted her head to one side and tugged on a strand of her hair. The corner of her mouth curved up. "You don't have a clue what I'm talking about, do you?"

"Not even a little bit." I grinned and shrugged. "But this is very entertaining."

She giggled. "For you to get some extra rest?" She spread out her hands and patted the cot we were sitting on.

"Oh." In the quiet, I looked around at the windowless room. It wasn't like I hadn't tried to rest during study hall before, but the only benefit of sleeping the way I did was to have some peace for my brain. With all the talking and goofing off going on in study hall, it didn't work. In here, it was quiet. It was genius. *She* was a genius.

She bit her lip and glanced from my eyes to the pillow behind me.

"It's perfect, Addie." I wrapped one arm around her and squeezed her close to me.

"Good." She relaxed against my body and put one arm behind my back. "I wanted to help you somehow."

How could she not know how much she'd helped me

already? I reached out, put my finger under her chin, and raised it until I could see her eyes.

"Thank you … for everything."

Her eyes and lips were so close I could feel her breath against my skin. I cleared my throat and let go of her chin, but she didn't move. There was a playful glint in her eyes, like she was teasing me, tempting me to just do it.

"You." She winked with a soft smile. "Are welcome."

I wanted so badly to lean in to her, to feel her soft lips on mine. But I couldn't. The last thing I needed right now was another complication, or to make Finn mad at me again.

Lying back against the pillow, I propped my legs across her lap. She was trapped. "So, is this the one that Jeff uses? Should we get some sanitizer?"

She laughed and leaned her forehead against my leg. "Yes, it's this one, but don't worry. I came in here with a bottle of bleach my first day as an aide. Nobody wants *that* in their sick room."

"Such excellent service." I fluffed my pillow and grinned up at her.

Her voice sounded sad when she spoke again a moment later. "Do you really think we can find out who is after Mia? Can we really help her?"

I didn't know what to say. Comforting Addie would be easy, but I didn't want to lie anymore. "I don't know. But I promise I'll do everything I can to make sure she's safe."

"I know you will." She turned to face me and her eyes met mine. "Promise to keep yourself safe too?"

Meeting her sad eyes, I lost all will power. In spite of the fact that I'd just vowed to tell the truth, I would lie through my teeth to say the words she wanted, to make her feel better. "I promise."

She smiled, and in that moment I knew the lie was worth it.

My eyelids drooped, so heavy that I couldn't keep them open anymore. I barely noticed when Addie slid out from under my feet and slipped through the door.

———————

An extra hour of peace per day didn't fix everything, but it helped more than I expected. I wasn't really less tired, but my brain seemed more functional.

On top of that, Addie coordinated when would be best for me to make eye contact with Mia, made sure she was in the right place at the right time, and distracted Mia right afterwards so she didn't get all freaked out about it.

Finn spread a rumor that I'd had eye surgery and my eyes were really sensitive to light. It made everyone stop looking at me weird for wearing sunglasses indoors, and the teachers even left me alone about wearing them in class.

I'd even made it to a few of Jeff's practices on days when Addie knew Mia would be staying late. Jeff seemed less frustrated now that I was showing up more often. It was a win-win.

My friends were amazing.

Even Mia's nightmare was improving—or at least my attitude about it was. While the dream was almost exactly the same each time, the difference was me: if I had to be in Mia's nightmare, I refused to just be the bad guy.

I could be the good guy too.

It was the only way I could fight my biggest fear. I wasn't most afraid of dying anymore. It wasn't at the top of my to-do list, for sure, but I was more afraid of the darkness within me. In Mia's dream, I could face it in human form. I couldn't affect her dream directly, but if I could convince her I didn't want to hurt her in the dream, maybe I could convince her in reality too.

My first time back in the nightmare, we reached the dead end of lockers and I watched from the corner, bracing myself for the pain and horror to come, waiting for the monster to light the match and show my face.

"Threatening someone isn't love," Mia spat out again.

"Maybe you don't know what real love is." He lit the torch with a sneer as my voice spoke the now-familiar words.

Mia cowered away from the flames and I made my way around to the other side of her. My jaw ached from clenching it. Determination flowed through me, alongside her pain and fear. This time she wouldn't have to face him alone. I grabbed her hand and squeezed. She stood frozen, watching the menacing flames move closer, but after a moment, I felt a small squeeze back.

I got closer to her shoulder and spoke low in her ear, not really sure what to say, but hoping somehow she would remember it.

"Mia, that isn't me. The e-mails aren't from me."

For a moment, I thought her eyes wavered to the side—a quick glance in my direction, but it was too dark to be certain.

Darkness reached out and touched her face. She cringed and he grabbed her hair, smashing her head into the locker. My head throbbed. Mia screamed and blood ran down the side of her face.

"You'll learn to love me and no one else."

I fought the disgust I felt at those words spoken with my voice. I squeezed her hand tighter, trying to think of some way to snap Mia out of her nightmare.

Her eyes turned to mine and time stood still.

"You're the monster."

Her whispered words were a wrecking ball hitting me in the chest. Every hope within me shattered as I watched Darkness enjoying the fear that sparked in her eyes when he moved his torch closer. I felt weak from her emotions. And helpless, unable to clean up the mess I'd made. Unable to save her, I dropped my hand to my side and sat down in the corner, defeat crushing me like a bug beneath a shoe.

This was a mistake. I couldn't do this again.

I tried to block out the scene around me. A shudder passed through me when I felt her fear as he touched the flames to her hair. Raising my gaze, I froze. My eyes locked on the one difference between this nightmare and the one before—Mia's hand—the one I'd been holding as I spoke to her. It was the only part of her body that moved. It jerked erratically, grasping this way and that. She was searching for something.

She was searching for me.

I jumped to my feet and grabbed her hand. Immediately a small amount of tension seemed to flow out of it. She held on so tight it hurt, but I didn't care. I enclosed her hand in both of mine and gave her every bit of strength I had left. After that moment, her emotions were dulled slightly, as if knowing she wasn't alone took the edge off. I knew exactly how that felt.

With my eyes closed, I stood at her shoulder and rubbed the back of her hand with both thumbs. I spoke softly, reminding her over and over that it wasn't real. It was only a nightmare. It would be over soon. Even as I felt a few drops of hot blood splash on my face and heard the hall echo with the clang of her head against the locker, I held on tight. My body shook with her pain, but I didn't let go. Her grip on my hand never eased, even after there was silence and the nightmare blurred into nothingness.

———————

My toes were nearly frozen when I woke up the next the morning. My window was pushed all the way up. I couldn't remember opening it, but I did remember feeling hot at some point. I shrugged it off. After experiencing Mia's nightmare this time, I felt almost hopeful. I needed to see if she would act differently toward me. I double-checked her schedule and got to school early, then convinced Finn to stand outside her first period class with me, explaining what happened as we waited.

She froze as she came down the hall, and stared at me.

Mia—dreams of the death of her parents ... and being murdered by me.

Her eyes were narrowed, but also filled with confusion. It was something. It was different, at least. Normally she acted like even the sight of me could hurt her. Not this time.

Someone ran into her shoulder and she broke eye contact with a little shake of her head.

Finn's eyes widened as she walked into the classroom across the hall from us without another glance. This could only mean one thing.

Mia remembered something. She had to.

"Some co-captain. Only shows up at practice when he feels like it." I heard Matt's murmur and turned to face him. Finn spun around, too, and as usual was ready to jump to my defense.

"Hey now ... ugh!" Finn's breath spilled out in a gush as we were both thrown against the lockers. Neither of us had seen Thor coming, but he walked through us like he was cutting through the streamer at a finish line. I heard his familiar low growl as he passed by with no apology.

It took a moment for us to figure out what had happened. Finn had a gash under his eye and blood running down his cheek. I sprinted after Thor, grabbed his shoulder, and yanked back as hard as I could. He lost his balance and went crashing across the floor.

"What's your problem?" I yelled at him as students scattered out of our way. Matt stood nearby, laughing, but made no move to step in for either side. Clearly our soccer team wasn't much of a team anymore.

Thor was on his feet in an instant. He was surprisingly fast. I knew that from soccer—it would've been good to remember it *before* I threw him to the ground, though. He had his massive hand wrapped around my windpipe in under a second. His momentum slammed me against the wall, and my feet dangled a foot off the floor.

Finn pulled on Thor's arm but before he could loosen it, Matt grabbed his shoulder and pinned him against the opposite lockers. "Stay out of this, Finn. We're just trying to teach our so-called *captain* what happens when he betrays the team."

The edges of my vision darkened, but I finally got one of my flailing feet braced against the wall and swung the other one full force into Thor's gut. He flew backward, catching Finn in his path and crushing him against the lockers. We all fell gasping to the floor.

The principal, Mr. Lint, pushed his way through the group of students surrounding the fight. I saw Blind Skull guy at the back of the crowd, but he was gone an instant later. Dude really had a knack for vanishing. Mr. Lint shooed the other students to their classes and didn't turn to us until most of them were walking away.

Mr. Lint tossed back his shoulder-length gray hair and shook his head. Something about his face and the way he moved always reminded me of William Shakespeare in a sweater vest. "What's going on here?" he asked.

"He attacked us," Finn muttered, clutching his side. "We were defending ourselves."

Not exactly true, since if I hadn't pulled Thor off his feet it wouldn't have gotten so out of hand. Still, I appreciated it.

"It was just a mistake, Principal Lint."

I whipped around toward the voice and found Jeff leaning against a locker a few feet behind me. I hadn't even realized he was there. I heard Finn release a gush of air and knew what he was thinking. The principal practically idolized Jeff. He would take whatever Jeff said as truth.

"A mistake?" Principal Lint raised one eyebrow. His gaze skimmed over the blood on Finn's cheek and shoulder and my footprint on Thor's white shirt.

"Yes." Jeff walked over to Thor and extended a hand. Thor took it and got to his feet. "Thor probably wasn't watching where he was going and accidentally ran into these guys. They thought he did it on purpose, and it kind of went downhill from there."

"Yes, well." Lint peered at us again. "I suppose I can see how that could happen."

Jeff walked over to me and helped me to my feet. He placed a hand on my shoulder. "And really, no one got hurt. So no biggie. Right, Parker?"

"Yeah, right." I shoved his arm off me and walked over to where Finn was slowly standing up. "Although I think Finn might need to see the nurse about where his cheek *accidentally* slammed into the locker."

Lint nodded and brushed his hands together. "Very well, then. Can you walk him to the nurse's office, Parker?"

"Yeah, no problem."

Liv Campbell walked past us in the hallway. Her cheerleading uniform went well with her peppy personality. She glanced around our group, then focused on me. I expected the smile she usually gave me, but instead she quickly looked away. Her expression was unmistakable—pure fear.

I cursed under my breath and shook my head. If she'd heard about the way I'd terrified Mia at the mall, probably half the school had. Perfect. Like everything wasn't complicated enough already.

We walked toward the nurse's office and the others turned in the opposite direction. Jeff shrugged, his smile tight but mostly genuine. He'd been right to step in. We all could've been expelled.

Finn wheezed as soon as Jeff and Thor were out of earshot, but he seemed to be okay. "This year just keeps getting better and better. Any minute now some dude is going to show up with a big check and some hot girls in bikinis."

I laughed and took his backpack from him. "I'm sure that's coming next."

"So, you know Matt and Thor want you off the team, right?" He grunted with a sideways glance in my direction.

I opened the door to the nurse's office and waited for him to enter. "I know."

He nodded. "Just checking."

NINETEEN

It felt weird to follow Mia around and try to make sure she *didn't* see me for a change, but I didn't know how else to find people to add to our list of suspects. Finn and I were parked across the street from the Green Leaf Medical Office Complex ... for the fourth time. It had been almost an hour since we'd watched Mia walk inside. A plaque beside the door read, *Dr. Clive G. Freeburg CHt—Freeburg Hypnotherapy Clinic.*

The wide window beside the front door of the clinic still had a few fake spider webs and miniature dancing skeletons decorating the corners, even though Halloween was more than a week ago. But at least it gave us a clear view of the reception desk and waiting area. From what we'd seen, there was no receptionist, just a heavy older man with a thin silver mustache and wire-rimmed glasses who opened the door for Mia when she arrived. His bald head shone in the fading sunlight, and he had a band of salt-and-pepper hair just above his ears. He always led her through a door to the right side. He was the only person we ever saw at the office. It was an easy bet that he was Dr. Freeburg.

Movement inside caught my attention and I watched Mia walk out the door with the therapist just behind her. They talked for a minute in the doorway. His hand rested on her shoulder, but as she spoke he slid it back and forth on her arm in a way that made me uncomfortable. He often stood a little too close to her in the first place, but this contact was just...something was up with this guy. Mia smiled and laughed, oblivious, but the way he was watching her reminded me of a fat guy hanging out at an endless dessert bar.

Finn yawned. "I don't know what hypnotherapy is, exactly, but this guy has to be doing something right."

"Yeah, she definitely seems better after every appointment."

"It's good. That first time, when she came out sobbing?" Finn frowned and shook his head. "There's just something about girls crying, man. I'm not a fan."

"Still, I think we need to put him on the list." I picked up the paper and scribbled in his name. It had a grand total of six suspects now: *Thor, Jeff, Chad, Mr. Sparks, Matt* (who we added after he took Mia out to a movie last week), and *Dr. Freeburg*.

Six—and none of them really seemed like an obviously threatening stalker type. If this were a game of Clue, we'd be getting our butts kicked.

"Oh, yeah. Definitely. He should get his own freaky list if you ask me."

Finn turned my car on and pulled into traffic, a few car-lengths behind Mia's truck.

"Agreed."

I propped my elbow up on the door and turned to Finn. Something had been bothering me, but I'd hoped we'd find answers fast so I wouldn't have to bring it up. That didn't seem to be happening, though. "Mia really seems sure I'm the one sending the e-mails."

"Well, you were acting pretty creeptastic for a while there." Finn didn't even take his eyes off the road.

"I know." I watched her purple pickup a few cars ahead and frowned. "But what if there's more to it than that?"

Now Finn glanced over at me. "Like?"

"I don't know." I shook my head. "It just seems like she *knows* it. Maybe it says something in the e-mail?"

"Why would someone want to make it sound like it was you?"

"Exactly what I've been wondering." Turning away, I rested my forehead against the window. "And more importantly, who would want to do that to me?"

Finn didn't respond, but when I looked over, I saw him tugging on his ear. He was thinking it over. That was all I could ask.

We followed Mia until she pulled into her subdivision, just to make sure she was heading home. Finn glanced at me and drove into a nearby driveway to turn the car around. I rubbed my eyes against the light of the setting sun. It felt so good to close them, so necessary. Two weeks had passed since Mia's first nightmare and there hadn't been even a hint of her peaceful dreams since. I craved them, both mentally and physically.

"You look beat, man. Want me to drive you home and keep your car tonight?" Before I could answer, he added, "I'll pick you up before school tomorrow."

"No, that's all right. Just drive to your house." I opened my eyes all the way and tried to look awake. "I can get myself home."

Finn looked doubtful, but he put the car in gear anyway.

———

I'd driven half of the way between Finn's house and mine before I recognized the black motorcycle behind me. In the glare of a streetlight I saw that same patch on his jacket. Blind Skull.

After all the time I'd spent following Mia, I knew how it was done. I wanted to be sure he was really following me and it wasn't just a coincidence, so I took a couple of sudden turns, and when he was still behind me, pulled into a nearby grocery store. I sat in the car until I saw him park a few stalls back and three rows over.

Who was this guy? What did he want with me? As much as I might deserve to be stalked after what I'd done to Mia, I was too tired to put up with this anymore.

I got out of the car, but instead of heading for the store entrance, I turned and walked directly toward him. He was quick, obviously watching me. Before I even made it past the first row of cars, he revved the engine and sped toward the exit.

Dad's voice echoed in my head. "The blind skull sees more than you think."

I stood for a moment, watching his taillight as he raced off into the dark. I couldn't help but wonder … what, exactly, did he see?

When I got back to the car, I added *Blind Skull* to the bottom of our suspect list.

———

If I didn't hurry, I was going to be late … again.

Grabbing a bagel from the half-empty bag on the counter, I pulled my backpack over my shoulder and was almost out the door before my mom's voice stopped me.

"Parker, wait." She was sitting in the corner of the living room in the dark. Weird. I'd thought she'd already left.

This didn't look good.

"I'm going to be late."

"You're going to talk to me." Mom reached up and flipped on a lamp on the table beside her. "And you're not leaving until you do."

My backpack slipped off my shoulder when I saw her. She was still in her robe and slippers and her eyes were swollen and puffy.

Mom—dreams of losing my dad ... and me.

"What's wrong?" My muscles felt leaden. I couldn't move. "Is it Dad?"

Her brow furrowed in confusion and she shook her head. "No." Her voice was stiff, distant.

I released the breath I'd been holding. I was a fool. He wasn't coming back. He was never coming back. "Then what's wrong?"

"Where were you last night?"

I shook my head. "What are you talking about? I was here."

"Stop lying!" She was on her feet in an instant. "I checked on you at four this morning and you were gone. Where were you, Parker? Where?"

Her one repeated word was like a lighthouse, slicing through the fog of my reasoning—my justifications. It shone like a high beam, vividly displaying the monster I'd become.

A memory of me, sitting in Mia's tree outside her window, hit my brain like a semi truck. The air caught in my chest and it took me a minute to breathe. It hadn't felt like a dream because it was no dream. I'd been sitting outside her window, watching her. I had no memory of going there, no memory of climbing the tree, and no memory of coming home.

That wasn't last night though, I reminded myself. Where had I been last night? And then there was the morning my window was open—had I snuck out that night as well? I closed my eyes and focused on keeping myself upright, on keeping my lungs breathing in and out as my brain flew into a state of total panic. What was happening to me? My life had become like watching myself in someone else's dream.

I'd lost control of everything—school, soccer, sleep, my whole life. Even my mind had started betraying me.

"Please tell me where my sixteen-year-old son needs to be at four in the morning, Parker, because I've been sitting here since then trying to figure it out." Her fists were balled up and she was walking back and forth between me and the chair. Even after Dad left, I'd never seen her this angry.

"Did you see me come back?" I asked, surprised at how calm my voice sounded. My mind scrambled for answers as I tried to keep from curling into the fetal position on the floor. *Where had I been?* The truth was simple and horrifying. I had no idea.

"No. When I came to check again, you were asleep. You must've come back in through your window." Tears rolled down her face, but she didn't seem any less furious.

"I just . . ." I crossed my arms, searching for an answer. Any answer but the one that I now knew was true. I could've been anywhere, doing anything . . .

To anyone.

"Don't think that gets you out of anything. I don't care if you weren't gone long. You don't sneak out in the middle of the night!"

"I just went for a walk, Mom. Relax."

Didn't she realize this wasn't helping? How was I supposed to panic about where I'd been when she kept freaking out?

She sighed and walked up to me until she was nearly standing on my toes. When she spoke, her voice was so soft and full of pain it felt like an icicle in my heart. "Do I really look that stupid?" Reaching out, she took my hand. "Parker, I know there is something going on. Something is wrong and I want to help you, but I can't if you won't talk to me. I don't understand what's happening. All I'm asking for is a little honesty. I promise I won't be mad."

It wasn't her anger that I was afraid of. She couldn't know the truth about me. She'd be so disappointed that I'd gotten so out of control. I couldn't be just one more person who let her down, one more burden. I'd fix this and handle it on my own.

"Mom, school is just stressing me out. I had to clear my head or I wasn't going to be able to sleep." I tried not to cringe.

"Have you even tried the sleeping pills Dr. Brown gave you?"

"They don't help, Mom." I kicked my toe against the carpet. "But it doesn't matter, everything is okay."

"No, it's not, honey. I know it's not." She gripped my arm and pulled me down closer. "I mean, if it's illegal—"

"Seriously? This again?" Jerking out of her grasp, I backed away. I couldn't deal with this, not now. "For the millionth time, I'm clean. Although I might as well start taking something if you're going to accuse me of it anyway."

"Parker, you need help," Mom yelled as I started to walk out of the house.

"No, Mom. Not from you I don't." I slammed the door behind me and left before I could hear her yelling or crying anymore.

I only drove a block before I pulled over and got out of the car. I was shaking, my world crumbling. The car was too small, the space around me so tight and confined. I had to breathe real air—fresh air.

I fell on my knees in the dirt behind someone's dried-up rosebush, two blocks from my house, and tried to understand how I'd somehow become a Watcher of my own life.

————

That night, I stared at my own eyes in the mirror on my dresser. Maybe if I looked hard enough I could see who I really was. I could almost see both sides now, the dark and the light, in constant battle. And I couldn't go back to what I'd been before.

Parker—dreams … doesn't dream, only lives at the expense of others.

What kind of creep sits in a tree watching a girl through her bedroom window? What was I becoming?

With shaking hands, I unzipped my backpack and pulled out the crumpled paper and a pen from the front pocket. As I touched my pen to the paper, my phone started vibrating on the table next to my bed. I picked it up and silenced it without even looking to see who was calling. I knew it was Finn and Addie, and I knew what they wanted.

I'd avoided them as much as possible at school today, but that couldn't last long. I had to accept the fact that if I didn't know what I was doing, if I was losing that much control, then I had no idea how dangerous I really was.

And I could never, ever forgive myself if I hurt them.

With a quick deep breath, I wrote my own name at the bottom of the suspect list. Every letter felt like a brand on my skin, like writing it out made it real. I stuffed the list into my bag, barely resisting the urge to erase my name and take it all back. All I could do was hope it wasn't true.

Glancing down at the dresser, I saw my dental floss sitting there. It bordered on ridiculous, that something so small and simple might be able to contain me. But if I tied my wrist to my bedpost, in the morning I would at least know if I'd gone somewhere or not. The floss wouldn't lie to me the way my mind could. From now on, I would know if I stayed in bed at night. It sucked that I couldn't trust myself anymore, but it was the only way to be sure.

————

Addie and Finn continued helping me make eye contact even though they could tell I was hiding something from them. It shouldn't have surprised me. They'd always been there when I needed them most.

Mia's beautiful dreams were still missing, but her nightmare continued to change for the better every night, and the pain dulled a little more. The beginning never changed;

as long as it was a memory, it couldn't. She cried in front of her burning house and I held her until she looked at me. It never altered.

One night, Mia's hand reached for me the moment we were in the hall at the school. When I grabbed it, she glanced at me in confusion a few times as we ran, but she never let go for the rest of the nightmare.

The next night, when we got to the end of the hall, she clasped my hand tighter. When it came to the point where she usually called me a monster, she didn't. Instead, she just bit her lip and cast a furtive glance in my direction. I murmured low in her ear, trying to convince her to fight back, to make the nightmare stop, but she gave a very slight shake of her head. Instead, she closed her eyes and tucked both hands into mine. The nightmare continued around us, but we refused to be a part of the terrible things her mind was doing to her.

It'd made a difference in real life too. When Mia glanced my way at school, she looked more confused than scared. Addie said she still wouldn't talk about me, but she didn't freak out the way she used to. Maybe I could convince Mia to trust me—both in her dreams and in reality—even if I didn't trust myself.

Although, why should either of us believe in me when the time lapses kept getting worse? The floss I used to tie my wrist to the headboard was intact for the first two days I used it; then I woke up the third morning and found it ripped in half.

The next night, I decided to try rope. It wasn't nearly as

easy to rip as the floss. I needed to be certain I wasn't merely breaking it by thrashing around at night. Maybe I was just a wild sleeper. I kept hoping the most reasonable explanation would be the answer here. That it wasn't what I feared. As I tried to relax my tense muscles, I kept telling myself it could be true. The rope would still be in place the next morning. I just wished I could make myself believe it.

When I woke up, yawning, I smiled at the weight of the rope still around my wrist. But as I lifted up my arm, my blood turned to ice. Just below the knot, the rope had been cut. I held it close for a better look; it was a clean cut. It hadn't been ripped apart or gnawed off.

Getting to my feet, I searched my nightstand for anything sharp enough to slice the rope in two. I'd put my scissors in the office the night before. I checked under the bed, in my backpack. There was nothing else.

I reached one hand under my mattress and it came to rest on cold metal. Swallowing, I pulled it out with one trembling hand. The dark-red box cutter still had the blade exposed. My breath caught in my throat. I dropped it on my bed and sat in my desk chair staring at it. I'd never seen it before. I didn't even know we owned a box cutter.

Wrapping my arms around my knees, I rocked back and forth, trying in vain to find any other explanation for it. Not the psychosis the doctor mentioned. Please, no. But I couldn't trust my own mind.

If I was inventive enough during my blackouts to do this, then it didn't matter whether it was floss or a thick rope. Until I was ready to ask Thor to sit on me while I slept, I'd get out one way or another.

I grabbed the box cutter off the bed, retracted the blade, walked into the kitchen, and threw it in the garbage. My hands wouldn't stop sweating. My pounding heartbeat made my head throb and I leaned my forehead against the cool glass of the dining room window. Something inside kept telling me to ask Finn for help, but I wasn't ready to tell anyone how much control I'd lost—not now, not yet. The thought of admitting it out loud scared me more than anything else.

———

I switched back to floss when I ran out of rope, which happens surprisingly fast when you cut it up into one-inch pieces in your sleep. Sometimes I woke up with my wrist chafed, like I might've broken the floss by thrashing around. Other times my computer monitor was on, not on screensaver, in the middle of the night. Once my window was open again and the bottom of my bed was covered in snow and footprints. I had no way to know what I was doing during these times—who I was with, who I could be hurting. Even following the snowy footsteps through the yard didn't give me any insight. Once they reached the shoveled sidewalk, I couldn't track them anymore.

By now, weeks had passed—Thanksgiving was coming

up soon—and I was on the verge of giving up on ever finding a way to help Mia. But then her dream changed even more. After the fire at her house, she stopped crying earlier than usual. She didn't glance up at me, and I knew why. For whatever reason, anytime she looked at me, the rest of the nightmare started.

"Parker?" Mia's voice sounded muffled against my chest. She was so full of conflicting emotions I felt guilty. My heartbeat raced. I'd never expected her to try to talk back.

"Yeah?"

"Which one are you?" It wasn't hard to figure out what she was asking.

"I'm not the monster, Mia." I pulled her closer. Her hands gripped my shirt tight. They were shaking.

"Then who is?" She glanced up at me and the nightmare shifted around us. Recognizing her mistake, she slammed her eyelids shut, but it was too late. The school walls closed in and I heard the footsteps of Darkness coming behind us.

I raced toward the end of the hall, practically dragging her in my wake. Only a moment, that was all I needed. Before he could catch up, I pulled her to face me and lifted her chin until she met my eyes again.

"I don't know who it is, but I promise you—I will find out." Her eyes flitted back and forth between me and Darkness as she nodded.

The nightmare went on, but this time he was different. It was still me, but my image flickered like static on an old

TV screen. Hope filled me when I realized that for the first time, she doubted.

Just when I was becoming convinced of my own guilt, Mia wasn't sure anymore.

TWENTY

"Are you sure about this?" Addie asked from her spot in the middle of my resident sick room in the nurse's office. "Today?"

Her eyes rarely lifted from what must've been the world's biggest first-aid kit. She had all one million pieces of it spread out on the floor in front of her. In the past five minutes, she'd packed, unpacked, reorganized, and was now packing it again—all while Finn walked around her in circles. They were making me dizzy. It looked like Addie's lower lip might start bleeding any minute from the way she kept biting into it.

"It can't wait any longer. It's almost Thanksgiving, and during fall break making eye contact with her will be even harder than it already is. We need to do it while this latest dream is fresh in her mind." I leaned against the wall and studied the popcorn ceiling. Maybe it was reckless, but we were running out of time.

My vision shook violently back and forth and I closed my eyes. Over the last few days, different parts of my body had begun having full-on mini-seizures; usually it was my eyes or my hands, but the other day my foot had gone crazy. The longer I went with less and less sleep, the worse they got. Mia's nightmares, while improving our relationship, were killing me.

"I told you about the dream last night." I shrugged, my eyes still closed. "Maybe it won't be as bad as we think."

Mia's dream wasn't the only thing that had changed for the better last night. The floss tying my wrist to the bed was in one piece when I woke up. Drawing in a deep shaky breath, I released it slowly. I'd stayed in bed. After everything lately, it seemed like a good sign.

Finn wouldn't stop pacing. His legs kept going like he was on a treadmill—if he slowed he might stumble and fly off the back of it.

"I don't know," Addie muttered as she struggled to wrap her thin fingers around an enormous stack of gauze pads. "She just started talking to me about the e-mails again. If we really want to help her, we can't afford to scare her off now."

"That's why you won't be a part of it." My eyes finally stopped their spasm and I slid to the floor, taking supplies from her hand and placing the pile in one of the containers.

"But things have been bad with her foster family lately. Mrs. Sparks is never home." Addie sighed and wrapped both arms around her knees, tucking them up under her chin. "I feel so bad for her. First there was the fire—which alone had to scar her for life—then, I don't know. It'd be so hard to get stuck in the middle of some family you don't even know."

"Do you think there is anything weird going on with Mr. Sparks?"

"No—from the way he acts, I think he cares about her. They're just really busy. Mia doesn't like to talk about family much, and she refuses to discuss her parents." Addie closed her eyes and shook her head. "No matter how many times I ask."

It was quiet for a minute before I reached over and closed the massive first-aid kit, stood, and pushed it onto the top shelf. "We're never going to figure out who's threatening her if we don't convince her to let us see the e-mails. I'm going to try to talk to her. I think after the dream last night, I might actually have a shot. If not, you're our backup plan."

I extended my hand to Addie. As she came to her feet, I waited until her hazel eyes met mine. "Remember, you know nothing about this. Play dumb and it'll be fine."

"No worries. She does that constantly." Finn's laugh sounded weak and robotic, but I still appreciated the effort. He got to his feet and stood next to her.

Addie smiled, then elbowed Finn in the ribs—hard—before looking back at me. "I just hope you know what you're doing."

Still rubbing his side, Finn led the way out of the office as the bell rang. His skin had paled and his voice wasn't as steady as usual. "So, the hallway behind the gym?"

"Yeah. Five minutes."

He gulped and nodded before turning and disappearing into the throng of students surging through the hall.

Addie grabbed my hand, squeezed it once, and whispered "Good luck" before releasing it, going back into the sick room, and closing the door behind her.

———

The old benches stacked in the hallway smelled like wood marinated in sweat and Gatorade. I perched on the edge of one, waiting. It was the reason I'd picked this spot. First, no one ever came here. The hallway dead-ended at the back entrance to the gym, so it was used to store old equipment. Second, if I sat on this bench, she'd never see me until they were already here.

Was it sneaky and underhanded? Probably. Did I care? No. I needed some place I could trap her for a few minutes. Just long enough to make her listen to me.

A shudder ran down my spine at the general creepiness of that thought, but I shrugged it off. I repeated the mantra I'd been practicing lately.

I'm not a monster. I'm not a monster. I'm not a monster.

Of course, it would be easier to believe that if I hadn't woken up all those mornings with the dental floss on my wrist ripped in half—but there were other explanations for that. There had to be. Ones that didn't make my hair stand on end. Ones that didn't end with me babbling nonsense in the corner of a white room with padded walls and an extra-tight jacket.

I took a deep breath. How could I figure out who was threatening her if she wouldn't trust me? Helping her was my goal. By definition that made it less creepy, right?

Footsteps sounded in the hallway and I froze, listening.

"And Addie said to meet her *here*?" Mia sounded more than skeptical.

"Yeah, I'm pretty sure it was here." I could hear the guilt in Finn's voice from down the hall. He was officially the worst liar ever.

With a shake of my head, I got to my feet, but I waited until their footsteps reached the end of the hallway before I stepped out.

Mia's initial reaction was pretty much what I expected. Her eyes widened and she opened her mouth to scream. I stepped forward and held up my hand. "Mia, I just want to talk to you for a few minutes. Please."

She glanced between Finn and me before she sighed, closed her mouth, and nodded. "There are students and teachers everywhere. They'll all hear me if I scream." She sat down on the bench and dug her cell phone out of her jeans pocket. With several glares at me for emphasis, she dialed 911 and left it open on her lap. "You have five minutes. Finn has to leave, though; I don't like being outnumbered. If you touch me, or even look like you're thinking about it, I'll scream as loud as I can and push *Call* at the same time. Got it?"

Finn's eyes were gigantic as he turned to face me. When I nodded, his breath came out in a gush. "Um, I'll go then. I promise, Mia, he won't hurt you. I wouldn't have brought you here if I thought there was any chance he would."

Mia turned her frosty gaze on him and shrugged. "You're his best friend. I don't exactly trust your opinion. Addie's going to kill you for bringing me here."

"Yep." Finn winced. "See you, man. Good luck."

"Thanks." I turned to take a seat beside her, but she cleared her throat and frowned, hovering one finger above the "call" button. With a jerk of her head, she indicated the opposite end of the bench. When I'd sat where she directed, she lifted her finger from the phone and turned her eyes back on me.

Mia was acting tough but it was hard to miss the tremor that ran across her shoulders. After the last week of dreams, it was painful to think I still scared her that much. I'd hoped it would be different now, but I couldn't hold on to that optimism while she looked at me like she thought I had a chain saw stashed behind my back.

"I need to tell you something, and it's really hard to believe, but it's true." I spoke soft and slow, keeping my hands where she could see them. I tried to remember all the pieces of the speech I'd run through a dozen times in my head.

"I'm sorry I've been such a freak—from pretty much the moment we met." I cleared my throat, trying to make the dryness go away. "You said I was on drugs once, and you were kind of right. I was addicted."

Mia's eyes widened and the flash of relief on her face gave me hope.

"The problem is that my addiction is you—or actually, your dreams." I shook my head as a wave of confusion and panic crossed her face. Everything was coming out all wrong. *My addiction is you?* Man, that phrase had "Things a Serial Killer Would Say" written all over it. What the heck was wrong with me? My brain and my mouth were refusing to communicate.

"What I mean is ... I watch dreams. I've seen yours— a lot of them. You used to have dreams all the time about these beautiful places." Now the words were tumbling out fast. Almost too fast to make sense, but at least I was kind of explaining. "And you were painting, or trying to paint, and you wore this white dress—"

Mia gasped and got to her feet, but I saw it coming and moved in front of her, blocking her path. I wrapped one arm around her back and covered her mouth with my hand. Her phone fell and clattered across the floor.

"Shh ..." The word slipped out of my mouth and a dark shiver ran through me. Terror poured from her eyes as she struggled against me, but I was so much stronger. It wasn't even that hard to hold her in place, and no one was here to help her—no one but me.

Horror filled me, and I felt sick at how close this situation felt to the one in her nightmares. I released her and stepped back. No, this wasn't me. I wouldn't let it be. I couldn't.

I fought the fire in my chest, forcing my lungs to breathe.

"I'm not done. You have to listen to me."

"No, I don't." She pushed against me, trying to get past. "I can't believe you talked to Dr. Freeburg. That's just—you're just—"

"What do you mean?" In my confusion she almost snuck past, but I grabbed her wrists and held them to my chest.

"Please, just listen to me. I know who Dr. Freeburg is, but I've never talked to him."

Mia leaned away with all her weight, frantically trying to wriggle her hands free. "Let go! All you've ever done is lie."

I brought both her wrists together between my hands and barely resisted the urge to pin her against the wall and force her to hear me. The darkness within me flared and I felt like throwing her away from me to keep it from gaining any ground. Her eyes flew up to mine and I stared into hers, trying to show her I was sincere. "Mia—I swear to you I'm telling the truth. What would it hurt to listen to me? I promise. I won't ask for anything more."

"Haven't you already done enough?" Tears welled in her eyes and my heart sank. I released her and sank down to the bench. She was right. I couldn't stand to see her look at me that way anymore. She stood frozen in place, so I made one final plea, my voice cracking with desperation.

"Please, listen, and then you can go. I promise."

Fear and pity seemed to have chosen her eyes for a battlefield. After a few seconds, pity won and she sat back down. "Fine, talk."

Straddling the bench, I turned to face her. I could see it in everything about her: this was it. The last chance I would ever get. I needed to make it count.

"I can prove it if you let me. I know about the nightmares too. I know about the monster you see—how he chases you and how you're afraid of fire. I know how he says he'll make you love him." I studied my hands and barely noticed how tightly they were clenched. I tried to remember everything, any small detail that might convince her to believe me. "I know in your dreams it's me, and I ... I beat you until you black out, but that's not me. I'm—I'm the other one."

My breath was coming out in panting bursts now, but I couldn't stop it. "And I know about your parents and the fire—how you were on the lawn crying. I'm so sorry—"

I stopped, wondering what I might have missed.

"Can I talk now? Are you done?"

I looked up at her, but her face was unreadable. I nodded. If what I'd said so far didn't convince her—nothing would. The fact that she'd listened this long was a minor miracle.

"I'm going to leave now, and you're going to let me." Mia got to her feet, and I stood too. Her voice was slow and deliberate, but her legs shook so bad she almost couldn't stay upright. "And you're never going to talk to me again."

Those nine words felt like a hundred very small and extremely sharp axes to my gut—each one drawing blood. Taking a faltering step back, I leaned against the opposite wall, fighting the urge to crumple to the floor. "So you don't believe any of it? How would I know all of that? How would anyone?"

"I don't know how you convinced Dr. Freeburg to tell you about my therapy, but this needs to stop right now or I'm calling the police. No more e-mails. No more talking to my therapist. No more getting Addie to tell you about my past or my family." Mia spat the last word out with venom so forceful it shocked me.

"What about the nightmares, the things the stalker said?"

My mind rebelled against the realization that she had an explanation for everything.

Mia reached into her backpack and shoved a crumpled-up piece of paper into my hand. "There is only one person who would know about those, Parker—the monster that sent them to me." She grabbed her phone off the floor, turned, and walked away.

My brain searched for anything else that could help. My voice trembled and I slumped down on the bleachers. "But ... I did it because I'm dying."

She didn't even turn around when she shouted, "Good!"

Her response echoed around me as everything seemed to move through a dense fog. I opened up the crumpled paper she'd put in my hand. It was a printed copy of an e-mail from Chipp8@gmail.com. My e-mail address was Chipp18. It said:

> *The fire will help me seduce you.*
> *It won't be long until we can be together.*
> *I'll make you love me.*
> *The fire will make you love me.*
> *If you don't, it means you're broken.*
> *I'll find a way to fix you.*

I dropped the paper to the floor. The pounding in my head was so loud I could hear every heartbeat like a marching band clanging in my brain. As I watched Mia's stiff form walk down the hall, I saw the shadow of someone following behind her. I took a step. It was him; it had to be. I had to warn her. As I opened my mouth to yell her name, the words caught in my throat and I choked on all the lies my life had become.

The shadowy figure stepped into the light. Tall, messy black hair, loose-fitting jeans—I recognized the familiar walk.

I blinked, knowing it must be my imagination. He nearly caught up with her before I finally rubbed my eyes and looked again. Darkness splintered into a thousand shadows before melting into the gloomy corners of the hallway.

TWENTY-ONE

The massive oak tree shuddered against the cold November wind. The few leaves that still clung to the branches were plucked off one by one, each spinning harder than the last as it skittered down the street in front of my car. I parked across from Dr. Freeburg's office again.

What I was hoping to learn from showing up here, at this point, I wasn't sure. I just wanted to talk to Freeburg. Mia had made it very clear in our conversation earlier that she already thought I had, so I might as well try. Maybe I could get a clearer idea if he was actually as creepy as he seemed to be. Maybe he had some of the answers that were out of my reach. After my plan to talk to Mia had crashed and burned, I desperately needed to cross a name off my suspect list, and if it couldn't be mine . . . well, then maybe it could be his.

I leaned the driver's seat back and closed my eyes to rest for a few moments, but it didn't help much. My headache was every bit as bad as it had been earlier, and it was getting worse by the minute. Each time I closed my eyes, I saw Darkness following Mia down the hallway. I'd seen occasional weird things before, but usually they were while I was in someone else's dream and were followed by a pink unicorn wearing a pin-striped suit.

This wasn't a dream, though. My mind had become my worst enemy. It was playing morbid tricks on me, and I didn't know how worried I should be. Blowing it off was the obvious option. It was easy. I was good at it. But I had a nagging feeling that seeing the shadow of me meant things were getting worse—more serious. As if losing time at night wasn't bad enough, full-blown hallucinations weren't something I felt prepared to deal with. Not now, not ever.

It was bad enough to see Darkness in Mia's nightmares, but to have him following me into reality wasn't an option. Yet what I'd seen *wasn't* real. I didn't want him to be.

He couldn't be.

I'd avoided thinking much about the e-mails, mostly because it confirmed my fears. Either someone wanted Mia to think I'd sent the messages, or I'd sent them during my lost time. I winced and focused on the first option. Who would want to frame me, though? Who hated me enough to destroy my life like this? I'd been thinking about it for a few weeks, but still didn't feel any closer to the answer. We had no real *suspects* there. Thor, Matt, and Jeff made more sense than anyone, but would they really be okay with terrifying Mia in the process of making me look bad? Worse still … what if it was my name on that e-mail because I *was* the monster who set up the account? What if Mia had been right about me all along?

Mia finally walked out of the office, chatted with Dr. Freeburg for a minute, and waved goodbye. He went back inside as she climbed in her purple truck on the other side of the parking lot. Ducking low in my seat, I closed my eyes and didn't move while she drove past. I didn't release the breath I was holding until after I heard her turn the corner. I was pretty sure she hadn't seen me. For the hundredth time in the last month, I was grateful my car was small and too boring to draw attention. Things were tense enough already.

I waited until I couldn't hear any more traffic before I sat up. The moment I did, I saw Blind Skull climb on his motorcycle, look straight at me, and peel out of the parking lot. I scrambled out of the car, but he was already so far down the road I could barely make out his receding figure.

I couldn't find him when I looked for him, but here he was in Dr. Freeburg's parking lot at the same time as Mia? That was just too much of a coincidence. A trickle of fear froze me from the inside out. If I hadn't already added him to the suspect list, I'd be writing his name at the top of it right now. I could think of only one reason for him to be here.

Dr. Freeburg caught my attention when he began shuffling around the reception area. Grabbing a coat, he flipped off the lights. I rubbed my hands together to warm them and crossed the street. I couldn't think about Blind Skull now. I had to find out everything I could about Dr. Freeburg and Mia before he left too. I'd just stepped up onto the curb when he pulled a small key from his pocket to lock the door.

I knew he wasn't supposed to talk to me about Mia, but if I could get him to tell me something—anything—it might help. Besides, the way he acted around her still gave me the creeps. He still stood too close for comfort.

As he turned away from the door, I stepped onto the middle of the step behind him, blocking his path. "Dr. Freeburg?"

"Yes?" He turned to face me, the pasty skin around his dirty brown eyes crinkled in confusion.

"I'm a friend of Mia Greene's. I hoped maybe you could help me."

"Oh, you just missed her. She left a few minutes ago. I'm sorry."

"No, I mean—I wanted to talk to you."

His eyebrows rose, but he didn't say anything.

I didn't really know where to start, but anything would be better than standing here stuttering. "She's tried to explain what you do—with hypnotherapy. But I'm not sure I understand."

"Ah, well, yes. Hypnotherapy is an underestimated art. There are so very many uses. Cognitive behavioral therapy, when combined with hypnosis, for example, can be instrumental in addressing issues like stress, anxiety, phobias." Dr. Freeburg slowly edged around me until he was out on the sidewalk and headed toward his car, but he kept talking. I matched his pace, trying to soak up any information I could. "Even panic disorders or insomnia have been found to respond well to treatment."

"Phobias, like with Mia and fire?"

He stopped walking and turned to face me. Frowning, he shook his head. "I can't talk about any specific patients, of course, but to answer your question about phobias—yes, any phobia has the possibility of responding to hypnotherapy."

I nodded, trying to piece together what this could possibly have to do with Mia's dreams. She somehow thought I'd heard about them from Dr. Freeburg. Did she have insomnia? "So, with the hypnotherapy, you could what? Help someone sleep better or—not have nightmares?"

"Well, dealing with phobias is a long and difficult process." Dr. Freeburg's expression was sad. "But as far as insomnia and other sleep disorders, hypnotherapy has varying degrees of success. With some, self-hypnosis training can work immediately, but with others it sometimes doesn't work at all."

"Self-hypnosis?"

"Yes. I usually train my patients to be able to hypnotize themselves. Particularly when dealing with insomnia or night terrors—issues that occur when I'm not present. It allows them to not only sleep, but to sleep in a semi-controlled, safe state. It's a difficult method to document, but I see quite a bit of success with it."

I felt my jaw click as my mouth dropped open. A light flipped on in my mind and suddenly everything made so much sense. Mia's painting dreams—the reason they were so repetitive, so unlike anyone else's. They were dreams induced by self-hypnosis.

"That's what Mia's dreams about the meadow and the

lighthouse and everything are, right? They're part of her treatment? She's hypnotized?"

Dr. Freeburg's brow furrowed. "As I said, I'm not able to discuss Mia's treatment with you."

"Right. I just know she has dreams like that—sometimes," I muttered.

We stopped beside a blue BMW in the parking lot. "Yes, well, I suppose you can ask her any other questions you might have."

"One more thing…it's not about the hypnosis or anything. Did she tell you anything about the threats she's been getting?"

The hypnotherapist turned slowly and leaned against the car. His expression was more guarded than it had been before. He seemed suspicious and oddly nervous…he looked guilty. "She discussed that with you?"

Out of nowhere, my left hand had another mini-seizure. It shook violently at my side and Dr. Freeburg got a good look at it before I stuck it in my pocket and pushed it down so hard that it mostly stopped.

"Well…" My mind scrambled for an answer that might both distract him from what had happened and somehow make him talk. I came up empty—there wasn't one. I decided to try the truth. "She mentioned she got some scary e-mails, and I'm worried about her."

"What did you say your name was again?" His eyes were glued to the pocket where my hand still jerked sporadically.

This was going downhill fast. I didn't want him to tell Mia I'd been here. "I'm Jeff—Jeff Sparks."

"That's odd. I've met Jeff Sparks before, since he brings Mia to therapy sometimes. And you're not him." Dr. Freeburg returned my gaze with cold eyes and I wanted to kick myself. Of course he'd met Mia's foster family. Real genius move on my part. I missed the days when my brain could keep up with everything happening around me...those were good times.

He pulled his cell phone from his jacket pocket. "I will give you thirty seconds to leave, young man."

Taking a few quick steps backward, I stumbled over the curb. "Right, well, thanks for your time."

I was halfway to my car when I heard him yell behind me. "And leave that poor girl alone."

The air slowly drained from my lungs once I got into my car and back on the road. Something about Dr. Freeburg felt very...off. I couldn't place it. He seemed to know his stuff, and had obviously helped Mia with her nightmares before I screwed everything up for her, but he made my skin crawl.

The sun was setting and shadows crept across the road before me. I felt the same gloom encroaching on my heart. I'd watch Dr. Freeburg's dreams tonight and see if they gave me a clue. If he knew something about the e-mails, maybe his dreams would show me the truth.

As I drove home, his last words rang through my head to the beat of the ever-present hammering. *Leave that poor girl alone.* My chest hurt as I drew in a slow rattling breath.

If only I could.

TWENTY-TWO

When I pulled into the driveway, Mom was already home. A little surprising since it wasn't even dark yet. She'd been working late a lot the past week or two, ever since our argument. Work and school made avoiding each other simple. We'd never talked about the fight again. We were both too busy pretending it never happened. But it's hard to stay angry with her when I know how easy it was for Dad to walk away.

He didn't even need a reason, and God knows I'd already given Mom too many.

I grabbed my sunglasses off the visor, pushed them up on my nose, and got out of the car. Retrieving my backpack from the passenger seat, I slung it over my shoulder and walked inside.

Mom stood in the kitchen slicing up carrots. Even when she was cooking, she still had on her business suit. Her jacket hung over the back of a chair at the table and her sleeves were rolled up above her elbows. Her short brown hair was pulled up in a clip and her reading glasses were pushed back on her head. Typical Mom.

The smell of her homemade chicken noodle soup filled every space in the house and made my stomach growl. It was my absolute favorite.

"Hey, Mom. That smells awesome." I grabbed a carrot and popped it in my mouth.

"Hi, bud. How was practice?" she asked without looking up.

"Fine," I lied and turned toward my room. Jeff never held practice on Tuesdays, and I didn't even have my gym bag with me. Of course, I'd missed most of the practices. When I'd stopped by Coach Mahoney's office as promised, I'd told him that I was taking a private soccer clinic at the college; he said that as long as I came to every practice once the season started, he didn't care. But I knew that soccer was just one more problem that would eventually come back up. It felt like everything I did lately was just putting off dealing with the inevitable. Mom, Coach, death . . . it would all catch up to me at some point.

A chill slid down my spine and I shrugged it off. As long as work kept Mom busy enough to keep her off my back, it was okay. I cracked my neck to ease some of the tension that built up there with every new lie I told.

"Where are you going?" Mom called down the hallway after me. "Dinner is almost ready."

"Yeah, I have a killer headache. I'm going to rest my eyes

for a minute." I shut my door behind me before she had a chance to respond.

I hadn't lied this time. My headache *was* becoming somewhat epic. But mostly I didn't feel like having the same old argument about wearing my sunglasses at the dinner table. I knew she considered it disrespectful, and having to come up with new excuses all the time made me tired. And tonight I really couldn't afford to make eye contact with anyone else. I needed to figure out what was up with Dr. Freeburg. If he wasn't the stalker, then I'd track down that Blind Skull guy and see what his dreams were made of. Not that I'd had much luck finding him so far.

I slipped off my shoes and leaned back on my pillow. Freeburg probably wasn't asleep yet, although I made him for one of those lame early-to-bed/early-to-rise types. Maybe I could relax in the void for a bit before I got sucked into his dream.

A light tapping on the door woke me up. I squinted at the clock; it had been about forty-five minutes.

"Parker?" Mom's voice whispered through the door. "Are you asleep?"

"Not anymore."

She opened the door a crack and I didn't have to fake my flinching reaction to justify hiding my eyes. A million light bulbs burst inside my brain at once and I threw my arm over my face.

"Sheesh, Mom, can you turn out that light?"

"Oh, sorry," she muttered and stepped inside, closing the

door behind her. Her voice warbled with that familiar worried tone again. "Are you feeling okay? You look terrible."

"Yeah," I said. "Migraine."

"Do you want some medicine?" she asked softly.

Dad used to get migraines all the time. It was one of the few things I remembered about him. So it made for a good excuse that she could understand, and it was pretty accurate at the moment.

"I can bring your dinner in here if you want," she added.

"That would be good. Thanks."

Mom leaned over and kissed my forehead in the darkness. "No problem, sweetie. Just feel better, okay?"

I nodded and rolled onto my side.

A few minutes later she was back with dinner and some ibuprofen. I kept my eyes closed tight as she moved about in the semi-darkness.

"Finn called three times tonight. He sounded worried." The way she said it seemed more like a question than a statement.

"I'll talk to him at school tomorrow."

"Addie called too."

"Okay."

"You aren't—I mean, are you two dating? Because that would be fine. She seems like a really sweet girl."

I groaned. "No, Mom. She's just a friend."

"Easy. I was only wondering." She leaned over and squeezed my shoulder with one hand. "Well, get some rest and holler if you need anything else."

Feeling guilty about my reaction, I wrapped one arm

around her shoulders. Somehow I had to make all the lies up to her, while I still had time left. She deserved better. "Thanks for dinner, Mom."

"You're very welcome." I wasn't sure why, but hearing the smile in her voice made me feel better than I had all day.

———

I rolled over again and squinted at the glowing red numbers of my alarm clock. It was almost midnight.

Sitting up, I drew in a deep breath and slowly let it out. My feet clunked to the floor and I tried to stand up when the dental floss tugged my arm back behind me. I yanked my hand around until I felt it snap and got to my feet. My head felt a little better, so maybe some water would help.

The house was silent. It'd been almost an hour since I'd heard Mom go to bed. I filled a glass with water from the fridge and walked back to my room. Halfway there, I heard a weird squeaking noise. Mid-step, I froze, listening for the sound again, but it was quiet. I walked in, shut the door, and then heard it again. It was coming from my backpack.

When I picked my backpack up, I felt the side pocket vibrating. Oh, my cell phone. I'd forgotten it was still in there. I pulled it out; the screen was filled with a picture of Finn wearing an enormous jack-o'-lantern over his head. Addie had taken it at Halloween last year. I flipped the phone open.

"Hello?"

There was a stunned silence on the other end before he

finally responded. "What. Is. Going. On?" He emphasized every word like it could be the most important one he'd ever said. I couldn't help but laugh.

"Um—mostly sleep. What are you talking about?"

"Dude. You talked to Mia this morning, then you disappeared and we don't ever hear from you again? You were supposed to give me a ride home from school, and you never showed. Addie and I have been calling you all night." In the background I heard Addie talking quietly. She was squeaking a little, the way she did when she was upset. Finn took a deep breath. "What happened?"

I winced. "Sorry about the ride. I totally forgot. I ended up going to talk to Dr. Freeburg, and—" I stopped, not sure what to say about Dr. Freeburg yet. It would probably be better to wait until after I'd seen his dreams.

"You talked to her therapist?"

"Seriously, Finn, do you listen to anything I say?"

"Hi, Parker, how are you feeling?" Addie's voice came through abruptly. She must've picked up the phone extension.

"Hey, Addie. I'm okay. Freeburg seemed to at least know what he was talking about." I scratched my head and yawned. "Oh, but I was wondering, do either of you know that new guy at school? Dark hair, wears a leather jacket with an emblem on the shoulder of a skull wearing two eye patches?"

"Oh yeah, and he keeps a parrot in his locker?" Finn laughed and then I heard a thud followed by, "Ow!"

"I think I've seen him ... but I'm not sure." Addie was quiet for a moment. "It's weird ... I can almost rememb—"

"Why are you asking about him anyway?" Finn interrupted. "Did Mia mention him?"

"No, I just keep seeing him around, especially when I'm following Mia. I just wondered if you guys knew who he was."

"You think he could be her stalker?" There was no humor in Finn's voice now.

"Maybe. I don't know." It was quiet for a few seconds before Addie changed the subject.

"So, what happened with Mia?" Her voice sounded soft next to Finn's. "I think she's avoiding me, so I'm guessing it didn't go well?"

Sitting on the edge of the bed, I secured a new strand of floss around my wrist. "Nope, it sucked. But I learned a few things, so it wasn't totally worthless."

"Like what?" Finn's voice echoed oddly, the way it does when there are two phones being used in the same room.

"Listen, can we talk about it tomorrow? I really need to watch his dreams first, and then I think I'll know more." I yawned and climbed under my covers.

"Whose dreams? Freeburg's?" Finn asked quickly. I knew they wanted answers before I hung up, but I just didn't have the energy.

"Yeah. I think it might help."

"Really? Why?" Addie sounded doubtful.

"I'll explain more tomorrow."

I could practically hear Finn shaking his head through the phone. "Random, but all right. Tomorrow though—you need to catch me up."

"Catch *us* up," Addie added.

"Promise. Good night, guys."

"Night." Their unison voices echoed the word until I heard two faint clicks and then silence.

TWENTY-THREE

It surprised me when the rippling sensation came and I slid into Dr. Freeburg's dream. I wasn't sure how long I'd been in my dreamless void, but apparently he was more of a night owl than I'd given him credit for.

The dream enveloped me and sounded like muffled air in motion, like a wind tunnel in an enclosed space. My nose filled with the odor of musky cologne failing to cover the smell of sweat. The slightly burnt scent of a car heater at full blast wafted over me. I was sitting in the back seat of Dr. Freeburg's car. He was parked, but I couldn't tell where because everything outside the car swirled in a white fog. I'd seen this before. It simply meant Dr. Freeburg's focus was elsewhere, so outside the car didn't matter.

The layers of the dream seemed to float through the fog like ghosts blurring in and out of the world around us: a shadow of an older woman discussing her finances, a young boy playing in a tree in a huge backyard.

In the front seat, Dr. Freeburg fiddled with his bow tie. He clipped it on, unclipped it, adjusted it, and clipped it again several times before he reached up and smoothed the sides of his hair back. Finally, with a nod, he opened the door and stepped out.

As his focus moved, I was jerked to a new spot outside of the car. We were parked in front of my school. I looked around in confusion. Every detail was exact, even down to a blackened dead spot on the grass to the left of the main doors. A kid in my chemistry class had mixed the wrong ingredients during the first week of school and picked that spot to dispose of his mistake.

My jaw clenched reflexively. This much detail had to be at least part memory, but the haze meant some of it was fantasy. The spot on the lawn proved he'd been to the school during this school year, and often enough to remember small details.

When I turned to the front steps and saw Mia jogging down them in a skirt shorter than any I'd ever seen her wear, I realized where the fantasy part was coming into play. I wondered what would happen if I punched a Dreamer inside their dream.

"Hello, Dr. Freeburg," she said with a flirtatious grin. "I'm ready for my appointment."

Okay, well, at least it wasn't a memory. I seriously doubted Mia ever acted like that with her therapist. Or with anyone really.

Dr. Freeburg nodded and cleared his throat with a stupid grin that made me want to puke. "My car is right over there."

The drive to his office took twice as long as normal. The sicko therapist couldn't keep his leering eyes off of her. Every time he moved the stick shift his hand grazed her thigh and she giggled. The car felt unbearably hot and my vision twisted, leaving the whole world skewed. I couldn't watch him live out his fantasies on Mia.

Without even thinking, I reached out for where his seat belt connected to the side of the car. I blinked twice when I realized I was pulling on it with all my weight, trying to strangle him. I released my grip, feeling ill. Dr. Freeburg coughed once, but seemed otherwise unaffected.

I stared down at my hands in my lap. The red stripes from my grip on the seat belt faded. What was I trying to do? Kill him with an aspect of his own dream? Was that even possible? Did the idea of him taking advantage of Mia in a simple fantasy affect me that much?

What scared me more was the hunger I felt burning inside. A desperate curiosity. A desire to see if it was possible. The darkness within me wanted to know more— wanted to know if I could physically hurt someone inside of their dreams.

I shivered and pushed the disturbing craving aside with as much force as I could manage.

We pulled into the parking lot and I reluctantly followed them into the building. Dr. Freeburg let Mia go up the stairs first. As she climbed, he stared at the back of her toned legs with unsuppressed desire. I couldn't even look at them. She had seriously nice legs, but the idea of having the same thoughts in my head as the therapist made me want to jump off a cliff.

His office was on the right. The room reeked of stale coffee and lavender from one of those plug-in air fresheners. The walls were painted in blue and gray tones, and a wide window overlooked the park on the other side of the parking lot. An enormous black leather chair sat across from a gray suede couch.

Mia immediately reclined on the couch with a seductive smile. But the doctor simply took a seat in his chair and she closed her eyes. For the next few minutes he talked in low, soothing tones, and she relaxed into a hypnotic state. Except for her ridiculously short skirt, I imagined this was exactly what happened when he used hypnosis during her regular therapy sessions.

I hadn't been expecting this. In the quiet, I listened to the cars passing on the street outside, feeling guilty for thinking so badly of him. The dream had become even clearer since he began the hypnosis. It had to be mostly memory now—too much detail for most fantasies. But which parts were fantasy? Besides Mia's ridiculous outfit, it was hard to tell.

I took in a deep breath and released it along with the tension in my body. This was even better than I'd expected. Maybe I could see aspects from her recent therapy sessions. Maybe I could learn more about the e-mails.

A small squeak interrupted my thoughts, and I turned to see Dr. Freeburg quietly pulling an ottoman from the corner to a spot next to the couch. He took a seat and I watched him place one hand on her ankle and run it slowly up her leg.

Suddenly, there wasn't enough air. I backed into his desk, searching for an escape. I wished I could open the window and jump out. A broken leg would've been worth it if it meant getting out of this dream.

No, not a dream. This still felt like a memory.

Mia's small trusting voice spilled secrets about missing her parents, feeling all alone, her foster family. All while his hands scurried like rats along her body. Mia flinched, and I heard his soothing voice telling her everything would be okay. There was nothing to be afraid of. She could trust him, and she would feel better after they were done. He would make sure she felt much better and happier—satisfied.

My breath came in shallow gasps. Dr. Freeburg had to be the one sending those e-mails to Mia—he *had* to be. But why would he frame me? His memory was blurred with my reality, and I couldn't think of anything else. I couldn't stand it. I couldn't watch anymore. I had to stop him.

My hands grasped around on the desk for something, for anything that could change what was happening. They closed around a small paperweight. It felt right in my hands, solid, like it had always belonged there. Fury drove me forward.

He was the monster, and I would end him.

I swung without thought, connecting with the doctor's head again and again before I glanced up at Mia. She was curled into a ball at the corner of the couch. Her shoulders trembled as she stared at me, the doctor's blood splashed in a rainbow of red droplets across her white shirt. I wasn't even sure how many times I'd hit him; it was like everything around me had frozen … everything but the rage boiling inside me.

Then Dr. Freeburg fell forward off the ottoman, and I was thrust out of his dream.

TWENTY-FOUR

I bolted upright, dripping with sweat. My fingers were wrapped up so tightly in my sheet that the tips were white and I couldn't feel them anymore. Disentangling my hands, I shook them back and forth. They tingled with stinging pains as the blood flowed back into them. The clock read 7:05 a.m. It was almost time for school, but I wouldn't be going. One by one, images from the dream infected my mind until it transformed into an oozing wound, disgusting and deadly.

What had I done? I knew it was only in a dream, but what if it had some effect on real life? I'd been able to break the barrier with Addie and Mia before, even if just slightly.

I snapped the dental floss still connecting me to my headboard and jumped up from my bed, tugging on some jeans and a T-shirt. My head was pounding with the same ferocity it had the night before, but I ignored it. Running through the kitchen, I grabbed my car keys and was shutting the back door when Mom walked out of the pantry, already dressed in her suit of the day.

"Have a good day at schoo—hey! Did you have breakfast?" She frowned and raised an eyebrow at me.

"Yep," I lied through the closing door, jamming my finger against the garage door opener.

As I backed out of the driveway, I saw Mom standing in the doorway. Even from the street, I could see the concern on her face. I knew there were frown and worry lines. It wasn't only me who was being affected … my life was hurting her too. It all needed to stop. I needed to make it all stop. Trying to smile, I gave her a quick wave and drove down the street.

The drive was torturous. Something dark and sinister had awoken inside my mind. I wasn't sure what I would find when I got to Freeburg's house. According to the Internet listings I'd pulled up on my phone, only one Dr. Clive G. Freeburg lived in the Oakville vicinity. If everything was fine and the dream was simply a dream, then I planned to confront him about the e-mails. It had to be him. He was a pervert.

If everything wasn't fine, and somehow my actions in the dream had followed me into reality, then I didn't know what I'd do. A twisted corner of my mind felt hopeful at this idea and I heaved the darkness back, along with the bloody visions plaguing my thoughts.

When I parked across the street, the doctor's house was as still as a coffin. The dark side of me shivered with pleasure at the thought, and I felt sick. Squeezing my eyes shut, I rested my head against the steering wheel for a moment. I couldn't—I didn't want to feel like this. It was time to face the truth before the menacing thing that stirred within me gained any more power.

I needed help. I'd never felt so out of control—so violent. There was a disturbing desperation to my dark side. It was determined to keep me alive—at any cost. I'd never imagined myself capable of some of the things I'd done over the last few months. Stalking Mia was terrible, but if I was losing control, I couldn't stop. And this was only the beginning.

I tugged on my black gloves, got out of the car, and made my way across the street to the house. The front door was locked, but I found a side entry into the garage that wasn't. Dr. Freeburg's blue BMW sat in the stillness. The house was so quiet. Impossibly quiet.

An iciness slipped through the concrete floor and wrapped around my legs, freezing them in place. I wanted to run, to get as far away from here as possible. Freeburg was probably sleeping in, that's all. I didn't join his dream until late last night. He must be tired.

My hands shook so hard that even sticking them in my pockets accomplished nothing. Quick breaths wouldn't slow as I fogged up the window on Dr. Freeburg's car.

A thirst started in my gut. A *need*. I didn't give them permission, but my feet shuffled from the garage, through the door into the house, past the kitchen, and up the stairs. Like I knew exactly where I was going. I was standing outside double doors that I was sure led to the master bedroom before I managed to slow my breathing a little.

This is stupid. I should leave. What will I accomplish here? I asked myself. If Freeburg was dead, did I really want to see that? If he was alive, then I'd committed breaking and entering, or at least entering, but illegal either way.

Hesitating, I took a step back and knocked a silver plate off a table in the hallway. It made a loud *clang* as it landed on the floor and then rotated slowly, like a top near the end of its spin. I put the plate back in place and forced my heart to stop pounding so I could listen for the sound of Dr. Freeburg scrambling out of bed.

Silence.

I turned to leave, willing my feet to run down the stairs, to get out, but they didn't listen. The darkness within pushed the rising need over my head like a tidal wave and I sputtered against the force.

I have to know.

With a single shove, both doors opened. In the dim light filtering through thick curtains, I saw Dr. Freeburg lying motionless in his bed. I watched him for twenty seconds without breathing. Waiting, watching—I needed to see the slight expansion of his side, the slight lift of his shoulder that would prove he was only sleeping.

But it wasn't there.

I stepped closer. He had one of those sleeping masks over his eyes. Moving around the side of the bed, I tugged up the sleeve on my right arm. I held my bare skin directly under his nose, waiting to feel the slightest push of warm, life-filled air. Nothing.

It had really happened.

I'd killed him.

My heart felt like an erratic jackhammer inside my chest as I stood beside the bed. I couldn't move. I couldn't think. I couldn't breathe. My chest hurt. So much pain. I was a killer.

I tried to look away, but I couldn't. My vision filled with the scene from the dream—it pounded me over and over the way I'd pounded his head with the paperweight. He was dead. The bloody misshapenness of his head, the rainbow of red across Mia's white shirt . . . there was so much blood I felt like I was drowning in it.

I extended one gloved hand and lifted the sleep mask. His dead eyes gazed at the ceiling above me. If it weren't for that gaze, I could've convinced myself he was just asleep—there was none of the blood from the dream. But he was dead just the same.

The world spun and came up sideways. I had no control. I didn't *want* control, not anymore. In a haze, I walked from the room. I could feel the blood smeared all over my hands—even though I could see the gloves still on my fingers. Had I touched Dr. Freeburg? I couldn't remember.

Looking up into the hallway mirror, I saw Darkness looking back at me. I started, surprised. But he moved when I moved, blinked when I blinked. We were one. He was inside of me, a place where I didn't even want to be anymore. I pulled my phone from my pocket to dial 911.

Darkness told me no—they would know I'd done it.

My mind rolled in horrified agony, trying to push away the images—the room, the words, everything. I retreated within my own mind. Letting my other side, Darkness, take over. Letting him close the phone, take me through the kitchen and out the garage door. Careful to leave everything as it was when we arrived, so careful. He walked calmly to the car, started it, and drove down the street. The street was peaceful, the residents so unaware of the murderer among them.

Murderer.

I snapped.

No!

I couldn't let this happen. What if I *hadn't* caused it? What if Dr. Freeburg just had a heart attack? He was overweight and older—that kind of thing happened every day, right? I couldn't let Darkness leave Dr. Freeburg's body like this. I shook my head. No, it wasn't just Darkness, it was me—Parker—it was *my* body, *my* mind. I pushed the evil away with every ounce of strength I had left. I wouldn't leave Freeburg like this. Who knew how long it would take for someone to find him?

A rush of adrenaline flowed through my veins and I felt more decided, more in control, than I had in a while. I was going to do the right thing. I tried to reach into my pocket to grab my phone, but my hand didn't budge. I focused all my energy on making my hand take out my phone, but it didn't obey. It remained on the steering wheel, following directions someone else was giving it.

"You don't want to do that."

I jerked my head around to the passenger seat and blinked several times, hoping the image would go away. It was me—but not me. It was Darkness. The circles under my eyes were a deeper shade than ever. My pale white skin made me look different—cruel, somehow. I couldn't breathe. Darkness had escaped.

"What's going on?" My voice was weak, just like me. I tried again to make my body obey—to place my foot on the brake, to pull my phone from my pocket—but nothing happened.

Darkness's laugh was so cold it hurt my ears. "Oh, come on. Don't be an idiot. If you're going to call the police, you might as well drive straight to the nuthouse from here."

"But he's dead. I need to call them. This might not be my fault."

He leaned forward and raised his eyebrows. "Oh, really?"

My voice sounded uncertain and hollow even to me. "Yes."

"How did the blood get on your hands?"

"It—it's not real. It's from the dream."

"Are you sure?" Darkness was watching me with mocking pity in his eyes. "Are you sure of *anything* anymore?"

I choked on the horrible thought that filled me. Darkness in the car beside me, the blood on my hands that couldn't be there—it had finally happened. I couldn't tell reality from dreams anymore. *Psychosis.*

"How could I have k-killed him? I was sleeping."

Darkness laughed and nodded sarcastically. "Good. You should practice that answer. Sure—of course, you were."

I shook my head violently, trying to remember anything

real that I could hold on to, but my shattered mind refused to help me. I could see the blood, feel the murderous fury. In my mind it hit me again over and over—like a song set on replay—the smashing. The heat. The blood. The way the dream ended, abrupt and jolting, thrusting me out.

I'd never been in a dream that ended from something I did before—it was unnatural. It only made sense that I had caused it to stop.

"Aw, don't take it so hard. We couldn't help ourselves. He was twisted. He deserved it. We never sleep. We aren't even trying anymore. Maybe we could get the rest we needed if you let us focus on *our* needs for once. But no, everything is about Mia, Mia, Mia." Darkness sighed and popped his knuckles exactly the way I did. "Frankly, I'm getting pretty tired of that little distraction. She could've been the answer—but no. She only wants to be part of the problem."

"No, no, she didn't do anything wrong," I muttered, trying to regain control of my mind, my car, my life.

"She didn't do anything wrong," Darkness mimicked. "You are so lame."

"Mia doesn't deserve this." I spoke low, squeezing my eyes tight for a moment and willing him to disappear. When I opened them again, nothing had changed. He was still sitting beside me, and the car was still driving down the road, oblivious of the madness inside.

Just like I'd been doing for months. Going through the motions, ignoring the signs, and now he was out.

Darkness folded his arms across his chest and looked at me like I was a confused child. "Besides, why do you care so much about being good? Following their rules? Why should we care about breaking the laws of a society that would toss us in a nuthouse for telling the truth? Or put us in jail for simply doing what it takes to stay alive?"

He leaned forward and I met my own piercing blue eyes. "These people aren't like us. They don't have the ability to understand. The only thing we need to worry about is keeping ourselves alive and getting them the hell out of our way. We'll do what we have to do. It's simple."

His logic made a perverse sort of sense. I was jumbled, lost, and oh so tired. I wanted to agree, to relax and let him take care of everything. Make all the decisions.

Until I thought of Finn and Addie—of the person I was around them.

"NO! It's NOT true!" I shouted, and he disappeared. I was alone in the car. I took a deep, ragged breath and reached for my phone again. This time, my hand obeyed. I pushed 9 and 1 then glanced up. A teenager was standing in the road, twenty feet in front of me.

I jerked hard on the wheel, and the phone flew out of my hand and past me into the back seat. It wasn't until I swerved around the person that I saw his face—my face—sneering back at me.

I looked ahead just in time to see the massive oak tree. Then everything burned in a massive flame of pain and went black.

TWENTY-FIVE

Bliss was hazy. It was my new home. I couldn't remember much about my old home. Just that it was bad—it was pain. Bliss was calm. It was restful and perfect.

It seemed to go on for days, weeks, months. It went on until time didn't matter. Time wasn't really a part of Bliss. Time was separate and overrated.

Sometimes words drifted in and out. Most of them I tried to ignore. They brought flashes of pain and torment. They ruined Bliss. There were only two voices that I wanted, two that didn't bring the torment. They brought memories of happiness, warm summers filled with laughter. Finn and Addie's voices didn't disturb the Bliss. They were good.

When I heard them, I wanted more. It was the only time I felt safe, the only time I inched closer to awareness and further from the Bliss. Eventually I got close enough that I understood them. Their words weren't buzzing noises in the background. They were clear.

I didn't know if I wanted to, but I was waking up.

"No, it was all true." The bitterness and anger in Addie's tone made me want to retreat back to the Bliss, but I couldn't—I'd come too far. "You don't know him—you've never known him."

"Why are you saying these things?" Mia's voice forced a dozen terrifying images through my head at once. I squeezed my eyes shut tighter, wishing I'd never come so close to the surface. "And why would I believe either of you anymore, after Finn lied to me—again—to get me down here? I can't believe you'd let him tell me you were in an accident, Addie."

"You'd be too stubborn to come otherwise," Addie groaned, and then continued. "And yes, Finn lied, but what Parker told you was the truth."

"How could it possibly be true?" Mia's voice sounded oddly pinched. This was hurting her.

"We don't know. He doesn't even know." Finn didn't sound much happier than his sister, but he was much calmer. "We're not lying that Parker's a good guy. He'd never hurt you—he'd never hurt anyone. He isn't your stalker."

More flashes of Dr. Freeburg slashed through my Bliss, and I retreated to a small corner of my mind, wanting it all to stop. This had been a mistake. All I wanted was for the Bliss to come back.

"Fine, okay. But it's bizarre, you know." Mia sounded resigned but wary. "Whoever is doing it obviously wants me to think it's Parker. Why would someone do that?"

"What do you mean?" Addie must have moved, because she sounded much closer than before. In spite of the painful memories, something in her voice made me glad I'd come back.

"They came from Chipp8@gmail.com. Eight is his soccer number, right?"

A stubborn shadow of doubt hovered over a corner of my Bliss like an ominous cloud. I stabbed at it with my thoughts, willing it to go away and leave me in peace, but like any cloud, stabbing at it was pretty useless.

Finn's breath came out in a gush. "Yeah, that's his number, but not his e-mail address. He set his up a couple years ago, when his number was eighteen. It's exactly the same, but with an eighteen instead of an eight. See? We told you it wasn't him."

The room fell silent for a moment before Addie finally spoke. "This is not a good thing, Finn." Her tone was hushed, worried. "Who would want to make it look like it was Parker?"

"If I knew that, I'd know who was sending them," Mia said, her voice trembling.

Then someone came in and ushered them out. From what the stranger said, she must've been a nurse. The giant, looming oak tree flashed through my mind, and I wondered for a moment how bad I was hurt.

———

I floated in and out for a while, bobbing back and forth between my own dreams and drug-induced nothingness. I tried to piece together why and how I was dreaming on my own again, but my mind didn't seem capable of holding onto one stream of thought long enough to reach a conclusion.

The bed pushed on my body in ways that were unnatural. Everything hurt as the pain dragged me inexorably toward full awareness. But my brain seemed to be worse than anything else. I felt pretty sure someone had taken it out, jiggled it around, and shoved it back in upside down. When I opened my eyes, light and dark were reversed, like one of those weird picture-editing programs had been set loose in the hospital.

I blinked several times before my brain seemed to straighten it out. Something itched on my face, and I raised my hands to try to scratch it. My right hand followed instructions, but my left hand was pinned against the bed. I scratched at my cheek with my right hand, and found a clear plastic oxygen tube across my face. Pulling it away, I rolled my head to the side, trying to figure out why my left hand wouldn't move.

There was a mess of wavy auburn hair and fingers tangled all around it. Both of Addie's hands were wrapped tightly around mine, and her head rested on the bed beside them. She was asleep. I blinked, trying to make sure I was seeing things right.

My fingers felt sweaty as a memory of my hands not responding when I wanted to reach for my phone in the car flashed through my mind. I carefully flexed my fingers, making sure I could still move them. Her eyes opened with the movement. I hadn't meant to wake her up, but the idea that I couldn't control one of my hands again was disturbing.

Addie sat up and blinked at me for a moment before squeezing my fingers so tight they hurt. "You're awake! Are you okay? You've been freaking all of us out for three days."

I tried to speak, but my dry throat wouldn't release the words until the third try. "I think so. What's going on?"

"Finn and your mom are out in the hall. You had a pretty bad concussion and you were in a coma, but they weren't sure when you might wake up. They kept talking about drilling a hole in your skull and stuff, but your mom wouldn't let them unless they could guarantee it would help. Your blood pressure kept spiking up and the monitors were going off and everyone kept freaking out and—and—"

Somewhere in the middle of it all, Addie started crying—not like the blubbering kind, but tears fell down her cheeks. I wasn't even sure she noticed. An ache deep in my chest throbbed with each teardrop. I felt responsible, and I didn't know how to make it better.

"I'm sorry, Addie."

Pathetic. The only thing I could think of to say was utterly useless.

She squeezed my fingers for a minute before she suddenly seemed to realize what she was doing. Her cheeks got red and she peeked down at my hand, but didn't let go ... and I really didn't want her to.

"How are you feeling?"

I stretched and felt pain twinge through every muscle. "Like I ran into a tree, I guess. That's what happened, right?"

"Yeah. Did you fall asleep?"

A vivid flash of Darkness sneering at me from the middle of the road tore through my mind and I couldn't help but flinch. "Um—yeah. I must have."

In the quiet room, my mind swirled through one messed-up thought after another. It felt dangerous for Addie to be here. I remembered the feel of the paperweight in my hand. I was dangerous. I needed her to leave for a minute so I could focus on what happened.

"Addie, can you please get me some water or something? I'm so thirsty."

"Sure. I'll be right back. And I'll tell your mom you're awake."

"Thanks. I really appreciate it."

Everything that happened before the accident flooded through my mind. Dr. Freeburg. All the blood. Darkness. I'd never called 911. I wondered who'd found him. Did the police know I was at his house? Had they even found his body yet?

Panic slithered down my spine as I reached for the bed remote and pushed the button that raised it to a semi-sitting position. The change in elevation made my head swirl, and the images spun like a hurricane. The cuff on my arm tightened, and it was more painful than I thought possible. One of the machines next to the bed started beeping and my brain felt like it might explode.

A nurse came into the room followed by Mom, Finn, Addie, and a policeman. My brain tried to make sense of that—a policeman? Maybe Darkness had been right. They believed I killed Dr. Freeburg. My heart felt like it was tearing a hole in my chest. Did I? Did I kill him? There was so much blood glistening on that paperweight. I could picture it in my hand. But I was asleep in my own bed when I held it. Nothing made sense.

There was a window to the hallway and I could see him there, watching me: Blind Skull. His dark eyes met mine, but I couldn't read any emotion in them. They were like my dreamless void—empty. I wondered if I looked that way to other people.

The nurse moved so fast that everyone else looked like statues. My mom, my friends, the policeman, and the stranger in the hallway—they all stood frozen in place while my life floated away. Maybe Blind Skull wasn't even real; maybe none of them were.

I glanced at the machine. A red number on one of the monitors was climbing: 138–142–150–154. I gasped, trying to force air through the fire in my chest and into my lungs, to stop the pain that engulfed me. The nurse pushed a button to lay the bed back and put the tube back against my nose.

"Take slow, deep breaths and try to stay with me, Parker."

"Parker? Is he okay?" It was Mom's voice, but I don't think anyone answered her. Addie stood beside my mom with her head buried in Finn's shoulder.

It felt like someone had placed a mallet inside my skull, and with every beep of the monitor, it pounded away. I moaned, reaching up with one hand to claw at it, to dig it out. The nurse said something about my blood pressure and heart rate, but I couldn't focus enough to hear her. Someone tugged at the IV in my arm, and within a few seconds everything smoothed out.

Bliss embraced me again, and the beeps got quieter. People talked around me, but I couldn't understand what they said anymore. And I didn't care.

———————

Mom's voice was always there. I'm pretty sure she didn't leave the room again. It drifted along with me like a raft. Something I could climb into when I was ready to leave the river of emptiness that surrounded me.

When I opened my eyes again, it was dark outside. Mom sat beside my bed, her cold hand resting on top of mine. Everything smelled like medicine and bandages and all I could hear was someone snoring.

Finn and Addie's dad, Mr. Patrick, was sleeping on the really uncomfortable-looking couch across the room. One of his legs was bent to fit at an awkward angle; the other hung off the end so far it nearly touched the floor.

Mom was watching the news on TV, but the sound was turned all the way down. I focused on the closed captioning running across the screen for a second but it made me dizzy. The tagline said "Black Friday" and they showed crowds of people shivering outside the Oakville Commons Mall.

Black Friday was today? I'd been unconscious through Thanksgiving? Not that we ever had much of a turkey day celebration, but it still sucked.

I glanced at Mom. In the flickering light of the television, the dark circles under her eyes mimicked mine.

"Mom?"

Her head whipped around and she whispered to me. "Parker?" She leaned over the bed, her eyes huge. "Do you know where you are, sweetie?"

"If it's home, I don't like the way you redecorated." My voice came out as a wheeze and I tried to smile for her.

Mom laughed and squeezed my hand, but I could see an edge of panic in her eyes. "You didn't do so well when you woke up earlier today. How do you feel now?"

"I'm fine, Mom." *Terrified to sit up again after what happened last time, fairly sure I'm a murderer, and did I mention I'm going crazy? But, besides that, fine.* "Was there a policeman here before, or am I hallucinating?"

How messed up is it that I hoped she'd say I had a brain tumor and was seeing things? Who hopes for a brain tumor?

"Yes. Officer Evans left a couple of forms for you to fill out."

I took several slow, deep breaths and pretended to find the Tide commercial on TV really interesting until my heart agreed to slow back down. "Do you know what he wants?"

"Nothing important. The tree you hit was on golf course property or something and he's trying to get details for the accident report." Mom shook her head and squeezed my hand. "I know it was an accident, Parker, but it was irresponsible of you to drive when you were that tired. You could've been hurt so much worse, or you could've hurt someone else."

I swallowed. The words "you could've hurt someone else"

echoed in my mind, accompanied by images of my hands covered in blood. I nodded. I couldn't think about that now, not with people here. Maybe not ever.

"I also, um..." Mom cleared her throat and looked down. "I wanted to say that I'm sorry."

"Sorry?" I turned to face her.

She scooted her chair closer and whispered, "I'm so sorry about our big fight, and I'm so sorry I accused you of taking drugs. When I thought you might not... when I thought of all the things I said..." Her shoulders trembled and she wrapped her arms around me.

"It's okay, Mom." I hugged her and patted her shoulder, wishing the worst thing I'd done was drugs. "You believe me now?"

"Yes." Her voice was muffled. "They tested your blood after the accident. I guess it's protocol or something. You were clean, just like you've said. I'm so sorry."

My gut tightened and twisted as she cried. "It's all right, Mom." I tried to shrug and glanced at the figure snoring on the couch, ready to change the subject. "Why is Mr. Patrick here?"

Mom pulled back, wiping her tears with a smile. "Finn and Addie wouldn't leave. He wanted them to get out of the hospital for a while. He promised to watch over you himself while they went to a movie. You're lucky to have such great friends."

"I know."

A petite nurse with short black hair came in, asked how I felt, and disconnected a few of the things they had me hooked up to. Then an older nurse brought in a tray with some soup so I could "see if you can hold it down, sweetheart." Mom turned back to the TV as the news came back on, and we sat in silence.

Eating food didn't sound that great, but I figured it was probably more because of the things that kept flashing through my head than anything else. I pressed my wrist into the table to stop my hands from shaking long enough to bring a few sips of broth to my mouth. I knew they wouldn't let me out of the hospital until I ate, and something about being here made me feel cornered, helpless.

Everything that had happened in the days before the accident was so surreal. My brain was finally giving out on me. The only thing that made me feel better was the fact that I hadn't seen or heard from Darkness since the crash. Although I had seen Blind Skull, and I was beginning to think maybe he was a hallucination too. Addie said she *might* have seen him, but maybe she didn't.

All I knew for sure was that several days in the hospital had meant quite a bit of sleep, and for some reason I wasn't seeing other people's dreams anymore. I'd even seen my own... at least, I think I did. Hard to tell when the drugs made everything so fuzzy.

Maybe it was over.

Maybe everything could be different now.

TWENTY-SIX

After twenty minutes of arguing, I finally convinced Mom to go home. She hadn't slept at home since the accident.

"And you're sure you'll be okay?" Mom wrung her hands together and looked from me to Mr. Patrick, who yawned and leaned against the wall.

"I'm sure. Now go and get some rest." I turned to Mr. Patrick. "Tell Finn and Addie I'll call them tomorrow?"

He nodded. "I'm happy to see you're awake and feeling better. You had a lot of people worried."

"Yeah, I'm an attention hog like that."

Mr. Patrick laughed. He looked a lot like Finn when he smiled.

It was silent for a minute as I raised my eyebrows and watched Mom. She fidgeted and turned her gaze back to the television.

"Mom? Going now?"

"All right, all right...I'll go home." Mom said, but she didn't move away from the bed.

"He'll be fine. They'll probably send him home tomorrow—and then you can hover all you want." Mr. Patrick inclined his head toward the exit and held the door for her. He seemed exhausted too. Mom kissed my forehead and finally walked out, Mr. Patrick right behind her. I sighed, relieved they'd at least get some sleep.

———————

All was quiet except the occasional beep of the machines and the rattling noise that sounded every few minutes as my blood-pressure cuff inflated. The TV was still on but muted. The flickering light made my eyes hurt. I stretched my arms and legs. Everything felt stiff, but moving was good. And I wasn't tired, not even a little bit. As I stood up, I secured the back of my robe so there would be no mooning on my walk through the hospital. Someone had put those lame blue hospital booties on my feet while I was unconscious. They looked ridiculous, but at least my feet weren't cold.

Slipping the cuff off my arm, I disconnected the heart monitors and the machines started alarming. I glared at the screen and tried punching a couple of buttons until I found the power switch. When I released a breath and turned around, I jumped. Three silhouettes stood in the open doorway.

"You going somewhere, Parker?" the petite nurse asked as she walked around the bed toward me and took my pulse.

I noticed her hospital ID for the first time: *Patti*. Finn and Addie waved from the doorway but didn't say anything.

"Yeah. Just a walk. I need to stretch my muscles, I think." I waited until she eventually released my wrist and looked me over. "That okay?"

Patti pursed her lips and nodded slowly. "Yes, but I want you to take it slow. Your friends and your IV stay with you."

Finn stepped over and grabbed the IV stand. "No problem."

"We'll make sure he's back soon." Addie walked over and linked her arm through mine, her expression worried. I glanced at Finn but he didn't say anything.

"Thanks." I shuffled toward the hallway. Everything ached, but before long my muscles relaxed and the worst of the kinks worked themselves out.

"So, what movie did you go to?" I didn't want to talk about anything that mattered yet, but I knew it was cruel to make them wait for long.

"She wouldn't go see kung fu." Finn glared at Addie. "Or *Terminator*."

"Don't act like I got my way." Addie leveled her gaze at him and he shrugged.

"So, what?" I laughed. "You saw something that neither of you liked?"

"It was that new alien one." Finn looked at me and grinned. "Don't worry, the humans won ... again."

"That's a relief." I rolled my shoulders, trying to release the tension.

Addie shook her head in mock sadness. "Poor aliens didn't even see it coming."

"Yeah, it was shocking, really. They were about to win and then we used our wits to pull this amazing turn-around at the end." Finn twirled my IV stand in a circle and then back again before my tube got all tangled up.

I laughed. "I think I've seen that one...about a hundred times."

Addie squeezed my arm. "Exactly."

We made it down the first long hallway before Finn's fidgeting became so obvious I decided to start talking and put him out of his misery. "I know you've got about a billion unanswered questions, so do you want me to explain or would you prefer to grill me?"

They exchanged a long glance.

"Not yet," Addie said. "You don't have to yet."

At the same time, Finn gave me a sheepish grin. "Well, now that you mention it..."

I chuckled for a moment, but my body ached with the motion so it was short-lived. Addie held tight to my arm and shook her head with a frown at her brother.

"Really, Addie. I'm strong enough, and you guys have been waiting days already."

I took a long, deep breath and told them what had happened—from my conversation with Dr. Freeburg, to his pervy dream, to getting in the car intending to confront him. I skipped over the part at his house, moving on to the accident with the oak tree. I didn't mention Darkness or attacking Freeburg in his dream—no sense telling them I'd dreamed of killing him and then found him dead. Not when I still wasn't sure what had happened. Reality was blurred, and at least some of the things I saw were impossible. If I'd been hallucinating, maybe Dr. Freeburg wasn't even dead. The empty hole in the pit of my stomach said otherwise, but I held on to hope like a vise.

Luckily, my friends were focused on something entirely different.

"Wait—so Mia's dreams aren't really dreams? Or what?" Finn's brow creased in confusion.

"Not sure. They start with some kind of self-hypnosis." I shrugged. "As far as I know, that's the only difference between her dreams and everyone else's . . . so it has to have something to do with why I can sleep in them. Dr. Freeburg said the brain works differently in a hypnotized state, and it must be related to that."

"The nightmares too?" Addie asked.

"I'm not sure. Nightmares can be repetitive, but I'm sure she was still trying to create the peaceful dreams." I let out a puff of air. "It's not like she's volunteering to have these nightmares, trust me."

It was silent for a minute.

"So then, theoretically, you could sleep in anyone's dreams —as long as they did self-hypnosis?" Addie glanced at me and then quickly away.

"I don't know. I guess that makes sense. I haven't been in anyone's dream since the accident, so maybe slamming my head really hard magically fixed it. If I'd known that, I would've crashed a car into a tree years ago. I've even had a few of my own dreams since I've been in the hospital."

"Your own dreams?" Finn raised both eyebrows so high they nearly touched his hair. "Who was the last person you made eye contact with before the accident?"

Now that the drugs weren't quite so strong, I thought back for a minute and then cringed, realizing why I hadn't seen anyone's dreams. It must be because Dr. Freeburg wasn't dreaming anymore. So I could sleep in Mia's dreams, or when the last person I made eye contact with, my Dreamer, was dead. Perfect. This was just what my warped mind needed—another excuse to hurt people.

Clearing my throat, I shrugged. "Can't remember. It's kind of hazy," I lied. "I guess it could also be the drugs."

"So you're getting real sleep, then?" Addie glanced at my face and pursed her lips. "No wonder you look so good."

Finn coughed and laughed at the same time, and Addie blushed.

"So healthy, I mean," she muttered.

I stopped walking as a bout of nausea hit me. I found a waiting area to the side and took a seat.

"Anyway, what about Dr. Freeburg?" Finn asked. I jerked my head up to look at him.

"What about him?" My palms instantly started to sweat and I wiped them on the front of my hospital gown.

"His dream was sick." Finn waited for me to respond, so I nodded. "Do you think he's the one who's been threatening Mia?"

"No." In the dream I'd thought it was, but this didn't

make much sense when I was awake. Maybe I couldn't blame anything on the man I might have murdered. Anyway, if he had been sending the e-mails, then I guess the problem had been dealt with.

I swallowed...hard.

Addie watched me closely, disgust curling her lip. "Why not?"

"I—I just don't think it was him. How would he know my name and soccer number for the e-mail address?"

"Maybe she told him about you—that you were following her?" Finn rubbed his chin with his left hand and grabbed my IV stand with his right.

I stood up again. "I think maybe I should go back to the room."

"Wait—how did you know about the e-mail address?" Addie got to her feet.

"Mia shoved one of the e-mails into my hand when I tried to tell her about my curse."

They exchanged another look, but I pretended not to see it.

"I'm sorry, guys, but I think I should go rest." Turning back toward my room, I waited for them to join me. They both nodded and said they understood, but I knew they couldn't, not really. I needed them to leave. I needed some time to think about everything, to come up with answers to satisfy myself *and* them.

Halfway down the hall, Finn's phone rang and he grimaced as he answered. I could hear his dad's voice, and he didn't sound happy. I glanced at Addie and she shrugged.

"We didn't exactly tell him we were coming here after the movie. We thought he'd still be here."

I nodded and Finn said, "Okay, okay. We're coming." Then he snapped his phone closed. "Dad's home. He says to leave Parker alone."

"It's fine. You guys go. I'll try to get some sleep."

"No." Addie shook her head with a frown. "Finn can get the car while I make sure you get to your room okay. It won't take much longer, and we promised the nurse we'd stay with you."

I opened my mouth to argue, but Finn passed the IV stand to his sister. "I'll see you tomorrow, man. Get better fast, okay? Hospital food sucks." He mock-punched my shoulder and walked past me to the elevator. "Five minutes, Addie."

He pressed the button, and a few seconds later the doors opened. As soon as Finn was out of sight, I grabbed the IV stand. Addie sighed and gripped my arm tighter.

"You know, I'm really all right. I can walk without you supporting me."

She flushed but didn't let go. And this was why I shouldn't be allowed around normal people—I hadn't meant to embarrass her.

Almost a full minute passed before she responded. "I know."

We walked in silence most of the way down the hall, but it wasn't uncomfortable. It felt so good to be close to her. I liked the way her cheeks got a little pink when she looked at me. The way her hands felt warm on my biceps. Addie made *me* feel better. Even my problems felt a little more distant when she was around.

With the curtains all closed, the room was mostly dark when we walked in. Only a small bit of light streaming out through the crack under the bathroom door kept it from complete blackness. When we got inside, I pushed my IV to the side of my bed and only turned around when I heard the door close. I squinted in the darkness, thinking Addie must've left. The intense wave of disappointment I felt surprised me.

But then I saw a few quick, silent movements in the shadows and she was in front of me. Her soft smile tugged up one side of her mouth. When I grinned back, she laughed. Placing one warm hand on my chest, she gave a small push with one finger. "You should lie down now."

I grabbed her hand and sat on the hospital bed. For a moment, she didn't move. My heart pounded in my ears, nearly deafening. I felt alive again.

She stood so close, her hand in mine. I wished the light was behind me so I could see her eyes. It was more tempting than anything to reach out and—but I wouldn't. Finn would kill me.

With a small sigh, she pulled her hand away and walked to the door. She turned on the light and came back to the side of my bed. She met my eyes, and the intensity in hers surprised me.

"I need you to promise me something."

"Sure." The word came out before I could even think about it.

"Go to sleep as soon as I leave."

"Why?"

"If you're still seeing dreams, I want them to be mine. I'm kind of curious…"

As much as I tried, I couldn't keep the smirk from spreading across my face. "Oh? Won't you feel all violated and stuff?"

The corner of her mouth lifted in a sly grin. "No. It's different if you're invited."

With a nod, I lifted my legs up on the bed and pulled the covers over them. This wasn't a hard request. Now that she wasn't as close, my heart slowed and I relaxed. Exhaustion rolled over me like a dump truck. My head weighed a ton. Only the expression on Addie's face kept me from lying back on my pillow and closing my eyes. I didn't know how, but I'd known her long enough to see how upset she was. A strange mixture of guilt and an intense desire to make it better washed over me.

I reached out and tugged on her fingers. "What's wrong?"

With one quick move, she sat on my bed and threw both arms around my neck. Without even thinking, I wrapped my arms around her and pulled her in tight. My breath caught in my throat and I was extremely aware of the way she felt against me. Her shoulders were shaking; I squeezed her tighter. I'd do anything to make her happy again.

"Addie? What's going on?"

"You have no idea. I thought—we all thought—you were going to die." Talking seemed to help, because she stopped trembling. Her fingers clung to my shoulders like they were her lifeline. I didn't know what to say, so I rubbed her back and let her talk. Her breath warmed my skin as she spoke against the thin hospital gown.

"And then you woke up, and I was there, and you seemed okay. And then you—you—" She shook her head and didn't finish.

"I'm fine. Everything is okay." I had no idea how to make her feel better. This was new territory and I felt unprepared.

Addie took a few deep breaths and my body moved with each one. Her scent—fresh citrus—surrounded me. I never wanted to let her go.

"Please, be careful. You need—I need you to be around."

I didn't know how to respond. Holding her felt incredible, natural. A thrill of excitement flowed through me at her words, but it was accompanied by dread. She was Finn's sister—that was serious betrayal. How could I fix it? I didn't want to hurt either of them. Or myself, if I was really being honest.

I took a deep breath, hesitating. "I'm not going anywhere."

She pulled away, smiled, and kissed my cheek. I couldn't think straight. Her lips were so soft. I could still feel them against my skin as I watched her stand up from the bed, turn off the lights, and walk out of the room. "Good night."

In the silence, my idiocy began to sink in. Over the past few weeks, Addie had become like another best friend. This—whatever it was—would probably ruin both of my friendships. It was already difficult to make myself stop thinking about being close to her again. How could I not wonder what it would be like to kiss her? Maybe I could talk to Finn. Would he really care?

Yes. Yes, he would.

I pushed my hands into my forehead and groaned. Leaning back into my pillow, I closed my eyes. As my mind drifted, flashes of Darkness and Dr. Freeburg plowed through it like an avalanche down my spine.

I jerked straight up in bed, knowing what I would have to do. I couldn't risk Addie. Somehow, I needed to stop whatever was happening between us before it really started.

Some kind of monster lived in my mind, and I deserved nothing from Addie. From anyone, really—Finn, Mia, even my mom. I didn't deserve their trust, not when I couldn't even trust myself.

I couldn't risk any of the people that meant the most to me, not until I could be sure about what had happened with Freeburg. Not until I knew that I was safe to be around.

TWENTY-SEVEN

I was in my familiar white nothingness for a while before I entered Addie's dream. We were surrounded by a shimmery silver mist with no walls, no ceiling, nothing at all, really—only mist. I could see the night stars peeking through when the air shifted. Addie sat cross-legged, looking up at them. She didn't move or even blink. Just waited.

A rolling wave of mist curled up and over her legs. A slight breeze lifted a strand of hair off her shoulder and flipped it over. After a moment she took a deep breath and sighed. I kept expecting something to change, but it remained the same.

Most dreams had something happening. The dreamer was focused on something else, someone else. But Addie knew I was coming, and she was only focused on me.

I'd never seen anything like it.

This wasn't one layer, like Mia's, but it wasn't a normal dream either. It was unique and amazing, just like Addie.

She was wearing navy shorts and a gray tank top that almost blended with the mist. I stood for a minute, not wanting to disturb her. Her long hair shimmered like dark copper in the starlight, and I could make out the sprinkle of tiny freckles on her nose. Looking at her made me understand why the word "beautiful" was invented. "Pretty" just wasn't accurate.

Walking over, I sat down beside her. The ground felt like a firm pillow, but I didn't pay much attention to it. The need to touch her was overwhelming, but my decision to distance myself from her made me hesitate.

In this dream, for this moment, maybe it would be okay. Here, we were safe. After this, I would stay away. I would protect her.

I would let go.

I took a deep breath and placed my hand on top of hers. Instantly she smiled, and my body warmed from the inside out. She wrapped her fingers around two of mine. I'd never noticed how much bigger my hand was than hers.

"Hi," she whispered. She still hadn't looked at me, like she was afraid I wasn't really there. "Guess you still have your curse."

I leaned forward until I caught her eye. "Looks like it." I watched the mist move through the dream around us. "This is different though."

"Is it? I was just trying to think calm thoughts while I fell asleep."

"Well, this is pretty calm." I watched the mist swirling around her. There were still so many things about this curse, and the dreams themselves, that I didn't understand. I'd never seen a Dreamer control a dream in this way. I don't know that anyone had ever tried, but still. She also seemed so aware, with none of the confusion the subconscious usually brings with it…she seemed almost awake.

She grinned. "Lie down."

I looked from her to the misty ground and back to her. What was she up to?

"Relax and lie down." Addie laughed. "I want to see if you can sleep here."

"Oh, did you use hypnosis?" I glanced around, certain she hadn't. Although it was similar to the stillness of Mia's painting dreams, I could feel a difference in my bones.

Addie leaned back and scooted closer to me. "No, but I was hoping maybe it might work with me too." Her mouth curved up at the corner in a cute lopsided smile. She tugged on my hand until I lay on my side facing her. "Could you please cooperate—just this once?" She batted her eyelashes and then stuck her tongue out at me.

I couldn't help but laugh. "Okay, but only this once. After that, I will be as uncooperative as possible."

"Deal."

I closed my eyes and tried to relax, but I felt Addie moving. She was careful never to release my hand, but she switched it to her other side and wiggled around a bit. Her hands were soft as silk as she passed my hand back and forth between hers. A minute later, she curled up with her back next to me and draped my arm around her waist. My heartbeat sped up enough that all thought of sleep fled my mind. Her hair smelled like it had at the hospital. The heat from her body next to mine felt like a spark; all it needed was a little kindling to scorch us both.

Warning bells went off in my head, telling me to move away, but I couldn't. I tightened my grip, pulling her closer, and she sighed. She fit perfectly against me, her waist dipped in a curve that was built for my arm to curl around. I rubbed the back of her hand with my thumb; everything about her was so soft.

It was just a dream. It was harmless.

"It's not working, is it?" Her voice sounded sad. I hated it so much I considered pretending to be asleep to make her feel better, but I knew that wouldn't do either of us any good.

I pulled in a deep breath, and slowly let it out. "No. I'm sorry. But it's closer to sleep than I've gotten before. You know, without the hypnosis thing."

She rolled over inside my arms to face me and my breath got stuck in my throat. Her lips, her eyes, her body—everything about her was so close. The situation had suddenly changed from a semi-harmless nap to something entirely different. The warning bells in my head turned to sirens and I started to pull away, but she wrapped her arms around my neck and held me in place.

With one small smile, she silenced the alarm, and it was over. I was done for.

Her feelings mirrored mine; I could feel them. A lightning bolt couldn't come close to the attraction, the electricity that flowed between us. My arms tightened, pulling her closer. In the last month, we'd become like magnets, and I couldn't keep flipping over trying to keep us apart anymore.

I lowered my head and gently brushed my lips against hers. The mist around us churned with warmth as her fingers curled in my hair and she kissed me back, pulling me closer. Any will I had left dissolved.

We became lost in each other. I moved my mouth against hers slowly, enjoying the moment. She scratched the back of my neck with her fingernails, and it was impossible to imagine ever willingly letting go. I wanted to kiss her forever.

The first explosion made me jump, and I tucked Addie's head into my chest out of instinct. I felt her giggling into my shirt, and she peeked out with one hazel eye and pointed up. The mist parted above us and I saw the stars exploding into fireworks.

I laughed and sat upright, still loosely holding her hand. She tried to pull me to her again, but I resisted. When she sat up, she was very quiet. As much as I wanted to keep kissing her, I couldn't. This was a mistake—an amazing mistake—but still a mistake. I could tell from the red creeping up her neck and the way she wouldn't meet my eyes that she already felt embarrassed, rejected.

I'd been lying to myself. Nothing about this had been harmless.

The more I let this continue, the harder it would be to stop. It had to end now. I wouldn't risk her, not Addie. She was too—I grasped for a word that would describe the mixture of fear, misery, and fury that ran through me at the idea of someone hurting her. But I came up short.

The fireworks stopped and the mist cooled. It was silent. This was fascinating. I'd never seen the setting in a dream mimic the feelings of the Dreamer so closely. I felt her emotions—disappointment, sadness, a touch of anger—but it was like the dream world around us felt it too. Even the murmuring from the other dream levels quieted. I didn't know what to say. I could feel how I'd hurt her and I didn't want to make it worse.

"Sorry," she said quietly. "I shouldn't have—of course, you don't."

I groaned and turned to face her. "I'm the one who kissed you, remember?"

"Then what?" Her big eyes stared at me, waiting for an explanation I didn't know how to articulate. How could I make her see all the reasons this wouldn't work?

"Well, you're Finn's sister."

Addie opened her mouth to object, but I plowed on before she could interrupt. "And I'm not good for you... Addie, I accepted that I might not live to see graduation a long time ago, and I don't want you to have to deal with it."

Her eyes widened and her mouth snapped shut. After a moment, she swallowed. "First, that's just an excuse and you know it." Her eyes glinted with determination in the twinkling starlight, but her expression was wounded. "Whatever we are to each other, if you... if anything happened to you... I'd *still* have to 'deal with it.'"

My word choices were never the right ones. The pain I

felt emanating from her surprised and scared me. I turned away but it was no use; I felt it in my core. My life had become like a black hole. I sucked at everything and everyone around me, taking pieces of them and ripping them apart. Why should my death affect them any differently?

Addie would be better off if she'd never known me.

The mist around us turned dark and blotted out any pinpoint of starlight coming through the clouds. I'd created this gloom in her life and I could never forgive myself for it.

"I need to leave."

She wrapped her other hand around mine and squeezed tight with both. "No. I think I know how to keep you alive. I could help you."

"How?"

"I could convince my parents I need to see a hypnotherapist." Addie shrugged nonchalantly, but I could see the red creeping up her neck and feel the heat in my own. "I'm sure I could come up with some issues that need to be dealt with."

I felt my mouth open and close a few times and finally clamped it shut. I couldn't trust what might eventually find its way out.

"Of course, I'd find a different therapist than—oh, I forgot." Addie stared at me, her skin paling. "Mia called on our way home. You might have been wrong about that doctor not being involved."

My brain sputtered into motion like an old car, lurching to life. "Wha-what do you mean?"

"I don't know specifics, but I guess he died a couple of days ago. They wanted to refer her to a different therapist."

Addie shrugged again. "Anyway, she hasn't received an e-mail since he died."

Darkness whispered from the back of my mind. There was still another possibility: if the e-mails were from me, I'd been in the hospital, unconscious, which would also explain why she hadn't received any more.

I hated that I could still feel him, even in Addie's dream. Darkness was weaker now that I wasn't as exhausted, but he was still there, squirming around in my head. Like a serpent waiting for the perfect opportunity to strike. He pulled on my thoughts, twisted my emotions. Darkness was part of me—the weaker part, the part willing to do anything to survive. The side of me that believed I could keep quiet and this would all blow over, all go away.

Mia might be willing to help me now. If not, Addie had just volunteered. I could live a normal life, and no one would have to know. No one would have to know I might have killed someone.

Even *I* didn't have to know, not for sure.

I jerked away from the dark tendrils warping my thoughts. I would never be like that. I refused to give in to the obscure and murky logic.

I had to tell someone, no matter how much I wanted to avoid it. Now, when I was stronger, when I had the power— now. I needed to tell Addie the truth.

"I know." I swallowed, trying to keep my throat from closing up and finishing our conversation for me.

Addie watched me, waiting. Her nose scrunched up. "You know what?"

"I know he's dead." I took in a deep breath and let it out slowly. "I saw him before my accident."

She opened her mouth to speak, but stopped when I shook my head.

"The last couple of months, things have been happening to me. Things I can't explain. I've been seeing things. They might be hallucinations; they might not. I really don't understand what's going on, but I'm losing control." I rubbed my wrist across my forehead. I couldn't look at Addie. Not while I admitted this. I'd seen her dreams; I'd felt her emotions. She saw something different in me than the truth, something better. She saw a lie.

As much as both of us wanted it to be true, I was no hero.

"I think I might've killed him."

Addie drew a sharp breath and squeezed my hand. "How could you think that?"

"It's not—I'm not always myself lately." How could I explain this to her? Addie's eyes were huge, and the brown and green swirls seemed to rotate in confusion.

"Freeburg was such a pervert," I said. "It made me crazy. In his dream, I hit him with a paperweight until he died and the dream stopped. When I woke up, I worried it might have been real, which is why I went to see him first thing in the morning. When I got there it was still early…and he was dead."

Her skin was so pale she blended with the mist around us. The only emotion I felt from her at that moment was pure shock. "He was murdered?" she whispered.

"I don't know. He looked like he was still asleep, but he wasn't breathing."

"How—" Addie cleared her throat and tried again. "How can you be sure he didn't just have a heart attack or something?"

"That would be quite the coincidence, don't you think?"

She stared at me, and her shock faded like stars before sunrise. "So, you attacked someone in a dream, which I've probably done a dozen times, and that makes you a murderer?" She shook her head and gave me a relieved smile. "No way, Parker. I don't buy it."

Every part of me threatened to cave in, to be happy and go along with it. To believe that my ability wasn't strong enough, that it wasn't possible. But I knew it wasn't the same thing.

This was the best thing I could do for her. To shatter any illusions she had about who I was—about what we could be together.

"That isn't all, Addie."

Her smile slid down her face like raindrops on a window, and the mist around us froze.

"The other me, from Mia's dreams—it's like he's real. He's a part of me, in my head, and sometimes he takes over. Once I found myself in a tree outside her window. I don't know how I got there. I'm losing it, Addie. I can't be trusted."

"No," Addie murmured. She shook her head and turned away, her entire frame shaking. Her anguish struck at my heart and plucked at my veins in a more painful way than I'd believed possible.

"Yes. I sat there, watching her. You need to believe me. I see things—things that I don't want to be real, that can't be. Like I didn't fall asleep at the wheel...I saw him, the dark side of me, standing in the road in front of me. Somehow I made myself get in that accident." I grabbed her chin and brought her eyes up to meet mine. "Whether I killed Freeburg or not, I tried to. Don't you see? In his dream, I wanted to. I'm not even sure which parts of his dream were memory and which were fantasy, but either way, I ended his life. I'm dangerous."

Her hazel eyes stared back at me, but instead of the fear I expected to feel, there was anger. They flashed, and the mist around me rumbled with thunder.

"No. I don't believe it and I never will. You're all kinds of messed up, but you aren't a threat to anyone but yourself. We're all dangerous. We hurt others all the time without meaning to. Even if you did kill him, you were in *a dream*. You could never know it would carry over into reality. You'd never hurt someone intentionally." Her jaw was set and she held my hand tight in both of hers. "I know you."

"How could you?" I sighed and pressed my chin into my chest. "I don't even know me anymore."

"Well, I do. So maybe you should trust someone else's instincts for a change." Her voice softened and her anger changed to kindness. "Let me help you."

Looking into her eyes, I knew she would never believe I could hurt anyone. Nothing I said would convince her of who I really was or what I was really capable of. There was only one thing left to do, only one way to protect her.

I wrapped my arms around her and pulled her into my

chest. The relief I felt from her was tainted by suspicion, and it almost made me laugh. She knew me better than I'd ever suspected—but not as well as she thought.

"I'm so sorry," I whispered into her hair, breathing in the scent of her, feeling her in my arms for probably the last time. She lifted her chin from my chest in confusion. I released the iron grip I was holding myself in and savored the moment. Her lips were so close and so perfect they dragged me in, and I kissed her again—there was a drive to it now, a need, an urgency. I hated myself for everything I'd done, hated Darkness for making it impossible for me to be with her.

Addie sighed and melted against me, both of us forgetting everything but each other. My blood pumped through my body with extraordinary speed, bringing every piece of me to life in ways I'd never felt before. The world, my worries, the dreams, all fell away until nothing else existed.

My breath came in ragged puffs when I finally managed to pull away. She smiled at me, and I felt her trust stab through me like a sword, opening me up and leaving my insides vulnerable and exposed. I tucked one tangled auburn curl behind her ear and kissed her cheek. "I'm sorry," I muttered against the soft skin in front of her ear. "Goodbye, Addie."

Then I let go and rolled quickly away from her. I couldn't risk her anymore—or Finn or Mia—any of them. I doubted I could find out the truth about Dr. Freeburg—I might never know if I caused his death, and I'd have to live with that.

There was only one way to know the truth about how dangerous I was: the threatening e-mails that were sent to

Mia. If I'd sent those, then I was beyond help, beyond control. I'd have to take some kind of action to be certain I couldn't hurt anyone ever again. I needed to know now, before I put my friends any more at risk.

"Parker?" she whispered. It only took an instant for Addie to understand. Tears poured down her cheeks. The mist formed solid clouds churning around us and the rain came. I was only inches away, but she couldn't see me unless I touched her.

The pain in her heart hit me with such force I gasped for breath. It was followed swiftly by a fear that I didn't understand. Maybe she was afraid of me. Even though I deserved it, it cut my soul. She was the one who had faith when I didn't. Knowing she was afraid filled me with a despair that threatened to break down my plan, if only to reassure her—to make her believe in me again.

"Don't leave me," Addie choked out in barely recognizable gasps. "Not like this, not by choice."

Her fear was of losing me.

I took both my hands and tucked them under my thighs, pinning them to the ground. Her emotions were shattering my resolve into a million pieces, but I couldn't let them take control. I would protect her.

Addie reached out with her hands and they passed right through me. It was nothing more than a warm breeze. I pushed down on my hands harder, forcing them to stay put.

I felt her shift in emotions before I even saw it in her face. She was angry. I could handle that. Let her be angry. Her anger didn't make me want to throw myself in front of a bus. After everything I'd done, to her and everyone around me, I deserved more than anger. I deserved hatred, but that didn't come.

She stomped around yelling my name over and over, along with a few colorful words I'd never heard her use in the real world. The rain had an occasional burst of lightning, but it didn't take long to fizzle out.

At the end, she curled into a small ball a few feet away from me and cried. It was miserable watching her, seeing the pain I could cause even when my intentions were good. Her feelings of abandonment were overwhelming. I'd felt this way when Dad never came back. It was the worst kind of pain I'd ever experienced. It was what Mom must've felt too.

And now I'd done it to Addie—I was no better than him.

I stretched out on the soft cloudy substance, only an inch away but refusing to touch her. I made myself watch the pain I'd caused. I deserved punishment for what I'd done, for everything I'd done.

The rain came in a steady downpour. I licked my lips and was surprised to find them salty. I couldn't tell if it was the rain or my own tears mixing with the water.

TWENTY-EIGHT

The morning sunlight streamed through the blinds of the hospital window. I rolled away from it and tried to close my eyes again, but the image of Addie crying appeared and they flew back open. With every blink, she returned. Her tortured face was imprinted on the insides of my eyelids like an after-image from looking directly at the sun.

I grabbed the remote and adjusted my bed to an upright position. The machines humming in the silence made me shiver. There was only one possible plan at this point. I needed to get home and get to my computer.

We're all dangerous.

Addie's words bounced around inside my head.

We hurt others all the time without meaning to.
Even if you did kill him, you were in a dream.

You could never know it would carry over into reality.
You'd never hurt someone intentionally.

She could be right. I hadn't believed it possible to hurt a Dreamer, and I still didn't know for sure if I did. It didn't matter, though; I'd never try it again. The question was—could I make that kind of promise? Even if I never hurt anyone, how much control did Darkness have over me? Could he hurt someone even though I didn't want to? I couldn't risk it.

The e-mails were truly the only thing I could think of, the only way to be certain of his power. Someone else could've created that address to frame me for stalking Mia. Or I created it—*Darkness* created it. Cold sweat ran from my pores at the thought. If I could access the account—if it was a password that only made sense to me—then I'd know Darkness was the monster chasing Mia.

And I'd have to deal with the horror I'd become.

I looked around at my empty hospital room. Usually I enjoyed being alone, but after Addie's dream it was like a unified confirmation from everyone in my life that I didn't deserve visitors. Like they all finally understood what I was and they wanted nothing to do with me. It didn't make sense, and I knew they didn't actually feel that way, but a big part of me was starting to believe they should. I tugged off the heart monitors and blood pressure cuff, everything that tied me to this place.

The machines went wild and the door to my room opened. Patti rushed in and gave an aggravated sigh when she realized I'd unplugged everything again. "You feel all right?" she asked, flipping off the machines beeping around me.

"Yeah. I'm fine. Just tired of being tied down."

My door swung open again and I barely suppressed a groan as Addie stepped through it. Her hair was slightly frizzed on one side, making it obvious she'd rolled out of bed and come straight here. Her eyes were red, puffy, and accusing.

Of course, the one time when it would have come in handy for someone to forget their dream, it was clear she hadn't.

"That's fine," Patti was saying. "You'll probably be going home in an hour or so anyway." She turned to Addie. "Let me know if he has any problems."

I snorted at the nurse's choice of words, and she glared at me. I held up my hands in surrender as she walked out the door.

Silently, Addie pulled a chair next to the bed, but I couldn't meet her eyes. The pain there sent ice shards through my spine and into my heart. For a few agonizing minutes, she didn't say anything. When her voice finally came it was hoarse and hollow.

"Don't *ever* do that to me again."

"Addie, you don't understand." My words came out more like a groan. I was protecting her, whether she could see it or not.

"Freeburg was the monster, Parker. Not you." Her voice was pleading. "You're not even sure if you killed him."

"And I'm the one who has to live with not knowing,

Addie—*me*," I mumbled without looking up. "Can you honestly say you'd be fine in my position?"

She fell silent.

"I need you to let me figure things out on my own for a bit." I stared at the divots in the white ceiling above me.

"It doesn't matter whether we're together or not." Addie leaned forward, trying to make me look at her, but I couldn't. I knew if I did, I'd give in. "Parker, you can't run away from this—not from me."

I gathered all the strength I had and withdrew all emotion from my eyes. If I had to hurt Addie to protect her, I would. Turning, I stared her straight in the eye.

"There is nothing between—"

The door to my room opened and my mom walked in with a stack of papers in her hands. She was followed by a much older man in a long white coat. I thought I'd seen him in one of my hazy awakenings.

"Oh, hello, Addie." My mom actually winced when she glanced at her. "Oh no, honey, you haven't been here all night, have you?"

Addie patted one side of her hair and shook her head. All at once, she seemed embarrassed. On the verge of tears, she reached down and squeezed my hand with a frown and a slight shake of her head. The message was clear—we weren't done. She glanced at my mom, then hurried from the room.

Mom raised her eyebrows at me, but I shrugged. She smiled and her entire body lit up.

"Good news." She indicated the doctor. "Dr. Rees says you're ready to come home now."

Dr. Rees walked over to the bed. He lifted up a miniature flashlight and checked my eyes, and then he hit my knees with his ridiculous little hammer. My leg jerked on command. As he spoke, he pulled off a couple heart monitors, removed my IV, and gave me a cotton ball to stop the bleeding.

"Are you feeling any pain, champ?"

I flinched. I hadn't been called "champ" since I was about six. The man meant well, but it grated on my already raw nerves. I needed to get out of here.

"Just a headache."

He nodded and looked me over one more time. "That's to be expected." He turned back to Mom and signed one of the papers she held. "He should probably stay down and rest for another week or so, keep the strain on his body to a minimum while his brain recovers."

I stifled a laugh and Mom sent me a look. My sense of humor was becoming as twisted as the rest of me.

"Sounds do-able." Mom shook his hand and he headed out the door. "Ready?"

"Ready as I'll ever be."

Sucking in a lungful of air, I ignored the ripple of terror that moved from my brain to my spine. This was it.

I stood up from the bed, forcing my feet to move. Mom stood in the hall while I got dressed and gathered my stuff. A giant bulldozer of pain crushed me when I picked up the get-well card from Addie and Finn.

It was time to stop hiding from my own worst enemy—myself. I needed to know if I was responsible for the threats Mia had received. Whether I'd killed Dr. Freeburg or not, I would find out if I had the strength to keep Darkness at bay, to keep control. If I didn't, then I had to be stopped.

I faced the empty hospital room and clicked off the light.

TWENTY-NINE

My fingers produced a strange rattling noise as they shook the keys. I couldn't make them behave. They didn't want to type the right combination any more than I did. When the keyboard shuddered off the desk onto my lap, I put it back and reclined in my chair, propping my bare feet up on the computer tower. I needed to calm down. There was no backing out now.

The phone rang in the living room yet again and I heard Mom pick it up.

"Hello?" she answered. "I'm sorry. Parker isn't feeling up to having visitors yet." I heard her sigh as she listened. "I know. I'll tell him you called."

Obviously it was Finn or Addie. She thought I was asleep or she might've come in to tell me they wanted to talk to me...again. It was the fifth time one of them had stopped by or called since I'd turned off my cell phone when we'd gotten home from the hospital that morning. But Mom didn't seem to mind screening their many calls and visits for me. There was some kind of unwritten rule that when your kid has a near-death experience, they get whatever they want for a while. And, really, wanting to be alone and get some rest wasn't asking for much.

I took three deep breaths and sat back up. Pressing my wrists firmly into the keyboard pad seemed to still the shaking a bit. One clumsy finger strike at a time, I typed the e-mail address in the login box. Each click echoed like a pounding gavel in my mind.

My soccer jersey hung from a hook on the back of my door. The eight was printed in ominous black over the vertical blue and yellow stripes. I omitted the 1 from my normal address, leaving only the 8. I tentatively tried to guess what Darkness might use as a password.

Darkness—no

Mia—no

Watcher—no

I only had one more guess before the security default would lock the account for an hour. Darkness laughed morbidly from the back of my mind. What else might it be? Out of frustration, I entered the password for my normal e-mail address: *s0cc3r*. One word flashed across the screen.

LOADING.

That single word sent me spinning, gasping for air. I jammed my finger into the power button on the monitor before anything could come up. Still, I could feel the secret e-mails tugging at me from behind the dark screen.

More air, I needed more air. I scrambled to my bed and slammed my fists against the window. Then I hit it with the only other thing I could reach, a soccer trophy from last year off my desk. Again and again, I beat the tiny brass soccer player against the glass until I heard it crack, and then it wasn't in my way anymore. The air in my room seemed impossibly thin; each breath was a struggle.

It was true. Darkness was the stalker. He'd sent Mia the e-mails. No, *I* did. Whether I was aware of him or not, could control him or not, he was me.

Images of the past few weeks floated like ghosts in the tomb of my mind, a barren wasteland where they hovered and plagued but never held still long enough for me to push them away. Flashes haunted me: Finn, his cheek already swelling as he glared at me from his locker; Mia, cowering with blood blossoming from her head; Addie, sobbing and screaming for me in her dream until her throat was raw.

Then the images burst through the flood gates I'd carefully erected to protect myself, one pounding over the next: Mia's parents melting in the blaze; Darkness standing in the road with his maniacal smile; me watching Mia through her window; Dr. Freeburg running his hand up Mia's leg; the bloody paperweight in my hand; Darkness bashing Mia's head until hot, red blood was all I could see. They wouldn't leave me. They were my constant company.

And there he was, leaning against the wall in the corner of my room. His cold eyes seemed to confirm everything I'd suspected for so long. My control was an illusion. He had the real power—always.

"So, now you think you know all my secrets?" Darkness sneered and shook his head. "You make things so easy."

Pounding sounded on my door. It was locked. Somewhere I recognized the sound of Mom's voice, yelling about a key. Mom sounded scared. I wondered if she knew she was safer out there than in here with me. Near the window I heard a horrible howling. It was outside, or maybe in my mind. Perhaps it was the sound Dr. Freeburg made when I killed him.

I leaned out the window and threw up into the bushes. The howling stopped. Only then did I realize that the terrible noise had come from me.

The door burst open and my mom was next to me, pulling me away from the window. She pushed me back on the bed, speaking in soft tones.

"Parker! Oh no, oh no." She grabbed a towel from the bottom of my bed and wrapped it around my hands. That was good. Someone needed to tie me up ... lock me away so everyone was safe. But it was just to stop the blood coming from the cuts on my arms. Why was I bleeding? Was it my blood or someone else's?

Didn't she know about all the other blood on my hands? The pain I'd caused? Couldn't she stop that?

"No. No. It's okay. Shh, it's okay." Her face was wet as she knelt next to me, warm brown eyes staring into mine. The muscle in her cheek flexed and I could see the fear behind her trembling hands. She was trying to be strong, always strong. "It's only a nightmare. It will pass. Shh."

I wanted to tell her to run, to get away from me as fast as

she could, but I was weak. Words were past me, so far away I couldn't reach them. My hands and arms were still bleeding a little. Blood covered me inside and out: my clothes, my sheets, my thoughts.

Darkness stood in the back of the room. He watched us. I closed my eyes and breathed the smell of my mom, a combination of peppermint gum and rose lotion that always signaled home for me. I tried to absorb it, willing it to wash all my thoughts away.

To wash Darkness away.

———————

My eyes were closed but I wasn't sleeping. Time was a distorted abstract that didn't matter anymore. The last two days I'd spent mostly watching Mom's dreams, watching the white walls of my void, or in bed pretending to be asleep. My mom's dreams were filled with worry about me. They tumbled me in guilt and refused to release me until morning. Still, they were better than the nightmare my life had become.

The bandages on my arms itched. My hands were healing faster, but there were nicks and scratches all over me. Half a cardboard box covered the hole where my window used to be. I could have just opened it. Not my most brilliant moment, or my sanest for that matter.

I'd caught up on my sleep during my hospital stay, so my more-rested mind refused to give up the way I wanted it to. It wanted a plan, and my tattered emotions couldn't present a valid argument against it. Denial was getting me nowhere.

Neither was bashing the window with a trophy, cutting my arms up, and puking—although it'd been worth a try.

One fact kept bobbing back up to the surface like a body that wasn't tied down properly. I needed to make my decisions now, when I was still rested. It was the only way to be sure I had control.

Sitting up in bed, I slipped on a pair of shoes. The house was quiet and I needed some fresh air to think. If I could sneak past Mom, or if she was out somewhere, I could go to the back porch and breathe for a minute.

I stood up and a shudder ran through me. It happened every minute or so, like clockwork. Nothing I did could stop it. My body wanted to rid itself of the foul creature inside it. It wanted me gone, and I wished I could oblige. I'd probably already killed one person, and the only thing I could do to even begin to make amends before I was gone would be to make sure I didn't kill anyone else.

I passed through the kitchen on my way to the bathroom. The note on the table said Mom went to the store, so I had a few minutes to myself. In the bathroom, I tried to keep my eyes closed as much as possible. One glance in the mirror brought on another shudder. My skin had a weird greenish tinge, and in spite of the extra sleep I'd gotten, my blue eyes were pale against the dark hollows beneath them. I looked like death. Maybe I was death.

Shuffling out the back door, I pulled out one of the black wrought-iron chairs on the deck and slumped into it. The metal was frigid even through my sweats, but my mind felt clearer and more focused from the cold. I rubbed my hands over my arms and wished the sun would come out from behind the clouds for just a few minutes before it set against the horizon.

Okay, no more stalling. I needed a plan. The way I saw it, I had three options. I could run away, confess to the police, or kill myself.

I rapped my knuckles against the iron tabletop and shook my head. I'd spent too long fighting to keep myself alive for suicide to ever sound like a good plan. Of course, if that was the only way to keep from killing again, from killing Mia, then I would do it. But I'd prefer the other options first.

Confessing came with its own set of problems. The more I thought about it, the more I thought no one would believe me if I tried to confess. There was no real way to prove it. My confession would be full of holes big enough to run a hearse through.

My chair creaked as I leaned back. Assuming they could try me as an adult and get me convicted—both of which I doubted—and that they didn't put me in the mental hospital—again, improbable—I couldn't even begin to imagine how horrific it would be to experience the dreams of other criminals every night in jail.

The wind picked up and blew a few leaves around on the grass below. I shivered. Part of me felt like I deserved to watch the dreams of killers and thieves, a fitting punishment. The other part knew it would make things worse. My gut instinct told me that Darkness would take over more and more every day if I was surrounded by criminals, seeing their dreams and feeling their emotions.

No. I'd rather be dead than alive with Darkness in complete control.

Standing up, I walked to the railing, resting my bandaged arms on the worn wood. I was left with only one option. Running away was an unknown, but at least it would keep the people I cared about out of danger. Maybe to the desert or out in the woods, somewhere I wouldn't be around anyone. My life, as I knew it anyway, was over.

I stood outside on the deck until my body ached from the cold, then came back inside to my computer and sat down. Emptiness filled me as I pushed the power button and the screen blazed to life. Every hope I'd ever had retreated to a safe place deep within as I opened up the first e-mail and started reading.

I kept expecting memories of the e-mails to surface now that I'd accepted the truth, but they didn't. I wasn't sure if I'd protected myself from them, or if Darkness just kept them private. Either way, I was grateful. Knowing he had that much power was enough. I didn't need to remember any more than that.

Over the next hour, I forced myself to read every depraved sentence I'd sent to Mia. Every word, every threat, every perverse declaration of love. I read them again and again until I was numb. They were filled with imagery from her nightmares—fire and blood. The only time she didn't receive one was while I was in the hospital. She must have been terrified—should still be terrified.

I checked the date on the last one against the date in the corner of my computer screen—yesterday. Last night, while

I'd been watching another of my mom's worried dreams, sleeping in my own bed for the first time in nearly a week.

I coiled into myself, pulling my arms in a tight protective ball around my head until my body stopped shaking. Even now, I had less control than I thought.

Opening the last e-mail again, I pushed all my emotions away as I studied it. It was the shortest of all, only six words long.

Time is nigh—time to die

I forced away the little voice in my head that rebelled against the idea that these were *my* words. I couldn't suffer under that delusion anymore. The intent was clear. Part of me, somewhere down deep that I didn't want to know about, wanted Mia dead—and soon.

But why? *Why* would I want Mia dead? She was the only one who could save me.

It didn't matter why. These weren't my motivations; they belonged to Darkness. It should be a relief that at least part of my mind still didn't understand the monster within me.

Then bubbles of fury broke through my numbness. He'd ruined everything. Stolen my last hope, my life, my friends, even my ability to die near those I loved. Darkness was my enemy, and I felt that driving desire to kill that I'd felt in Dr. Freeburg's dream. I knew if I could, I would act on that instinct. I would kill Darkness. He was dangerous—to me and everyone around me. My eyes dropped to my hands. I gripped the keyboard in front of me so tight that the skin under my thumbnails turned purple.

But how do I fight an enemy that is inside me?

My anger exploded like a volcano and I threw my keyboard against the wall. Keys popped off like shards of glass, shooting across the room with lethal velocity only to bounce harmlessly to the floor—just like me. I had an enemy and I wanted to destroy him, but there was nothing I could do about it. I was powerless.

I turned off my computer and the lights as if in slow motion. Closing the door, I locked it and crumpled on the edge of my bed like wadded paper.

Accepting the truth brought a certain peace. When I had no power, why should I fight?

In the stillness, I let my mind go blank. My will retreated. No matter what death held, could it be worse than this?

The garage door opened and I heard Mom shuffling around the kitchen. Soon I would leave, and she would be alone. Images of her pain when Dad left pierced my mind like daggers, each one drawing more blood than the last. I sat up, taking a quick breath and letting the oxygen mend the wounds in my brain.

I couldn't let her believe that I'd abandoned her too. Finn, Addie—none of them could think that. This was something I could control. I wouldn't let Darkness hurt them any more than he already had.

There was a knock on my door, and I opened it. The worry lines on my mom's face were too painful to look at, so I wrapped one arm around her and pulled her into a hug. She relaxed against me and laughed.

"Thank God," was all she said. Her relief made me want to smile and scream at the same time.

"I love you, Mom."

"I know, honey. I love you too." She sighed. "Everything is going to be okay."

Mom patted my back with her hand and I felt about five again. Somehow, I knew she was right. For those I loved, I would fix things—the only way I knew how. I would tell them why I had to leave. How I felt about them. How sorry I was.

I would tell them the truth.

THIRTY

I stayed up late writing the letters. There were four in all: Mom, Finn, Addie, and Mia. The first three told them how important they were to me and my reasons for leaving, and the one for Mia was an apology that didn't even begin to make up for what I'd done to her.

I was emotionally drained but not tired when I finished. Mom had gone to bed hours earlier, and I couldn't help but smile at the thought that her dreams should be happy tonight. She deserved that—one night of happiness before I destroyed her by running away. I hoped once she read the letter it would help, but I wasn't going to lie to myself. She would never be the same again, and it would be my fault.

The kitchen was quiet as I grabbed a drink from the fridge. I pretended not to hear his voice the first time he spoke, but Darkness was nothing if not persistent.

He laughed. "You forget. I'm in your head. I know you can hear me."

I drew in a deep breath and turned to face him. "Hearing and listening aren't the same thing."

He was leaning against the wall on the other side of the kitchen. I hated how confident and relaxed he looked.

Darkness—dreams of complete control.

His grin turned to a scowl at my words. "Where do you think you're going?"

"Somewhere else." I rolled my head back and forth on my neck. Just like Darkness, the knots never seemed to go completely away.

"Really?" His eyes glinted. "You should know there is nowhere you can run that is far enough to escape me."

"I'm not running from you." I glanced at the letters I still gripped in one hand. "I'm running from them."

"Who do you think you're kidding? You think leaving this town will help? You use freaking dental floss to keep track of me, but you still don't have a clue what I've been doing." His fists were curled up by his sides and he seemed ready to pounce. "You're so stubborn, so sure you're right about everything. Maybe if you'd just relax and hand over control for more than five minutes, I could keep us alive."

I locked eyes with him, struggling to keep my voice steady. "That will never happen."

"Eventually I won't need your permission." Darkness stepped around the corner toward me, his entire frame shaking with anger. "And next time, you can count on the fact that I'll go farther than some stupid girl's backyard."

I blinked and he was gone. I pushed my palms against my eyes, letting out a huge breath. At least I now knew he hadn't gotten very far when he took over. Of course, with the damage he'd done just by writing a few e-mails, I didn't feel very reassured.

The counter before me had row upon row of messages with my name on them. Most were from Addie and Finn. I couldn't say goodbye to them. Maybe I was a coward, but they were the only ones who knew enough to talk me out of going.

And I cared too much about them to let that happen.

My muscles were all kinked from my writing session. I flicked my right wrist back and forth. Glancing back at the messages, a green one from Jeff caught my attention. I picked it up. It was from a few days ago. He'd scheduled a captains meeting for the soccer teams on Tuesday morning—tomorrow. If I didn't come, the team was planning to make Matt the co-captain instead. *Final Warning* was written along the top in Mom's curly handwriting.

Interesting that she'd never mentioned the message. She probably didn't want to stress me out. That didn't matter now, but ... it said *teams* ... that meant Mia would be there too.

Something inside me had balked at the idea of leaving without apologizing to Mia face-to-face. I wanted to tell her she wouldn't have to be afraid anymore, that once I was gone, she'd be safe. I hesitated. What was wrong? Was it me, or Darkness? I stared at the green paper for a few minutes, but I didn't feel that sinister pull I had so many times before. I nodded. This time, it would be okay.

School was still out for fall break, so no one would be at school except us. Jeff had unlimited access to Coach Mahoney's keys, and it would be the perfect opportunity to give Mia her letter, say I was sorry, and then leave—no risk of running into Finn or Addie, either. They would all be safe, and I would be far away. Maybe I could even tell Jeff I was sorry for being the worst, most unreliable co-captain ever. At least he wouldn't have to share that spotlight anymore.

I started to formulate my plan. Tomorrow morning, I would convince Mom to go back to work. Then I'd make sure the letters got where I needed them to go while still giving myself time to get as far as possible before Mom even knew I was gone. It was better this way; the sooner I left, the less time I had to change my mind.

My backpack was all I could take. I didn't have a car anymore, since the accident, and someone would probably notice me lugging my suitcase around. Dumping all my school stuff out, I started with the letters, tucking Mia's envelope carefully in an outside pocket. I placed the rest on my desk. I'd have to leave them on the counter for Mom and ask her to deliver them for me. Inside these small white rectangles was everything I would leave behind for the people I cared about the most. My life and reputation sealed neatly in an envelope.

———

"Are you sure?" Mom frowned and shifted her weight from one pink slipper to the other. I'd bought her those for

Mother's Day. It gave me an uneasy feeling knowing they would probably be the last gift she ever got from me.

"Positive." I put my hands on her shoulders and turned her toward her closet. "You've stayed home for days. Your clients are probably homeless now because of me."

"They're fine." She laughed but stopped resisting. "Are you sure there isn't anything you need me here for? I can really stay home."

"For the seventy-fifth time, yes, I'm sure." I grabbed her cell phone off the nightstand and placed it in her hand. "And if there is, I can call you."

Mom glanced at the phone and nodded before turning back toward the closet. "There's no school today. Will you at least have Finn come over and stay with you?"

I shook my head without even thinking, and she sighed.

"You two aren't fighting again, are you? He and Addie both seem really worried about you."

Their worry felt like a punch to the gut. "I don't need a babysitter. My head hurts and I want to sleep today. I'll invite them both over later tonight after I get some more rest, okay?"

Mom nodded and grabbed an outfit out of the closet. "I'm sure that will make them feel better."

"I'm going to make breakfast."

She dropped the clothes on the bed and stepped toward me. "Oh, why don't you let me do that before I go?"

The exasperated sigh that gushed out of my mouth was followed by instant guilt. She only wanted to take care of me, and I was about to rob her of the ability to ever do that again.

"Okay ... thanks." I smiled and followed her back to the kitchen.

———————

I couldn't remember the last time I'd had pancakes. It wasn't that I was pancake-deprived, but it'd never been memorable before, I guess. This time would be branded on my mind forever. Mom joked and laughed about how much syrup I used, and the way they melted in my mouth made me smile. The essence of the happiness I would leave behind—the opposite of where I planned to go.

My experience on the city bus was just the reverse, smelling like tar and garbage. My backpack was so full and heavy it felt ready to explode. I couldn't fit it under a seat, and I kept hitting people with it when I stood. Everyone around me was hostile and angry. I missed my car.

I couldn't have taken it with me anyway. I'd seen enough fugitive TV shows to know cars were easy to track. After I left school, I'd head to the bank to withdraw the money from my savings account. Mom and I had been putting money in it for college. Mostly Mom, but I'd put in a little from lawn mowing every summer since I was ten. It wasn't enough to last forever, but it would get me by for a little while.

After that would be the truck stop. Dad told me once that it was the best place to start a new life. Ever since he disappeared, that idea had stuck with me. If that's where he started, I would start there too.

He used to talk about Arizona a lot. How the caves

were cool during the day, and, with the right supplies, warm enough to survive at night. I wasn't sure when I'd decided to look for him, but it just felt like the right thing to do. Maybe he had the answers I needed. Maybe he wasn't even there. If not, at least there wouldn't be as many people around to hurt, in the desert.

I wondered how many hours it would be before Mom found my letters. They were so stark against the dark-green countertop. They looked almost clean … but I knew what they held was anything but. Better that she knew why I was leaving, that it had nothing to do with her; yet that didn't mean it wouldn't be painful.

After two stops, the bus pulled over at the corner near the high school and I got out, ignoring the grunts from the people I accidentally hit with my backpack as I passed. The school looked deserted, but I knew the door by the gym would be unlocked for the meeting.

Jeff always held his meetings in the shop room. I listened for voices, but I couldn't hear anything. I was a little late, as always, but I didn't care. It's not like I came to plan game strategy. A million different ways to apologize to Mia tumbled through my head as I stepped into the room. Then everything fell away.

Mia sat on the floor in the corner, wearing dark blue jeans and a pink T-shirt, her arms wrapped tightly around her shoulders. Flames flickered in the wastebasket in front of her, and her eyes spilled terror as she focused on the blaze. A stream of blood dripped from a nasty gash near her temple, down her cheek.

No, no, no—this is not happening, my brain screamed. I took a step back from the nightmare in front of me. It was impossible. How could Darkness have done this? I'd missed no time this morning.

It didn't matter. I wasn't Darkness right now—I would help her.

I took one hesitant step forward and something slammed into my head, crushing my skull until I could see nothing at all.

THIRTY-ONE

Before any sound came the pain, like someone had hit the back of my head with an axe and then left it there, embedded in my brain. Noise only made things worse. Every word, every breath, every cough sliced through the back of my head instead of taking the normal path through my ears. I couldn't make out any specific words, only the sharp throbbing.

The smell of smoke invaded my nose and I remembered Mia in the shop room. What happened? Did Darkness take over again? No, that wouldn't be this painful. I tried to open my eyes, but they weren't ready to cooperate. I could tell I was upright, and the seat I was in felt worn and familiar; it felt like one of the bright orange chairs we sat in for shop class. My hands—my hands were tied behind me.

I couldn't have done that. Darkness wouldn't have done that. Someone else was here.

I forced my eyes open, trying to see the piece missing

316

from the puzzle around me. I blinked a few times until my vision focused. The only thing I could see was Jeff's light hair and the back of his jersey as he knelt before Mia.

"Jeff?" I coughed and pain shot through my head. "Help her."

He turned from Mia, and the grin on his face seemed bizarrely out of place. It was more than happy—it was victorious. The shock hit me as I looked at the scene from her nightmares and realized the truth.

Darkness wasn't the stalker. *Jeff was.*

I hadn't lost control, at least nowhere near as much as I'd thought.

Relief washed over me, just long enough for me to realize I now had something to live for.

"How? What...what are you doing?"

"Enjoying myself." He remained crouched, but turned his whole body toward me. I leaned back out of instinct; he looked like an animal ready to pounce.

I needed to slow him down, make him talk...and buy myself some time to think. "I don't understand."

"Such a fool." Jeff got to his feet and sneered. "You still haven't figured it out?"

I recognized his emotions immediately: hatred and disdain. He oozed smugness and power. He was feeding off my stupidity, Mia's fear, and loving every second of it. I didn't know who this guy was—what had happened to my old friend? But my instinct told me to keep feeding him what he wanted, to play dumb and let him revel.

"Figured out what?" I let my legs tremble in spite of the piercing vibration it created in my head.

Shaking his head in disgust, Jeff turned and stoked the fire. A few embers flew up and Mia whimpered. "See, Mia? It's like I told you. You don't want someone that stupid."

No one spoke for a moment. The only sound was the crackling fire as I struggled silently against the ropes tying my wrists together.

"It's okay, though. We'll be together, and then you will be gone … and so will he."

My whole body went cold at his words and I stopped struggling for a moment. "Where, exactly, are we going?"

Jeff stood with a smile and pivoted slowly to face me. "Depends. Do you want to know what the police will think happened, or the truth?"

"Let's start with the truth."

"Well, I get to do whatever I want with you and Mia before you both die."

"Die?" I swallowed, and Mia curled deeper into a ball in the corner.

"Of course, it won't be that hard to believe you're a stalker *and* a killer after the way you've been acting." He walked closer to me and I stopped fighting against the ropes.

"A killer?" I stared into his eyes. The inhuman coldness I saw there was terrifying.

"Of course—Mia's killer. I tried for a while to get her to turn you in for the way you were acting, but she wouldn't. I think it's better this way, actually … at least for me it is."

Jeff laughed and slammed his fist into my gut. "She

fought you—she's very strong—but in the end, you overpowered her."

I doubled over, trying to make my breath come back as the pain ripped through to my spine. Gasping in air, I stared at Mia, but she didn't move a muscle. She was practically catatonic. Her eyes were trained permanently on the flames before her, barely blinking. I could see from her arms and legs that she wasn't tied up. Only the fire kept her prisoner.

Jeff followed my gaze and his face hardened. He wrapped one hand around my throat and lifted my face to his.

"Don't look at her!" he screamed as he tightened his grasp, blocking my airway. "Never look at her!"

Releasing me, he walked away, his fury cooling instantly and his crazy rage replaced by a knowing smile. "Don't you know that's what got you in trouble to begin with?" His fists hung by his sides as he backed away from me. "If you'd left her alone in the first place, then she wouldn't have been so distracted. She would have paid attention to me. Everyone would have paid attention to me. And none of this would have happened. Of course, with you here now—this is even better."

"I don't understand." The rope binding my hands together wasn't budging. I stopped and tried to think of another plan as I waited for Jeff's response.

"Oh." His eyes were wide, his voice condescending. "Let me help you understand, then. By the time I finish with you, you'll wish you'd died in your sleep like her freak therapist."

"Dr. Freeburg?" I asked, my mind whirling.

"Yes, Freaky Freeburg. If he hadn't died, he'd be the

one here. You should've seen the way he touched her. It was disgusting. As if she could be interested in an old fart like him." Jeff's eyes filled with fury. "Then there was you, following her around and watching her all the time. Neither of you could respect what was mine. But now you will. Today, I'll help Mia realize I'm what she wants."

He turned his back on me and moved the flaming metal garbage can closer to Mia. A small cry escaped her lips and she pushed her body farther into the corner. "No one ignores me, Mia. No one."

Jeff spun toward me, his eyes hard and angry. "This is my school. And you don't get to share my glory. I made our team a winning one. Not you. I turned soccer from a sport into a lifestyle. Not you. Mia is mine, and you can both burn in hell if you think I'm going to let you have her." Then he gave a crazy laugh and pointed to the flame. "Burn, get it?"

"Did Thor help you with all this?" I had to keep him distracted. Every time he met my eyes, I saw it. That desire to kill, to cause pain. I needed to keep him focused on gloating over his victory. I had to keep him away from Mia.

"Thor? You think that moron has the brains to pull off something like this?" His laugh was ice cold. "He's my permanent alibi. He already kept me from getting in trouble when Liv and that other whore started yelling rape, and he'll keep me from getting blamed for this."

I coughed. "Rape?" Liv … the fear I'd seen in her eyes in the hallway. She hadn't been afraid of me—she'd been afraid of Jeff.

His eyes glinted in the light of the fire. "They wanted it." A sneer twisted his lips and his eyes looked wild. "Just like Mia will."

Turning, he walked toward her. "You want it, don't you, Mia?" He grabbed a paper from a nearby table and lit the corner. He knelt before her and touched the flame to her calf. I fought the rope that bound my hands as she screamed.

"Stop it!" I yelled as loudly as I could, trying to draw his attention back to me.

"Don't tell me what to do. Never tell me what to do!" Whirling, he dropped the paper in the trash. In an instant he was on me, hitting me over and over. My world filled with the metallic taste and smell of blood.

Time passed through a haze as I tried to make my brain refocus. Whether from the hour or the worsening storm, the light coming through the high windows was dimmer than when I'd arrived. Snow fell outside—that much I could tell. It was hard to remember what had happened, though—hard to remember anything. Jeff added a piece of wood to the garbage can, and then he sat beside Mia and ran his fingers down her hair.

He turned to face me, his expression hard, cruel. "I downloaded this neat little tracking program to tell me when someone logs into my account from another computer. I noticed you finally accessed my e-mail. It took you long enough. That was pretty much genius, don't you think?"

I met his eyes and tried to nod, but my head refused to obey and fell to one side.

"You're an easy target, Parker. Always so trusting." Hatred filled his eyes, but his mouth twisted into a smug smile. "You really should've taken those password security recommendations more seriously."

I remembered that Jeff had sat next to me in computer lab last year. He must have seen my password back then, and I'd never seen any point in changing it. He was right— I'd been a fool. I'd accepted the fact that I was guilty of everything and stopped searching for the real threat.

I'd made a mistake, but I'd be damned if I was going to let Mia die because of it.

"Of course, I considered using your real e-mail, but I couldn't risk you finding out too early and ruining all the fun." Jeff laughed, sat on the floor beside Mia, and held her hand in his. She was helpless, and he was psycho. It made me furious, and the instant he glanced my way, he could see it.

"You know she isn't yours now." His eyes flashed with arrogance and fury.

"She was never mine," I growled out between my bloody teeth as Jeff ran his hand up her arm. "But she isn't yours either."

"Yes she is." His head whipped back around to face me. "Her hands aren't tied, but is she telling me to stop?"

He was staring at me like he seriously expected an answer. I opened my mouth but nothing would come out.

"I can do anything to her." He moved his hand to her opposite cheek and lifted her hair away from her ear. "I can touch her and kiss her." He nibbled on her ear for a moment and then bit her until a few drops of blood came out and she flinched. "I can hurt her. Anything I want and she will let me. That's how I know she's really mine."

My hands gripped each other so tightly behind me I thought I might pull something, but I didn't say a word. I kept my face neutral. I wasn't going to play into his twisted thrills.

Mia's whole body shook as Jeff kissed her neck. He pulled the neck of her T-shirt down, his hair falling around his face as he kissed her shoulder. She might not have been saying no with her voice, but her body was screaming it. It horrified me, but I didn't let it show. I couldn't—not now, not when she needed me most.

"Whatever, man." I shrugged. Everything felt a little clearer; my brain was responding faster with every minute he wasn't attacking me. "You're sick, but she's not my problem. Do whatever you want with her."

Jeff raised his head and stared at me. Something about my statement seemed to make him unreasonably angry. "What do you mean? I've seen you following her. You want her too. I've *seen* it."

"I did at first." I met his eyes and didn't even glance at Mia. "But I was just curious. I haven't even seen her in weeks. She's exactly like every other girl."

"You haven't seen her because you were in the hospital. Do you think I'm stupid?" He snarled and stood up. "Free-burg thought I was stupid." He paced around the room, his motions tight and rigid like a furious robot. "He was like you.

Both of you, staring. She didn't want you or Freeburg. Mia didn't want you. You were just a distraction. Distracting everyone from me."

Staring at the snow out the window, he muttered, "Like Mom, always distracted from me, no one notices. But not now. Not this time."

He spun to face me as though just noticing I was there again. "You love her, and you kept her from me. Don't lie. I don't like liars." He grabbed a chisel from a nearby workbench and lifted it as he walked toward me. His eyes were glazed over and focused at the same time—I saw a need for violence in them that I never could have imagined.

"Okay, I lied," I shouted as he closed in. "I love her."

He froze and dropped his arm. Peace filled his expression and he grinned. "I knew this would be fun."

In the silence, we heard a door slam somewhere in the school. The wind picked up outside. I could hear it whistling through the walls—maybe a gust had closed the door. Jeff placed one finger to his lips and held his chisel up again. I nodded and he slipped out of the room.

Now was my chance. It might be the only one I would get.

I sawed my wrists back and forth; they were raw and bleeding from my efforts, but the rope still wouldn't give. My legs weren't tied down. Maybe if I caught him off guard I could kick him.

I glanced at Mia. Her shirt was crooked, her shoulder still exposed. But she didn't even seem to notice. Her eyes were glued to the fire still crackling in the trash can. Why hadn't the fire alarm gone off? Looking around, I saw the smoke detector hanging useless on the ceiling. A window at the top of the wall, above Mia's head, was open, and most of the smoke was escaping there.

I inhaled the stinging, hazy air. I needed to get through to Mia. It was our only hope.

"Mia." She jerked at the sound of my voice but didn't lift her eyes from the flames. "Mia, I know you're scared, but I won't let the fire hurt you."

No response for 1 … 2 … 3 … Then a slight shake of her head. She could hear me.

"I won't let the fire hurt you like it did your parents." I could hear something in the distance—a shout and then silence. "You have to trust me, Mia. I won't hurt you."

Mia stopped shaking and took a deep breath, but she still couldn't drag her eyes away. Behind the silence of her response, a weird shuffling sound came up the hallway.

"I'll do everything I can to help you, like in your dreams. But you have to let me."

Mia's eyes flitted to mine for a moment and I thought I caught a slight nod, but then she glanced at the door behind me and her eyes went straight back to the flames. I hoped it would be enough.

I could hear Jeff grunting behind me but I couldn't see him. "You know, if you untied me, I could help you," I said.

His laugh was brittle. "I doubt you'd want to do that."

He finally came into view, and I saw why he was struggling. He was dragging someone along the floor behind him. The body was half-rolled in a mat, the head covered in a black snow cap. It was agonizing, only being able to see a portion of the person at a time, but by the time Jeff dropped the mat, I could see the blood-soaked shirt that read *The police never think it's as funny as I do.*

My gut clenched, and suddenly I couldn't make my body respond to any of the orders my brain threw at it. I couldn't breathe, I couldn't think. And the painful vacuum in my chest convinced me that my heart had refused to beat.

"Your little boyfriend doesn't look so good, Parker." Jeff stood in front of me with his hands on his knees. The smirk on his face made me gag.

Finn was dead, or dying, and Jeff was enjoying it. I couldn't stand to see his face anymore—not ever again. He was close now … close enough …

When I kicked hard against my chair, flipping it up in the air and connecting my shoe with Jeff's face, it felt eerily similar to an extremely solid soccer ball. He lurched backward and sprawled across the floor, and I crashed down too, landing on my bound wrists.

I felt two snaps in my left arm and yelled out in agony. I thought I would pass out from the pain, but Mia yelled something. Not words, actually; more like disjointed sounds. I rolled the chair toward her and my hands went oddly numb.

Jeff was out cold, blood flowing freely from a deep gash on the side of his head. When he fell, he'd knocked over the garbage can, and pieces of burning wood were scattered around the room. A couple were already burning themselves out on the concrete floor, but one had landed in the wood bin and the fire had started to spread.

"You–you–said–ahh–you–Parker." Mia was breathing so fast her skin was stark white and her lips had a strange bluish tint to them. I knew if I couldn't calm her down she wouldn't be conscious for long, and then ...

Well, then we'd all burn.

"Mia, I need you to come to me." I spoke through gritted teeth, trying to forget the agony in my arm. She shook her head, her breathing actually speeding up more. "You need to take slower breaths. Everything is okay now. We're leaving, okay? I need you to come untie me and then we'll leave."

She seemed uncertain, but she glanced at Jeff's limp form and her breathing softened a little.

"There isn't any fire between you and me. Can you come over here so we can go?"

Mia glanced over at the fire and froze, her body trembling so hard I thought she might fall over.

"Mia!" I shouted, and her eyes turned back to me. "Don't look at the fire. Look at me. Keep your eyes on me. Like the dream, okay? It's just us and we're going to get out of here alive."

She nodded and crawled toward me. By the time she made it across the first few feet, her breathing had slowed even more.

"Great job." I spoke slowly and calmly, focusing on Mia and not the fire spreading from the wood bin to the desk. It moved fast, greedily consuming the papers and wood projects waiting to be graded.

"Can you focus on my hands? We need to untie them so we can leave."

She moved around behind me and gasped. "One is br- broken."

"I know. We need to go so I can get it fixed, okay?"

"Okay." I could hear her sobbing as she scooted over to reach my ropes. With every tug, pain shot up my body and through the top of my head. I bit my tongue so hard it filled my mouth with blood. I couldn't risk a scream escaping and frightening Mia back into her frozen state.

The room was filling with smoke now and I could feel heat waves pulsing from the blaze at the other side of the room.

"G-got it." Mia tugged one last time and my hands were free. We got to our feet as smoke spilled out into the hallway and the fire alarms finally went off. Mia crouched down and covered her ears, her body racked with sobs. I rushed over to Finn. He was still breathing. A deep cut leaked blood from his stomach. Jeff must have stabbed him with the chisel.

I glanced down at my arms. My left one was useless. It was bent at an angle that looked so wrong. My right one was weak too, and my wrist had been rubbed raw, but there was no way I would leave Finn or Mia behind.

Pulling Mia to her feet with my right hand, I raised her chin until her eyes were level with mine. "We're leaving now. I need you to hold on to my shoulder so you don't hurt my arm. Okay?"

"Okay." She nodded and coughed. The smoke was getting too thick. "G-get me out of here."

Mia grabbed onto my left shoulder and I dragged Finn's rug toward the hall with my good arm. I'd gotten the rug halfway through the doorway when it stopped moving. Ducking low, I covered my mouth with my sleeve and peered through the smoke.

Jeff smiled back at me from the shop room. Blood ran down one half of his face.

"I'm ... not ... done." His voice was low, gravelly. Mia whimpered into my shoulder.

"Mia, I need you to keep going." I squeezed her hands and placed them on the rug. "I need you to pull Finn outside. I promise I won't let Jeff get to you."

Her eyes swirled with terror as they met mine. "You want me to leave you?"

"Yes." I nodded. "Now go!"

I jumped over the rug without touching Finn and slammed my body into Jeff's as hard as I could. The hit knocked him on his back, and as we slid across the floor I glanced behind me to see Mia pulling the rug into the hall. Even through the smoke, I could see how hard she was shaking. But she was still doing what I'd asked.

Jeff's fist connected with my face and it felt like my cheek exploded. Then he was on his feet, and I saw him pull back to kick me. I rolled aside and out of the way. Every movement made my broken arm scream in agony. He was coughing, and he staggered to one side. Keeping myself low to the floor, I waited. I could breathe; he couldn't.

I found a piece of wood nearby and held it tight in my good hand. If I was going to get out alive, I needed to make my move. But I couldn't just run. He'd come after us once already, and I had to make sure Mia had enough time to get Finn out.

It felt like everything had slowed down, and I took a deep gulp from the disappearing pocket of fresh air. I watched Jeff bend his knees and duck to get below the smoke. His crazed eyes met mine. I saw in them what I'd seen in the eyes of Mr. Flint so many weeks ago, when he'd killed his wife, and in the eyes of Darkness. Jeff would kill me without a second thought if I let him.

He lunged toward me as I swung, and I felt my makeshift weapon connect with his head. The sickening, solid thud reminded me of the way it felt when I'd hit Dr. Freeburg with the paperweight. I pushed aside the thought and watched Jeff stumble forward. I scrambled back, but when I saw that his eyes were closed and he was heading directly toward the fire, I dropped the wood, reached out, and grabbed his shirt.

He turned to face me, blinking in confusion. His pupils were different sizes and he glanced down to where my hand was gripping the fabric. His face filled with anger.

"Stop, Jeff!" I pleaded with him, seeing him start to pull away.

"Shut up and get off me." He shoved against my shoulder and I lost my grip. I stared in horror as he walked backward into the flames.

I couldn't watch. I turned my back, ducked low, and ran out the door as his screams echoed behind me.

———

I was halfway down the hall before I saw them. Mia was on her knees, still trying to pull Finn as her shoulders shook with sobs. Finn was heavy, and it was clear Mia couldn't breathe. I could barely breathe myself and I wasn't trying to lug another person around. My vision was already getting blurry and my throat burned from the smoke. The nearest doors were the ones by the gym, but they were still about ten feet away. We had to make it. After all this . . . I wouldn't let them die now.

I knelt beside Mia and she turned tear-filled eyes on me. "You're here."

"Not for long." I grabbed the opposite corner of the rug with my good hand and ducked even lower for one more breath of clean, cool air. "Let's go."

"Thank you," she choked out. Then we both pulled as hard as we could, toward the cold snow and fresh air outside.

THIRTY-TWO

By the time we got out, sirens were sounding in the distance. We collapsed onto the snow, both of us gagging and coughing out the smoke that permeated our bodies. As soon as the spasms stopped, I checked on Finn. He was still breathing, but it made a weird rasping sound. There was so much blood. Careful to avoid my broken wrist, I took off my sweatshirt and secured it against his wound.

I couldn't take anymore. I buried my face in the snow, letting the cold seep in through my blistered skin. After all that, was it not enough? Would Finn die anyway?

There was a soft tug at my shoulder and I sat up. Mia wrapped her arms around my neck and pulled me close. "Thank you," she whispered, hot tears burning on my cheek. "I'm so sorry I thought it was you."

I didn't know how to respond. There was really only one answer.

"Me too."

We held each other as the fire spread deeper into the school. Ashes mingled with the snow and fell on us as we coughed and cried until the paramedics arrived and pulled us apart. One of them inspected my arm, but I jerked it away.

"I'm fine. Help him!" I pointed toward Finn, even though two paramedics were already hurrying him toward one of the ambulances on a stretcher. I only caught pieces of words—"loss of blood," "uneven breathing," and "John Doe." The ambulance sped away immediately, its siren blaring through the frosty air.

I couldn't feel anything anymore. I could barely think. Dread coated my veins as I wondered if he would make it. I didn't think I could take the answer right now. Only one thing seemed important enough for me to try to speak.

I turned to the paramedic next to me. "His name is Finn Patrick," I rasped. My throat felt like I'd swallowed a dozen hot coals. "He's my best friend."

She nodded. "I'll let them know."

It was getting dark. The sun was probably setting even though it hadn't really made an appearance all day. Half the school was ablaze but I kept my back to it. Every time I faced it, I could feel the heat and smoke on my skin again. People parked along the street, milling about in groups and speaking in hushed tones.

"Were you the only ones in the school?" a firefighter asked Mia. She stared at him, and then I heard a rough sob escape her lips.

"There was one other guy, in the shop room," I gasped, against the pain in my throat. "He started the fire."

Two firemen headed back into the school. The paramedic nodded and pushed me back onto a stretcher. She jabbed an IV in my arm and set an oxygen mask over my face. She kept talking to me, but I couldn't answer questions anymore. I closed my eyes and tried to picture Addie's dream, tried to feel the cool mist instead of the hot, choking smoke. I tried to picture her smiling instead of crying. Then I slipped down into my familiar void.

———

Every piece of me itched and ached simultaneously. I wanted to roll over to ease the irritation, but my left arm was bound tight and held in place. I blinked and saw I was back in the hospital. As my eyes focused, they came to rest on Mia. She wore a hospital robe and was gripping my free hand.

"M—ah?" My vocal cords were so painful they felt like flames licking my throat.

She turned to face me. It was the first time in months that I'd seen her eyes without fear in them.

"No, don't talk. Here, have some ice to suck on. It helped me a lot." Her voice was hoarse too, but nothing like mine. She had a small oxygen tank beside her and a tube beneath her nose. A bandage covered the gash on her forehead.

I took the chopped ice and sucked on a few pieces. They brought instant relief, and I relaxed back into my pillow.

Memories from the school came to me and only one thing mattered.

"Finn?" I managed to choke the word out.

"He's going to be okay. They gave him some blood and removed his spleen, but he's fine."

I released the breath I'd been holding and all my tension flowed out with it. Mia and Finn were okay. Everything was okay.

"They're trying to get ahold of your mom, but before she gets here, I want you to listen. Please?"

I nodded, and she continued. "I thought about what you told me—about the dreams. I remember everything, I think. And what I didn't remember, Finn and Addie told me about. I really owe you." Her voice was quiet, but her eyes held mine.

Was she crazy? Of course she didn't owe me. I shook my head, but Mia frowned until I stopped.

"Yes, I do. You saved my life." She squeezed my uninjured hand and smiled. "Now I'm going to save yours."

I waited. I couldn't really talk anyway.

Mia pulled on one strand of singed hair as she spoke. "I want you to watch my dreams. And not just tonight . . . every night."

I opened my mouth and got out the one word I really needed to say: "No."

I couldn't let her do that. Maybe I wasn't as bad as I'd thought, but I still wasn't normal. I'd probably killed Dr. Freeburg. I didn't send the e-mails, but Darkness was still real. Mia was sitting here, volunteering to be the answer I'd wanted her to be—and what Darkness still wanted her to be. I could feel his delight, see him laughing in the back of my mind. He enjoyed it; he was the reason I'd sat outside her house in the middle of the night. He'd caused my accident. I wasn't safe and I wouldn't risk it.

Her jaw tightened. "Yes."

"No."

She groaned. "Come on, don't you see? It will help both of us."

I opened my mouth to argue again, but her last sentence stopped me. I waited for her to explain.

"I need you to be there." Her cheeks flushed. She looked down and fiddled with the hem of her hospital gown. "You helped me even when I thought you were a monster. You can help me face my nightmares when they come, and when they don't—I can help you stay alive."

I didn't know what to say. I didn't trust myself, but how could I refuse to help her? I glanced over at my arm, at the cast that went up to my elbow. Our lives had been filled with such carnage since we'd met. What if it happened again?

Mia stared into my eyes and I could tell she saw my uncertainty. "Parker, I'm so tired of being afraid ... aren't you?" Her eyes welled up with tears, and I knew I'd agree. I had no defense against that. I was tired of being afraid of myself, of Darkness, of my future.

I squeezed her hand with a small nod. This might be the worst plan ever, but I'd never know until we tried it.

A smile spread from her lips and up her face until I half expected it to burst out the top of her head. She leaned over and kissed my cheek. Her lips felt warm and soft on my skin.

Just hours ago, Mia couldn't even trust me. Now she was kissing my cheek? Telling me she owed me? My entire world felt upside down.

"I want my life to be normal someday, and I think you can help me do that," she said. "Who knows, maybe I'll even be able to paint again." Her expression was sad, but hopeful. "It used to be my favorite thing, until all my paintings burned with...with..." She stopped and took a deep breath. "Anyway, I better get back to my room now. I'll see you later."

She walked to the door. Other than having a slight limp, a bandage where Jeff burned her leg, and some blisters, she looked like she'd made it out okay. She stopped in the doorway and watched me for a minute.

"Thanks again, Parker."

I swallowed a piece of ice and nodded.

Before the door even shut, Addie pushed it back open. I smiled even though it hurt my scorched skin.

"Addie." My throat was feeling better already—still raw, but much improved.

Comfort filled me as she entered the room, until she turned to face me. Her eyes were puffy and swollen and all I could think of was Finn. I sat straight up in bed and the world skewed oddly to the right.

"What's wrong? Is Finn..." My voice sounded low and foreign. My head spun. I couldn't finish the sentence.

Addie shook her head and gently pushed me back against the pillow. "No. He's okay."

She sat in the chair Mia had just vacated and I reached

for her hand, but she pulled it away. It felt like a dagger slicing clean through my heart.

"What's wrong?"

She reached into her back pocket and pulled out three white envelopes. The letters I'd left on my kitchen counter. The one marked *Addie* was open.

"Did you get those from my mom?" The fear that my mom had read her letter hit my chest with the weight of a continent, making it impossible to breathe.

"No." Addie sighed, her eyes accusing. "I went to check on you this afternoon, and when you didn't answer the door—well, I was tired of you avoiding me."

She glanced back at the door to make sure no one else was coming in. "I took your spare key from under the gnome in the garden and I went in. Only you weren't there. I saw the letters on top of the message about the captains' meeting, so I called Finn and asked him to go find you before you left. An—and now—"

Her voice broke with a sob and I grabbed her hand again. This time she didn't resist.

"I'm so sorry, Addie." I pulled her closer and wrapped my right arm around her.

"You were just going to leave?" Her muffled question came through the fabric on my shoulder. "How could you do that?"

"I felt like I had to." I squeezed her closer. "I thought I was putting you in danger. I'm still not sure that anyone is safe around me."

She sat up and gaped at me in shock. After a few blinks she managed to speak. "So are—are you still leaving?"

"No." I answered immediately, but she didn't look relieved. I wasn't entirely comfortable with the decision, but for now it felt like the right one.

"How am I supposed to believe you?"

"I'm telling the truth." I stared her straight in the eye and waited a moment before finishing. "I can't promise that I won't leave in the future if I feel like it will keep everyone safe, but I'm not leaving now."

"I knew the truth about you." Addie stood up from her chair and touched my hair with her fingers. "Even when you didn't, I knew the truth, and you wouldn't listen." She turned toward the window and walked to open the blinds. Her movements were jerky, like a wounded animal.

Addie was so kind and sweet. She believed in me—always—and all I did was disappoint her. My heart throbbed in painful bursts and I resisted the urge to clutch my chest. I'd been a terrible person, but maybe I could be better. Addie deserved better.

"I know. I'm sorry." It was lame, but what else could I say? I couldn't promise to never leave again, because if she was at risk, I would. "All I can say is that I'm sorry, Addie."

"I know." She sighed and walked closer. Leaning over, she kissed me. Her lips were gentle and loving, even more incredible than in her dream, but when she pulled back her eyes were the opposite—miserable and defeated. "But I don't know if that's good enough."

She sat in the chair beside me in silence. Everything felt

wrong, and yet nothing was wrong—nothing I could fix right now, anyway. After a few minutes, she changed the subject.

"Jeff is dead, you know." The hatred in her voice surprised me, but I wasn't sure why. It made her sound different, not like the Addie I'd always known. But she'd been through as much as the rest of us. Jeff had tried to kill her brother, her best friend, and me. I guess we were all a little different now.

"Yeah, I figured." I was surprised at how little the confirmation of his death affected me. Numbness spread through me and my brain ached. I didn't want to think anymore.

"Mia told the police what happened, about the e-mails and Finn. What Jeff did . . . "

One massive weight lifted off my shoulders and I took a deep breath. It felt good to hear that Mia had told the police who the threats were from, but the other issue was still there. Dr. Freeburg would never really go away. The weight of taking a life—it would always be there.

"Do you feel guilty that he's dead?" Her eyes bored into mine.

I blinked at her.

"Jeff, I mean."

I wasn't sure how to feel about one more death when there was already blood on my hands. "He was seriously messed up," I said. "And he was the one who started the fire that killed him. Besides, I could only get two people out, and I could never regret saving Finn and Mia."

"How is it different with Dr. Freeburg?"

"He wasn't trying to kill me, for one thing."

She crossed her arms over her chest. "And who knows

how many girls he might have hurt in the past? And the future."

I opened my mouth and then closed it again before finding the argument I was looking for. "He could've gone to jail instead," I said, my voice barely above a whisper.

"Yeah, but how could you prove it? Mia says she doesn't even remember."

She wasn't making me feel any better. I shrugged, the weight of the discussion heavy on my shoulders. "I don't know, Addie."

She squeezed my hand. "Even if you did kill him, you can't change it. All you can do is make sure it doesn't happen again."

I stared into her eyes and wished I could have the same faith in me that she did.

Addie cleared her throat and smiled, but it didn't reach her eyes. "Mia's going to live with us now."

"Really?" I hadn't thought about it, but of course Mia needed to find another home. The Patricks were perfect.

Addie swung her legs over the arm of the chair and leaned against the opposite side. "Yeah. They were going to put her in a group home, but you know my mom. She'd never let that happen."

"That's awesome. Your family is amazing. You know that, right?"

"Yeah." Addie grinned and looked like her old self for a moment. "And don't *you* forget it."

The door to my room opened and Mom rushed in and hugged me, her skin pale and eyes wide. "I'm so sorry I didn't get here sooner. I was with a client and didn't realize my phone was on vibrate...a-and I'm so glad you're okay, honey."

"I'll be back in a bit," Addie whispered, then gave me a little wave and walked out the door. My chest ached. I didn't know if things would ever be the same between us. I knew that it was probably for the best if it ended now, with Finn and everything, but I didn't care. Addie made me happy when no one else could. She made me feel like I could be as good as she thought I was.

My mom kept circling around my bed, tucking in blankets and fluffing my pillow.

"I'm fine, Mom."

"I know, but this is crazy. I mean, Jeff Sparks? I can't believe it." She hugged me again. This time she didn't seem to want to release me, but the position I was in made my broken arm ache painfully.

"Yeah, it's definitely crazy." I pulled away until she let go and sat down next to the bed. "Did you talk to Finn or his parents?"

She nodded but didn't say anything; her eyes were locked on my cast. When I cleared my throat, she jumped.

"I'm fine." I watched her until she raised her eyes to mine and smiled.

"Sometimes I forget how much you're like your dad."

Now it was my turn to stare. She never mentioned Dad—ever. I'd tried to get her to talk about him before, but she always said it didn't matter.

It took me a second to respond. I was afraid that if I

asked the wrong question she'd decide she didn't want to talk about him. "How much?"

"Quite a bit, actually. You look like him, but lately, you're acting like him. More worried about everyone else than yourself."

"Dad was like that?" I asked, surprised. It seemed to contradict almost everything I knew about him.

She laughed and squeezed my arm. "Leaving wasn't the only thing he ever did, you know."

I nodded. I'd been prepared to leave for my own reasons this morning, and none of them were because I was unhappy. Maybe he had his own reasons for leaving, reasons I'd never been able to understand before.

"I guess him leaving is the main thing I remember."

A slight frown crossed her face. "Maybe I'll have to do something about that."

Mrs. Patrick opened the door. "Can I come in?"

"Of course." Mom stood and gave her a hug. Finn and Addie's mom had obviously been crying, but her mouth curled up in a smile.

"I wanted to say thank you." She walked to my bed and gave me a gentle hug. "Thank you for getting Finn out of that school. Mia told us what you did."

"You're welcome." I ducked my head a little. "I would never have left him there."

"We know. That's what makes you who you are." She rubbed my head and smiled. "Finn wants to see you. Do you feel up to it?"

"Always." My body disagreed, but I didn't care. When I

got to my feet, the room spun a little and the nurse brought in a wheelchair even though her expression dripped disapproval.

We passed Mr. Patrick in the hall. Mom and Mrs. Patrick stopped to talk to him and Addie stepped over to push my wheelchair.

"Finn is fine. Just remember that when you look at him," she whispered by my ear. "He's kind of—"

Addie froze just short of Finn's doorway, and a movement at the end of the hall caught my eye. It was Blind Skull. Just walking toward us like we were old friends. I blinked, but he didn't disappear or even fade into the shadows like he usually did. I let out the breath I was holding and looked up at Addie.

"You, uh … see him, right?"

Addie nodded but didn't look at me. When he came to a stop beside us, her brow furrowed. "Where do I know you from?" she asked.

"That doesn't matter now." He turned his eyes on me. "I need to talk to you, but not here. It's not safe here."

"You've been following Mia." I forced myself to keep my voice level. Now that I knew he was real, I wanted answers. "Tell me why."

"No." He bent down a little closer and met my eye. "I've been following *you*."

"Me?" I glanced up at Addie, but she was still staring at Blind Skull with confusion. "Why? Who are you?"

"I was hoping we were wrong and I could leave you to your business, but there's no use denying it anymore." He glanced up and I saw Mom peering past the Patricks, watching us with a strange expression on her face. "Name is Jack. Your dad sent me to talk to you, to teach you."

I felt like I had the wind knocked out of me. "M—my dad?"

"Like I said, this isn't a safe place to talk. I'll be in touch. It seems impossible for you, but at least try to stay out of trouble for a few weeks." Jack pivoted and walked quickly away. He disappeared around a corner just as Mom patted Mrs. Patrick on the shoulder and started toward us. Her brow was furrowed and she looked puzzled, but then the nurse came up with forms for her to sign.

I released the breath I'd been holding and glanced up at Addie.

Her lips squeezed in a tight line, but she shook her head. "Tomorrow. We'll worry about it tomorrow. No more today." Her eyes met mine and I felt the vibrations of her shaking hands through the back of my wheelchair. "Okay, Parker?"

"Yeah, okay." There were no answers today. Not now. Right now we just needed to see Finn.

Addie pushed my chair into his room and I forced myself to breathe normally. Finn was beyond pale. He was practically invisible against his stark white sheets; only his freckles stood out dark in contrast. He looked like some kind of polka-dot person, and it made my stomach turn. Addie walked out and shut the door behind her.

Finn smiled as I sat forward, and it transformed him. I felt better. He was weak, but still the same old Finn.

"Hey, man. I was going to lie, but I can't." I shook my head. "You look terrible."

"I know." He nodded with a grin. "I did it on purpose."

I blinked. "You what?"

"I figured if I looked bad enough to make you feel guilty, then you'd stop excluding me from all the excitement." He wheezed and clutched his side.

"Mission accomplished. The excitement is all yours." I smiled, then winced. "Now stop looking like crap so I can go back to ignoring you."

"Sounds good to me." He drew a ragged breath. "It's not worth feeling like this."

I laughed, and we sat there for a minute.

"So, I hear you pulled some kind of crazy hero crap back there." He only seemed to be able to keep one eye open at a time, but he was really trying.

"Oh yeah?"

"Yeah, running out of a burning building, pulling two injured people out to safety, with a broken arm and all." Finn's chuckle turned into a weird snore/snort thing before he opened both eyes wide and continued. "Promise me something."

"What?"

He smiled in a totally drug-induced, dreamy way. "Make sure someone totally ripped plays me in the movie."

I laughed. "Deal. You get out of the hospital and I'll let you pick the whole cast."

"Count on it," Finn mumbled. His eyes fluttered closed and he snored almost immediately. For some reason, his drug-induced narcolepsy made me feel so much better. Finn wouldn't be Finn if he didn't snore.

I wasn't sure what would happen with Addie, but we'd figure it out. And with Mia's help, I wouldn't be dying anytime soon. There were so many things I didn't understand, but I had time now. I would make Jack answer all my questions. I would find out about Dad—why he left, if he was a Watcher too, and every other damn thing I'd been waiting to ask for nearly five years.

"Everything is going to be okay," I said aloud to the silent room. I wanted the reassurance to convince myself, because even now, I could feel him.

Darkness sat in the stillness of my mind, watching for the perfect moment. The moment when he could voice his warped opinion like an oar dipped in the river of my decisions, awaiting the time when he could use my weakness and the tide to throw me off course.

But I was strong, and he was weak. I knew that now. As long as I kept getting rest by watching Mia's dreams, my future would be what I wanted it to be.

Acknowledgments

Without the assistance of some incredible people, *Insomnia* never would have made it from the realm of dreams into reality. First, to my incredible Agent Mafioso, Kathleen Rushall—you always believed in me and this book even when I wasn't sure anyone should. Thank you, Kat! To Taryn, Danielle, Brandy, and Kalah—thank you for helping the world find me. To my editor, Brian Farrey-Latz, thank you for wanting to help bring this book to life. To you and the rest of the team at Flux, especially Mallory and Sandy, thank you for making every step easier. Special thanks to Heyne Fliegt and Newton Compton for wanting to bring Parker's story to new places.

A special thank you and I love you to Ande, Cameron, and Parker. Thank you for putting up with my laptop following me around the house. Your hugs and kisses give me the strength to keep going every day. To my mom, Wendy Chipp, and my sister, Krista Poll—thank you for Girls' Cruises, always being willing to read, and helping me get so much better. To Grandma and Grandpa V—we love and miss you every day. Thank you to all the readers in the world, especially Carrie, Stephanie, Faith, Chantele, Nichole, and Nick. And thanks to Kamakea Kauwe for being the best target audience/ neighbor ever!

To some freaking amazing authors: James Dashner, Jennifer Bosworth, Elana Johnson, and Carrie Harris—thank you for taking pity on a lowly debut and sharing your kind words. You guys rock. Lastly, thank you to my amazing friends in the writing community (both in Utah and online) who help me celebrate and identify both my weaknesses and strengths. To my girls: Kasie West, Candice Kennington, Natalie Whipple, Renee Collins, Michelle Argyle, Sara Raasch, and L.T. Elliot—I know I wouldn't be the writer I am today without you. Thank you!

© Michelle Davidson Argyle

About the Author

J. R. Johansson has two amazing sons and a wonderful husband who keep her busy and happy. In fact, but for the company of her kitten, she's pretty much drowning in testosterone. They live in a valley between huge mountains and a beautiful lake where the sun shines more than three hundred days per year. She loves writing, playing board games, and sitting in her hot tub. Her dream is that someday she can do all three at the same time.

Visit the author online at www.jrjohansson.com.